D0401608

Secrets, Lies, & Crawfish Pies

A Romaine Wilder Mystery

ABBY L. VANDIVER

HENERY PRESS

Copyright

SECRETS, LIES, & CRAWFISH PIES
A Romaine Wilder Mystery
Part of the Henery Press Mystery Collection

First Edition | June 2018

Henery Press, LLC
www.henerypress.com

Trade Paperback ISBN-13: 978-1-63511-346-4
Digital epub ISBN-13: 978-1-63511-347-1
Kindle ISBN-13: 978-1-63511-348-8
Hardcover ISBN-13: 978-1-63511-349-5

Printed in the United States of America

Secrets, Lies, & Crawfish Pies

The Romaine Wilder Mystery Series
by Abby Vandiver

SECRETS, LIES, & CRAWFISH PIES (#1)
LOVE, HOPES, & MARRIAGE TROPES (#2)

To my sister, Robbie,
who I recently lost and who was always on my side.
I'm happy you got the chance to know that
this writing endeavor was a tribute to your only son.
And to her son, my nephew,
Romain Wilder Ramsey, who we lost a long time ago.
I love you both to the end of time.

ACKNOWLEDGMENTS

First, I want to thank my mother because I love her and because she made me who I am. She encourages me still and makes me want to be a better person even though the only place she can now be found is in my heart.

I want to thank Erin George, who got me started on this road, her guidance and encouragement is what made me want to make this a reality. Thanks to everyone at Henery Press who took to my idea for this cozy mystery and gave me a chance.

I also want to say thank you to Kathryn Dionne, my soul sister, and Laurie Kincer, Specialist extraordinare of Cuyahoga County's Public Library's Writers' Center. Both women are especially important to me in my writing endeavors and have been an inspiration and sounding board in my many, many moments of despair—thank you!

And last, but certainly not least, my grandchildren from whom all my love springs from.

Chapter One

"I talk to dead people."

I heard my auntie's voice. Although I couldn't see her, I'd know that drawl anywhere. The voice came from the middle of a small cluster of people at my "Here's-To-The-Next-Chapter-in-My-Life" soiree. The group's attention seemingly rapt with what the dear old woman had to say.

But my spry eighty-two-year-old auntie was anything but a "dear old woman." Her voice, loud enough to carry across the room, had alerted me to her disastrous intentions. I knew I needed to get to her before she got to the next line of her signature icebreaker.

"Oh, no you don't!" I huffed under my breath. I wasn't too keen on letting my small-town roots be extorted, especially since everyone in the room thought I was from a culturally inclined, arts laden, big city haven–I had told them I was from Houston.

Gossip, I knew, traveled just as fast among Chicago's upper crust as it did in my actual hometown of Roble in East Texas, one hundred seventy miles from Houston. Current population nine hundred and eighty-three. I rested assured, as I flipped my long, straight as a bone, black hair, that the population would soon be back to nine hundred and eighty-*four*, because I was, without a doubt, sending my auntie back posthaste.

Anxiety simmering, embarrassment teetering, I clutched my highball glass tightly in hand, gave a tug on my mini, off-the-shoulder Tadashi Shoji blush-colored cocktail dress, and headed off on my mission. I wended my way through the small dining area of my Sheridan Park apartment packed with doctors, lawyers, and judges, all my closest friends, to stop that party wrecker before she uttered another word.

My auntie had positioned herself at the far end of the living room and I could just picture her, the words tumbling out of her mouth with ease, a spark of mystery in her eyes as they met with those of each person in her audience, pausing to make sure they heard every word she said. She always planted a pause between the opener and the clincher of her two-liner. I had come to believe that she had it timed for maximum effect. I could almost hear her count between beats. I knew I didn't have much time.

In my rush, I bumped past one guest, nearly making her spill her glass of red wine. I spun around and, holding my glass up in the air, I was able to steady her hand before it splattered onto the newly shampooed Exotic Sands-colored carpet. That would be all I needed, an extra expense to have it cleaned again before I moved out in three days. But in saving it, I backed into a short man who stood eye level with the double-D bosom of a woman in a low-cut dress he'd been ogling all night, driving him, nose first, right into them. Although I don't believe I'd have been remiss if I said that he may have added a little momentum to the push I gave him.

A flash of red swam up the busty woman's face starting from her bejeweled neckline. Eyes bugged, she screeched out her disdain. His eyes just as wide, but it was a cheesy grin that curled around the edge of his mouth as he let out a satisfied sigh.

"I'm sorry," I mouthed and saluted her with my whisky tumbler as I backed away, only nanoseconds left to get to Auntie. Whirling around, I landed at my destination, blew out a pent-up breath and reached an arm out to grab her.

Too late.

"But not to worry," Auntie was saying. She wiggled a finger. "Because they talk back to me."

A collective gasp spewed forth and everyone turned to look at me.

"She owns a funeral home," I said with a nippy grin and transitory chortle, as if that could explain the lunacy that came out of her.

Dressed in a satin, cream-colored blouse and a black taffeta skirt with a crinoline slip, Auntie sashayed away from her spectators, my hand gently grasping her thin arm. The fullness of her skirt made a swishing sound with each step she took, announcing our hasty getaway. I guided her over into an unoccupied corner, away from the prying eyes of my guests to try out Plan A: Reasoning with her.

Born Suzanne Arelia Sophie Babet St. Romain, she married and became a Derbinay, a name she still wore proudly nearly fifty years after becoming a widow. She was the woman who raised me from age twelve after my parents died. "Auntie Zanne" to me, short for Suzanne, "Babet" to everyone else. Tonight, however, I was being reminded of who she truly was–a little troublemaker.

Five-foot three, short-cropped white hair–tapered in the back and puffed high on top–she was loaded down with bangles and bobbles and a smile just as fake as a pair of Louboutin's sold online from China. Auntie Zanne's distinguished, Louisiana mixed-race French Creole beginnings had morphed into Big Texas attitude and small-town intrusiveness over the last fifty years.

"Auntie," I said once I had her quarantined. "You have been at it all night. You've been like a little bee." I let my fingers flutter in front of her face. "Buzzing around, causing a commotion. People will think I come from craziness."

"I've been up to what?" she asked, her forehead crinkled, her accent exaggerated. "I have been doing no such thing. I've just been trying to help you entertain your guests."

"Trying to ruin my reputation. That's what you've been doing," I said. "And you know it. I wouldn't be surprised if you'd mapped out your entire foray into dismantling my life at the same time I was mailing out the guest list."

"Pfft." She waved her hand. "I did not." She tried to look as if she didn't know what I meant, but I knew that it was all an act.

"You know I have a different kind of life up here," I said, my eyes darting around the room to make sure no one was listening. "I'll never get the job I want in this city if one word gets out about you!"

"You won't have to worry about that," she said matter-of-factly. "You won't be around them—or here—much longer. Mark my words."

Mark my words.

I flinched as that phrase leapt from her frosted, rose-colored lips. I didn't know why she thought I wasn't going to be around much longer, but I did know whenever she made such a pronouncement, somehow, whatever she was referring to eerily came true.

"I just bet," I said, nervously shaking off her warning. I licked my lips and tried to muster back up a little bluster. "I saw you talking to the Chief of Staff over there-"

She cut me off. "Is that his name?" Nose scrunched, she acted as if she smelled something bad. "Chief-of-Staff?"

"No." My words came out in a puff. "You know it isn't."

"How am I supposed to know that?" she said. "That's all you call him every time you talk about him."

I blew out a breath. "Dr. Hale," I said. She rolled her eyes. "Okay. Alexander Hale." Her eyebrow arched higher. "Alex," I surrendered, lowering my voice. "I need a recommendation from him—from Alex, if I want to get a prominent position in another hospital. He has connections. I hope you haven't ruined that for me."

At forty-*ish*, I didn't want to start all over in my career.

"I don't think I have," she said measuredly. "I think you'll be fine." She patted me on my arm and turned to step away.

I pulled her back. "What did you say to him?"

She turned her head up to me, pulled me in close like she had a juicy secret, and nodded knowingly as she spoke. "I prepared a truth serum."

A sickly moan bubbled up out of my throat, and my eyelids went aflutter. I let my head roll back and stared at the ceiling, my imagination conjuring all the things she could have had him drink unwittingly.

I just hoped she hadn't given him anything that would kill him.

I rubbed my temple, giving myself a circular massage, and shifted my weight from one sore, high-heel clad foot to the other. "Did you really put something in his drink?" I looked into her eyes trying–hoping to detect a lie. "Please, Auntie. Please! Don't tell me you're going around pretending you are capable of some kind of magical hocus pocus. Telling people you have powers. You promised, Auntie."

"Why would I tell him that if I wanted him to drink a little brew I'd made?" She frowned at me, her voice loud enough to draw attention. "That would defeat the purpose. You know, the element of surprise."

"Oh, goodness, Auntie!" I swiped my hand across my forehead. Tears of frustration and disquiet stung as they welled up in my eyes. I fanned them with my hands hoping the tears wouldn't spill onto my perfectly MAC made-up face. "I need that man," I said earnestly.

"You ain't said nothing but a word," she said. "And from what I gather, that need goes much deeper than you getting a reference for a job."

That caught me by surprise. I stood up straight and swept the hair off my face.

How could she know?

She didn't know.

She *couldn't* know.

"He didn't tell you that." It came out more like a question than a statement.

She raised an eyebrow and gave me a look that said she knew whatever it was the two of us were trying to hide.

"You don't have any truth serum, Auntie Zanne. There is no such thing." I took a big gulp of my drink, trying to calm myself, and dabbed the liquid from the corner of my mouth with the tip of my finger. "I really shouldn't be talking about this to you, but..." I made my voice even lower and sidled up next to her ear. "He's married," I admitted. "But he's separated, and we are keeping our relationship quiet. No one knows about it. I *know*, emphasis on that word 'know,' Auntie Zanne, he wouldn't ever tell anyone about us. Especially someone whom he doesn't know." I widened my eyes at her to make my point. "I don't care what you think you gave him."

"*He* didn't tell me. I only spoke to him because I wanted to see what kind of man he is," Auntie said. "The truth serum was for you." She tapped the edge of my glass. "Seems like it worked." She gave me the eye. "Wanna tell me, Miss Romaine Wilder, why you're dating a married man? That's not the kind of girl I raised. Or maybe I'll give Mr. Chief-of-Staff over there some of my potion and see what he can tell me."

I threw up a hand in surrender.

There was no stopping her.

On to Plan B.

Without saying another word, I took her by the hand and led her into the cluttered, left-over-food-filled kitchen. "Can you just stay in here?" I tried to put a little niceness in my voice, but it probably just came out whiny. "Just until everyone leaves?"

Of course, asking her to stay put was like asking the sun not to shine, but my plan was meant to appeal to her idiosyncrasies.

Auntie Zanne had a phobia about clutter. "A place for everything, and everything in its place" was built into the very fiber of her being. Disarray was one of the many things she couldn't "abide by." I knew she wouldn't leave that room until everything was cleaned well enough to sparkle.

And I was going to do my part to help her stay put by making sure a steady stream of dirty dishes found their way to her—no one was going to use the same glass, plate, or spoon twice.

I dumped the rest of my drink in the sink and set the glass on the counter, nodding at it with my head, setting her to her task.

Before pushing my way through the kitchen door and back to my party, I turned and, tilting my head, I pointed a finger at her, silently telling her to behave.

That, I knew, really would take some magic.

Chapter Two

I stood in the entryway of my apartment with the door to the coat closet open and stared at my reflection in the full-length mirror. All my things packed in boxes and being loaded onto the moving van, a storage facility their new home. I was going home with Auntie Zanne.

I looked like a little lost child.

Hands at my sides, shoulders slumped, just two days after my happiness-infused get-together, I could feel the life I'd so meticulously built for myself slithering away from me.

"Just for a little while," I told the mirror image of me. I ran my fingers through my long hair, then down the front of my size six frame. "You'll be back with a job, back to the big city in no time at all." I leaned in close and tugged at the corners of my cocoa-colored eyes, then ran my fingers along my cheek, smoothing out the thin lines that had started to crease into my creamy-colored skin.

My lone suitcase and duffle bag, brimming over with the things I'd need for what I hoped to be a short stay, waited patiently for me in the corner by the front door.

In an abrupt downsizing, it had been nearly two months since my government job gave me notice, my subsequent job search not even garnering a callback from any of my inquiries. And, I found none of the multitude of those I called my "closest" friends could help. Then came time to renew my lease, a year's commitment with no hope of having a way to pay.

And to make matters worse, it was then that the new man in my life for the past three months, Alex Hale, prominent physician and apparent concealer of truth, told me that legally he wasn't available to make any promises to me. That truth was a harder pill to swallow than being unemployed and homeless.

I wish my auntie really did have some kind of truth potion, I thought. Then I could see what else he was keeping from me.

Without an idea of what to do after my world crashed in on me, my auntie showed up out of nowhere as if she knew my life had hit a snag.

Still, Alex made a good show of caring about me and I certainly liked him. A lot. He was handsome, enjoyed wining and dining me, and had a reputation as a skilled doctor with an affable bedside manner. He had taken time to help me pack, took me out for my last evening in Uptown to a blues club, and had even stopped by on his way to the hospital to assure me that he loved me and would help find me a job in Chicago. By then, he promised, he would be in a position to make a commitment to me and we'd be together.

His words sent my eavesdropping auntie into a coughing fit, but I held on tight to every one of them. I had to. It was the only thread of happiness I had left to cling to in what had become my unraveling life.

"Hey kiddo," my auntie said, walking back inside the apartment. I shut the closet door, giving her a weak smile, and tried to put my mind back on the task at hand.

"Are the movers almost finished?" I asked.

She had been following the movers in and out with every load— supervising, fussing, and generally getting in their way.

"I've never seen such healthy grown men move so slowly," she said. "I've got things to do back home, and I don't want to miss my train. You know I just can't abide being late. I've had to watch them like a hawk."

"They don't need your help."

"They need all the help they can get," she said, then switching in an instant from complainer to beseecher, she lowered her eyes and gazed up at me. "Speaking of help, I sure could use yours when we get back."

"Help doing what?"

"I am up to my knees in getting this year's crawfish festival planned. I figured since you're going to be home, you could help me."

Just then, the realization of what going back and getting embroiled in the life of Roble meant hit me like a brick. I raised my sad eyes to meet Auntie's. I blinked them hard and tried not to cry.

"I don't know, Auntie." I sniffed. "I don't think I'll be around long enough to help."

"Oh, look at you, darlin'. Now don't look so sad." She put her arm around me and gave me a squeeze. "It'll be alright, you'll see. Hey!" Her attention averted from my woe-is-me pity party just as quickly as the tears had welled up. "We're not paying you to turn in circles," she yelled, leaving me to continue her harassment of the movers. "Pick up that box and get a move on!"

The world moves on...

I swiped at my eyes, blew out a breath, and took my bags out to the front stoop of the apartment building. Uber was giving us a ride to Union Station. Amtrak was taking us to Texas.

The sunny early June day smacked me in my sullen face as I walked out the door. It made the concrete pavement glisten, and the neighborhood I'd adopted look cheerful. Bursting at the seams with architectural charm, it was the type of place people dreamed of living in.

I plopped down on the stoop and straddled my legs over my luggage. I rested my elbow on my knee and put a fist under my chin. I looked for the last time at my street filled with old houses, many of them listed on the National Register of Historic places. Uptown Chicago was gentrification with a big dollop of diverse flavor. Best known for its music venues, it was a place after my own heart. I had wandered down the street many an evening, following the call of a world-class jazz club, Theater Corner.

"Finally!" Auntie said. She stepped out on the stoop and poked her knee into my back. "Let's get a move on. Isn't that your Hoover driver?" She pointed to a black Kia Optima.

"Uber," I said, moving out of her way. She stopped on the step two down from where I sat, her big tapestry purse clutched at her side.

"What kind of word is that?" she said. "Ooober. And whatever happened to neighbors giving neighbors a ride? Thank God time has stood still in Roble."

I let out a moan. Just what I needed to hear.

"Well, c'mon," she said and gave my arm a yank. "Let's get a move on."

I felt twelve years old again, my feet dragging as I ambled over to the car, pulling my bags behind me, not wanting to leave. Back then it was Beaumont, Texas, where I had lived with my parents. After they died, Auntie Zanne was the first to arrive. She planned the funeral, buried her baby sister and her sister's husband, and took me home to live with her. I felt lost and numb, but too young to protest or put up a fight even if I had had the strength to. In the end, my life in Roble with my auntie turned out well. I couldn't have asked for a better childhood. But all that uncertainty I felt when Auntie Zanne stepped in to whisk me away, I was feeling at this moment.

Auntie Zanne practically had to get behind me, push me to the car, and then into Union Station and out onto the platform. Once it was time to board, I climbed into the train, tucked my bags underneath the seat, and plunked down. I leaned my cheek on the cool glass of the window in the air-conditioned Sightseer Lounge car where Auntie Zanne insisted we sit.

I cried as we left the Windy City and traveled through the farmland and rolling hills of Illinois. But by the time we crossed the Mississippi River and rode through the elevated plateaus of the Ozarks, my auntie had scooted in close to me and prodded me out of my mood, chatting me up with her plans for the 25th Annual Sabine County Crawfish Boil and Music Festival. As a board member of the Tri-County Chamber of Commerce, she was in charge, and that put an excitement in her that notched up with every mile we put behind us.

Full of life and animated, I listened as she rattled on about the East Texas "big" event. I smiled at her—so much energy, she didn't look or act anywhere near her eighty years. A Texas transplant, she loved their traditions.

In the late forties, her parents had moved their three girls, Suzanne, Carmalice, and Gabriela, from Louisiana to Texas after Naomi Drake became New Orleans' City Registrar for the Bureau of Vital Statistics.

In her zeal to impose a strict binary system of people either being black or white with nothing in between, Drake denied mixed-race French Creoles' distinct classification, something they coveted. She systematically applied hypodescent rules, lumping white and mixed-race Creoles into the same pot with Negroes.

Naomi Drake's race flagging began with her having her employees comb records to conduct her own style of genealogical assessments. If a person who identified as white had a surname common to blacks, or if obituaries listed a decedent as having black relatives, family members having services at traditionally black funeral homes, or burials at traditionally black cemeteries, she changed their race, no questions asked. And if a person didn't accept her new assignment, she would refuse to release the birth or death certificates.

That didn't sit well with the members of the French Creole community, and a mass exodus commenced. Some left to reestablish their own segregated community and others to find work. But the majority moved to Texas, settling in Houston and the cities that made up the Golden Triangle—Beaumont, Orange, and Port Arthur.

The St. Romains settled in Beaumont and resumed attending Mass at the Roman Catholic Church and speaking French. Everything was good—at least for a little while. It wasn't long before young Gabriela died and my grandparents— heartbroken, so the story goes— followed shortly after. A tragedy that drove my Auntie Zanne to hastily marry a man with distant French kinfolk and move to Roble to start a funeral home. I glanced over at her. She had dozed off and was snoring lightly. Auntie Zanne's fair skin was smooth, and nearly wrinkle free–no sign of all the history that she'd lived through. She was pretty, my auntie. Even at her age she still looked a lot like Lena Horne in her prime. Ah, but the voice of that songstress had gone to my mother, Carmalice, the middle child and, as my auntie often told me, the one with all the spunk.

My mother spoke French, had a beautiful singing voice that she offered almost exclusively to the choir at church, and she made the best gumbo in all of Louisiana and Texas. But even with my mother's love of everything French Creole, it was the blues that stole her heart. A guitar player by the name of Earle Wilder, to be exact.

My parents met at a bus stop, were married within the week, and had me nine months later. Momma, in naming me, took her maiden name, St. Romain, since there were no family members left that would carry it on, took the "saint" off the beginning and added an "e" at the end to match the spelling of her and my daddy's names. Carmalice, Earle and Romaine, one happy family – our house always full of music and laughter.

Until tragedy struck again.

I let out a sigh.

By the time our train rolled past the piney woods of East Texas, low hanging clouds tinged in a grayish ash had opened up and plonked a torrent of rain and wind down on us.

"Wake up, Auntie," I said, gently shaking her.

"I wasn't sleeping," she said, her eyes snapping open. "I was just resting my eyelids."

"Well, tell your eyelids their rest is over. We're here."

"We're here? Well, that wasn't a bad ride at all," she said, patting her hair back in place.

"Who's coming to get us?" I asked as we left the platform and got a glance out the front door of the station.

"Rhett Remmiere," she said and waggled her brows.

I chuckled. "Am I supposed to know who that is?" I asked.

"He's French. Someone for you to talk with."

"I can speak French to you if I want someone to converse with. All I care about is if he's punctual. I'm ready to get in out of this rain."

"*Voilà*," Auntie Zanne said and pointed.

Mr. French Guy, just coming in the doors, was tall and well-built, dressed in torn jeans and a black T-shirt, with a pair of round wire-rimmed glasses. He donned a pair of ratty tennis shoes that showed he had stepped through puddles instead of over them.

"Hey!" Auntie Zanne yelled out and waved. He couldn't have missed us. The station in Nacogdoches wasn't much bigger than a Lakeshore East studio apartment in Downtown Chicago.

"Hey, Babet," he said smiling. He walked over to us. "Looks like you brought a bunch of rain back with you."

"Wasn't me," she said. "It wasn't raining in Chicago. Was it Romaine?"

"Nope."

"Romaine," he said and let his eyes trail the length of me. "So, you're the doctor?" There was no sign of a French accent.

"I am," I said.

Seemingly, what he'd seen wasn't what he expected. But I didn't have the strength to say anything else or to prove my worth to him.

"Okay," he said and slapped the palms of his hands together. "Let's try and see if we can run between the raindrops out to the car."

Auntie Zanne laughed so hard at his comment that she tickled me. She couldn't have thought him that witty. He smiled. I was sure he knew that he hadn't been.

* * *

Wipers slapped across the windshield, barely keeping the road before us visible as we made our way east on State Highway 21. A wind had picked up and the rain beat against the branches and leaves of the trees and ricocheted, splattering hard against the car. It reminded me of driving through a car wash.

The usual forty-minute drive from Nacogdoches to Roble took a little over an hour. But even through the pounding rain, the large Greek Revival-style plantation with the sprawling oak trees on Grand River Road that Auntie Zanne and her husband had turned into Ball Funeral Home & Crematorium emerged beautiful and stately. Built in the mid-1800s with its white pillars, black shutters, and arched roof, it had been one of the largest cotton plantations during its time.

"What is she doing?" Auntie Zanne asked as we neared the house.

Josephine Gail Cox, my auntie's oldest friend, and frequent resident of the county's mental health facility, was standing in the middle of the driveway. Yellow plastic rain jacket on, her soaked thin dress clinging to her bare legs. She stood sentinel, re-angling her body every now and then so the heavy rain wouldn't pummel anything vital.

"Pull under the carport," Auntie Zanne directed Rhett. "Let me see what in tarnation is wrong with her."

Rhett did as directed and drove slowly up the driveway, running up onto the grass so as not to hit Josephine Gail or splash her, not that she could have gotten any wetter. He pulled up and parked next to Jack Russell, Auntie's Jack Russell Terrier, who watched Josephine Gail from a sheltered distance. Auntie had so named the dog because, as she said, that's what he was. According to that logic, I had told her, we'd all be called Man and Woman. And even with that she didn't stick to the name she'd chosen, he was J.R. to all of us.

We opened the doors and got out of the car. J.R. didn't know who to scamper to first. He turned in circles and scuttled from one side of the car to the other. He hadn't seen me in two years, and Auntie in two weeks, but in the end, I won out.

"Hey boy!" I said and stooped down to pat him. He turned on his back, demanding I rub his belly. "Yeah, I'm happy to see you too. Good boy."

"Josephine Gail!" my auntie called out to her friend, but she didn't answer. Didn't even give a look our way.

I stood up, ready to go and see about her, but Rhett volunteered before I could.

"I'll go and get her," he said.

"Good," Auntie said, then muttered, "I just hope she isn't getting sick again."

Reaching inside the double glass doors of the house by the carport, Rhett retrieved an umbrella and splashed his way down the drive to usher Josephine Gail back into a dry place. But it was easy to make out by her body language–side-stepping cover from the umbrella twice, her fists balled down at her side and eyes fixed straight ahead–she wasn't budging.

At the same time that Rhett made it back to us to give his report, the sheriff's car, silent red lights flashing through the dark rain, raced into the long driveway. It splashed through water as the tires came to an abrupt halt a good thirty feet from where we stood. The car door swung open and the sheriff bolted out into the rain and jogged, swerving around and hopping over puddles, past Josephine Gail to where we had gathered underneath the awning of the carport.

You would have thought a shoot-em-out bank robbery was in progress.

My first cousin on my father's side, Pogue Folsom, was the law in Roble. But with a population of not even nearly a thousand and zero crime rate, he was more public servant than protector. Not long elected, doing welfare checks, retrieving cats from trees, and setting up blockades for the annual crawfish festival made his sheriff title almost inconsequential. But he had worked hard to get where he was, and I was proud of him.

"What's going on?" Auntie Zanne asked Pogue, raising her voice over the wind and rain. "What are you doing here?"

"There's a dead body in there," Pogue said, pointing through the double glass doors. He pulled off his hat and brushed beads of water off it.

"Of course there is," Auntie Zanne said, sucking her tongue and rolling her eyes. "It's a funeral parlor. I've got lots of dead bodies in there."

"Only this one..." Pogue said, his voice getting louder over the bash of thunder and a crackle of lightning, popping as it smacked the ground, "...was murdered."

Chapter Three

"What do you mean murdered?" Auntie asked Pogue once we had gotten Josephine Gail to move and the five of us retreated inside. We stood pushed together in a small, tiled area of the add-on entryway, J.R.'s tail wagging as he went from one person's leg to another. "Don't come 'round here starting trouble, Pogue Folsom," Auntie fussed. "I'm just getting home and I need to get settled in. I've got a festival to finish planning."

"Josephine Gail called me," Pogue said in his defense, his drawl thick as molasses. "Said she had a dead body that didn't belong here. She thinks there has been a murder."

"Murder!" Auntie Zanne said. "There you go saying it again. I can't abide by such language in my place of business. Who is it?"

"I don't know," he said and shrugged. "I'm only repeating what she said." He nodded toward Josephine Gail.

Everyone turned to her. Water dripping off her, hair clumped together, eyes glazed, she was as stiff as a dead body herself and wasn't offering any information.

"I'll need to ask you some questions, Josephine Gail," Pogue said, pulling a notebook out of his shirt pocket. "Then, I'ma need you to show me that body."

"Well, you are just going to have to wait," Auntie Zanne said. "Look at her. There's more water on her than there is in the Sabine River. I'm gonna get her dried off before I let her do any talking."

Auntie put her arm around Josephine Gail's shoulder. "Help me, Rhett." She started up the five steps that led to the main floor. Coming around the other side of her, Rhett grabbed a hold of Josephine Gail's other arm to help steady her. "She's probably in shock from seeing that body," Auntie said.

Pogue looked at me, a big grin on his face. I just shook my head.

"Doesn't Josephine Gail work here?" he asked, still grinning. "Seems to me she'd be used to seeing dead bodies."

"Wipe that grin off your face, boy," Auntie said over her shoulder. "I know without looking at you you're looking like the cat that caught the mouse. Don't think 'cause you made Sheriff you can come in here bossing folks around."

"No ma'am," Pogue said, grin getting even wider. He thought himself clever even if Auntie didn't.

She got to the top of the stairs with Josephine Gail and turned around to look at us. "And, Mr. I'm-the-Sheriff, are you implying that I have murdered bodies in here all the time?"

"No ma'am." Pogue shot a look over at me.

"Good, 'cause I don't. And that's probably what's giving her a shock. The killer could still be around. Rhett, you give the place a once-over after we get her settled." Auntie gave her friend a squeeze. "C'mon, Josephine Gail, you'll catch your death of cold with all those wet things on. Romaine'll take a look at you, make sure you're alright. Pogue," Auntie waved her hand toward the back, "go get a blanket out of the hall closet and bring it to me. Matter-of-fact, bring me two and a few of them white towels. We're going to the kitchen. I'm gonna make something hot for her to drink."

We watched them amble off and Pogue turned to me. "Didn't get a chance to say a proper hello to my favorite cousin," he said and wrapped his arm around me.

"Hey cousin," I said and hugged him back. "How's your momma?"

"She's good. She's already trying to get me to drive her over to

San Augustine to go to Brookshire Brothers' grocery store so she can make you some jambalaya."

"Tell her if she's gonna make me some of her jambalaya, I'll drive her over there myself."

"I sure will tell her that," he said.

"Where are my blankets, Pogue?" Auntie's voice came booming out from the kitchen to us.

"I better get them," Pogue said and gave me another hug. "Good to have you home, Romie."

"Good to be home," I said. "And, yes, you better hurry up or there might be another murder around here."

When J.R. and I got to the kitchen, Auntie had turned one of the kitchen chairs around to face the stove and parked Josephine Gail in it. She was keeping an eye on her as she busied making one of her cure-all potions. She had filled the teapot, set it on the stove and was hunting through the many small spice bottles she kept for just the right root or leaf, or whatever it was she was going to use to resurrect Josephine Gail.

"What I'd like to know," Pogue said, coming into the room with the blankets, "is how an extra body could have gotten in here."

"That's easy," Auntie said. She took one of the towels and used it to dry Josephine Gail's hair and clothes. "We got them from the Hollerbach Funeral Home over in Sunrise. They had a fire and needed some place for their bodies."

"And you just took them in?" Pogue asked.

"Of course I did," she said, sucking her lips. "Death don't stop for nothing and nobody. And we in the NFDA have an obligation to the families we serve and to each other to get the job done no matter what." She looked at Pogue. "You should know that."

Auntie had not only been a member of the National Funeral Directors Association for half a century, but had been the president of her region for eighty percent of that time.

"The question you should be asking," Auntie Zanne continued as she poured hot water into a cup, "is what you are going to do about the body that doesn't belong here." She raised her eyebrows.

"Whether he was murdered or not, he's still got to be readied for burial."

"There's a lot to be done before we put him in the ground," Pogue said. He narrowed his eyes at Auntie. "And I do know what to do."

"Well, first thing we need to do is make sure he isn't one of the bodies from Hollerbach," she said. She sat down next to Josephine Gail and started spoon-feeding her some of the piping hot concoction she'd made. "Rhett, go get that list they sent us and let's see if we can't account for all the bodies. Most of them have already been buried, I'm sure."

"Okay," he said. "I'll do a walk-through while I'm at it."

"If he isn't from Hollarbach, then me and Romaine'll take a look at the body and see if we can't determine the cause of death."

"You'll do no such thing," Pogue said. "Doc Westin is the medical examiner for Sabine, Shelby, and San Augustine Counties. Appointed by the County Commissioner Court. That's his job."

"I know who he is," Auntie said. "ME for the Tri-County area for as long as I can remember. But he isn't here."

"He's over in San Augustine County taking care of some business. That's the only reason he isn't here now." Pogue sat at the kitchen table and pulled out his notebook. "As soon as he can get this way, he'll check out the body."

"You gon' wait till then?" Auntie Zanne asked. "That body will rot and stink up my whole place. We don't have any idea how long it's been here."

"The doc won't be long." Pogue held up his head and inhaled. "I don't smell anything. I think that we should be good until he gets here."

"You think *we* should be good?" Auntie popped up from her seat where she'd been nursing Josephine Gail. "*We* don't do the thinking around here," she said in a huff. "This is my funeral parlor and *I* do all the thinking."

"Well, I am the law around here and—"

"Don't you say it," Auntie warned.

"And I...I have to take care of this, Babet." His voice squeaked as he tried to stand his ground. "You know I do," his voice had changed from demanding to a plea for understanding.

"Why can't Romaine take a look at the body for you?" she said, not backing down.

"She may be a medical examiner up in Chicago," Pogue said giving me a look that told me he wasn't trying to be mean. "But if it is a murder, her testimony wouldn't hold up in court because she's not licensed here."

"Oh, hogwash," Auntie Zanne said before I could speak up in my defense. "She is more of a legitimate doctor in Texas than you are a sheriff, that's for sure."

"I am licensed here." I finally got in a word between the two of them going back and forth. "Did my residency in pathology and fellowship in forensic pathology over at Houston Methodist. You know that."

"He also ought to know that you keep up your medical examiner's license here, too," Auntie said. "That's why you came home two years ago, to take those continuing learning classes."

"Continuing education," I corrected.

She nodded her head. "And her board certification, in forensic medicine, Mr. I-Am-The-Law, is good anywhere."

Pogue couldn't say anything after we double teamed him with my credentials. And to be honest, I wanted to have a look at a corpse that was able to make its way to the inside of a funeral home before its death had even been called.

"Fine. If Josephine Gail isn't confused and the body isn't from Hollarbach, Romie can have a look at it," Pogue acquiesced.

"Good," Auntie said. "Just hold on and let me get some more of this tea into her. Rhett should be back with confirmation and then we can go and see what we can see."

"Who exactly is Rhett?" I asked. "I thought he was just someone that was picking us up to give us a ride home."

"No, darlin'," Auntie said. "He is my right-hand man around here. I'm grooming both him and Josephine Gail for the funeral business."

"Isn't Josephine Gail too old to start learning a new trade?" I asked.

"No," Auntie Zanne said.

"She's in her seventies," I said.

"Haven't you heard?" she said. "Eighty is the new fifty, so that makes seventy the new thirty."

"I don't think that's how it goes, Auntie."

"Sure it is. Josephine Gail is practically a spring chicken."

Pogue and I had to duck our heads and cover our mouths so she wouldn't see us holding back our laughter. For someone who worked with death on a daily basis, she was quite optimistic about immortality.

"And," she was still talking. "I wouldn't have needed Rhett, except my business is booming. People are dropping like flies. I swear, you'd think the world was ending and they were trying to beat the rush."

"And you've even got non-paying ones dropping in," I muttered.

"That's just what I was thinking," Pogue said.

"Just the two of you hope you live as long as me." She pulled the blanket up tighter around Josephine Gail then looked at us. "Okay. Let's take a look at the squatter." She pointed at J.R. "Be a good boy and stay here and watch over Josephine Gail."

He barked out his reply, then went and laid at her feet.

Rhett met us as we headed out of the kitchen. He had found the body.

"Is he one of the bodies from Hollerbach?" Auntie asked.

"As far as I can tell, he isn't," Rhett said. "I couldn't find two that were on the list, but seems like I remember their funerals."

He led us into a small room that was used for those that didn't have much family to speak of, or enough money for a package deal. But when I saw the body, I wouldn't have ever been able to guess he hadn't been readied by a licensed mortician.

The squatter was a middle-aged white male. He was dressed in a suit that was a couple sizes too big and hastily put on, but he had been carefully placed in a casket, hands holding onto the bedding and showing little signs of decay.

"Do you recognize him, Babet?" Pogue asked.

"Why would I know him?" Auntie said. "I've been gone for two weeks. At least a million people have died in that time."

"They didn't come through here," Pogue said.

"And if they had," Auntie countered, "I still wouldn't have seen them. I was in Chicago."

"I need some latex gloves," I said, interrupting their banter.

"I've got some." Rhett pulled a pair out of his pocket.

I gave him a look that said I was impressed with his readiness.

"I was just inspecting the bodies," he said. "I couldn't touch them all without gloves."

I nodded and turned my eyes to Mr. Dead Intruder to start a visual examination. "I really can't tell much without cutting him open," I said.

"Doc Westin'll do that," Pogue said. "Just see what you can see now."

The first thing I did was lift his head from the pillow to see if there was any trauma. I didn't see anything obvious but noticed that the body felt firm. I pushed in on the cartilaginous parts of the corpse—the ears and nose. They appeared somewhat brittle and discolored.

"There isn't much desiccation," I said, announcing my observation without lifting my head up.

"Be careful," Pogue said. "I don't want to lose any evidence."

"I do this for a living," I said. "I know how to preserve evidence."

I placed my finger over one eyelid and rolled it back. Then the other.

I glanced at Pogue. "Blue eyes," I said.

"Good observation. Important, I'm sure."

I didn't miss the sarcasm in his voice.

I didn't comment, I only nodded. I couldn't let him break my concentration.

Color of the irises was only a side note to me opening the dead man's eyes. I was looking for evidence of strangulation or asphyxiation. But his corneas were clear and the conjunctivae–the mucous membrane covering the eyes was free of petechiae. Those purple and red spots would have meant broken blood vessels. They were often present when there a restriction of blood to the head from choking or pressure being placed around the neck. Them not being there was not conclusive, but it pushed me more to want to search for the manner of death.

I took one hand at a time and checked his nails. Underneath for material, on top for break or chips, signs of a struggle. Then the skin for any marks, scars or even tattoos.

Nothing.

I unbuttoned the suit jacket and then the shirt.

I ran my hand over the man's chest to feel for any breaks or lumps in the skin. It was cool, smooth, and firm.

"What is he saying to you?" Auntie asked, leaning over from behind me, peering at the body.

There went my concentration.

I looked down at her. "He isn't saying anything, Auntie. He's dead. Even though you've said it a hundred times, it doesn't make it true. Corpses don't talk."

"Sure they do." She sucked her tongue. "You never talk to the people on your autopsy table?"

"No. I don't. I talk into the microphone."

"Well, you should try talking to them. You'd be surprised at what they have to say. You could learn a lot." She nudged me over with her hip and bent down toward the body, nearly touching her face to his exposed stomach. "You gotta use your ears," she said.

"That's your nose, Auntie," I said. "Are you going to talk to him or smell him?"

"That's enough," Pogue said. "From the both of you. No offense, Romie, but we've got a coroner. Just button him back up."

"Okay." I did as he asked.

"Did you find out anything?" Pogue asked.

"I did," Auntie said, raising her hand.

"I was talking to Romie, Babet."

"Well," I said pulling the dead guy's suit jacket together and securing the button. "I couldn't find any visible signs of trauma."

"That's all you got?" he asked.

"It was just a visual exam, Pogue. Nothing in depth." I turned around and looked at him.

"Okay," he said. "Let's just go see if Josephine Gail is ready to talk."

Although I was intrigued and would have loved to have more of a look around Dead Guy, I had no intentions of stepping on my cousin's toes. I wouldn't be around long enough to mend any bridges with family.

I put my hands up, surrender-style. I stepped away from the body.

Auntie Zanne didn't move. Pogue looked at her, then me.

I reached out and pulled Auntie Zanne over next to me. Then I looped my arm around hers to keep her anchored and out of the way.

"All yours," I said.

Chapter Four

Sunlight was streaming in through the light fabric covering the window over the kitchen sink. The rain storm had passed and there was a peacefulness surrounding it. But there was another storm brewing inside our walls.

We put our John Doe into the cooler and headed back upstairs to the kitchen. When we walked back into the room everything was still and quiet, including the occupants.

Josephine Gail and J.R. both had their heads down, eyes open wide and there wasn't a wag or a peep coming from either one of them.

Josephine Gail, I believed, was in shock. I think that J.R. just wanted someone to rescue him.

Auntie Zanne leaned in and whispered in Josephine Gail's ear. Then she bent over and scratched the top of J.R.'s head.

"Good boy," Auntie said. "You are released of duty." J.R. stood hesitantly. He gave a wag of his tail and looked from me to Pogue back to Auntie Zanne as if he wanted to be sure. "I'll take care of her now." His tail went into overdrive. He gave out a bark and scampered out of the room.

"Even the dog doesn't want to be around to hear you dig into Josephine Gail," Auntie Zanne said.

"It's my job," Pogue said. "I just need a minute with her."

"I'm not leaving," Auntie Zanne said. "And Romaine," she

pointed at me, "is her doctor. They've got privilege. Or something. So, she's staying, too."

Pogue huffed.

He pulled out a chair facing it toward Josephine Gail and sat down. He matched her gaze and held it as if he were trying to read her thoughts. After the quiet moment between them, he reached out and touched her. She didn't move.

"I need to ask you some questions," Pogue said gently. "You up to it?"

She nodded.

He licked his lip and didn't let his eyes stray from hers. "When did you find the body?" he asked.

Josephine Gail lowered her eyes. I saw her taking deep, quick breaths, and her hands, which were placed in her lap, began to tremble. "When I called you." Those were the first words I'd heard her utter since we'd gotten back. And they emerged seemingly with trepidation.

"That was the first you saw of it?" he asked.

"That's what she said," Auntie jumped in.

"Babet."

Auntie held up both her hands. "Just trying to keep this moving. She's liable to shut down any minute."

"And what does that mean?"

Auntie cupped her hand aside her mouth and in a loud whisper, enunciating each syllable, said, "Her depression."

"Whose benefit was the whisper for?" Pogue asked, obviously annoyed. "Everyone could hear you."

"Just didn't want to say it out loud," she said and shrugged. "Not something that should be discussed. It's a disease you know."

Pogue huffed. Again.

"Do you know how he got into the casket?" Pogue asked.

Josephine Gail slowly shook her head tugging on her bottom lip with her teeth.

"She said, 'no,'" Auntie-The-Translator said.

"Thank you, Babet." Pogue's sarcasm filled the room.

"You're welcome," Auntie Zanne said. "But that question seems obvious. I mean someone had to put him there. He couldn't have gotten there by himself."

"Babet. I can't do this with you here." He stood up and faced her. "I'm going to have to ask you to leave."

"Leave?" she sputtered out. "You can't ask me to leave my own house."

"Not the house, Babet. Just the room."

"I can't leave Josephine Gail," she said pouting. I thought she'd be angry and flat out refuse. Instead she acted as if he could tell her what to do.

"I'll be here," I said, speaking up for the first time during Pogue's scant questioning. "But I don't see how Pogue'll get through this with you here answering everything." I pulled up a chair next to Josephine Gail and ran my hand across her still damp back. "Is it okay if I stay in Auntie Zanne's place?"

Josephine Gail's eyes slowly went up to Auntie's. She held them there for a moment then let them fall back down to her hands. She gave a single nod of her head.

The pain showed in Auntie Zanne's face. Her eyes were pleading. I knew she didn't want to leave her friend to agonize through the questioning. I understood that making someone who suffered from depression do anything was tasking and could sometimes make things worse.

I had known Josephine Gail for as long as I could remember. Even before I came to live in Roble, I could remember her and Auntie Zanne being friends. And I'd seen Josephine Gail depressed before too–plenty of times.

When I was younger and she'd get that way, my auntie would take me when she'd go to visit. The house would be dark, clothes and dirty dishes everywhere. We'd take her food and straighten up her place.

Auntie would be so gentle and kind with her, treating her like she was a sweet little child. Oftentimes Auntie Zanne would make Josephine Gail a lavender bath and help her in the tub to soak, squeezing the water from the sponge over her hair and down her back. She'd sometimes sit her in a chair and brush her hair with deliberate, tender strokes. We'd always put clean sheets on her bed before we'd put her back in it, and then Auntie would feed her.

We'd never stay long because Auntie would say that people suffering from depression don't like having people around, and they don't like to talk. Then she'd say, "Depression is contagious, and we can't afford to get it because we have to stay strong, so we can help Josephine Gail."

Now Auntie Zanne left the kitchen with reluctance, her eyes brimming with tears and her face filled with the same distress as what was etched into Josephine Gail's.

I wasn't sure, though, that her leaving was going to help. People who suffered from depression were unmotivated to talk. But I didn't suppose that Pogue knew that because Auntie's leave seemed only to empower him. He changed tactics.

"Did you kill that man?" he asked, his voice harsh. Changing his demeanor, he sat up straight and stiffened his jaw. "Is that why he was here, Josephine Gail? Because you did it and put him in that casket?"

I saw sudden alarm wash over Josephine Gail and her face go pale. She seemed to shrink—her shoulders slumped, she wrapped her arms around herself, folded her legs together and began to rock back and forth in her seat.

"You may as well tell me, Josephine Gail." Pogue leaned in close to her, taunting her. "Tell me how you killed him."

She slowly shook her head back and forth as if she was trying to keep Pogue's words out.

"Why did you kill him?" Pogue squinted his eyes. "Did you stab him? Is that what happened? Or did you take that shotgun you keep that belonged to your daddy and do it?"

"Pogue." I said. "Don't."

"She knows something, Romie." He turned and looked at me. "I know she does. And she is going to tell me what she knows."

"You're not asking her that," I said. "You're accusing her of doing it. That's not right. It's not the right way to go about it."

He looked up at me as if contemplating my words, then turned back to her with even more determination in his eyes. "Did you do it, Josephine Gail? Did you kill that man and put him here because you thought Babet would help you cover it up?" He shook his head. "She can't save you, you know." He seemed to be angered at the thought. "Not if you did it. I'm the only one that can. But only if you tell me the truth."

Josephine Gail closed her eyes, and I could imagine the black hole that she had disappeared into somewhere deep inside, because we didn't hear another peep from her.

Chapter Five

Our house on Grand River Road had always been divided, in a real sense and in a figurative one.

There was the "primary" business. Ball Funeral Home & Crematorium. It was settled, impassive, presented by a constant hush and much formality. Alive only with the vibrant woven Axminster carpets, papered walls, alcoves, podiums and rows of gold painted Chiavari chairs that adorned the various Chapel Rooms—all appropriately named.

And then there was the part that was immersed in notoriety and commotion. The living quarters.

Before I moved away, a lot of the hubbub was my life at odds with Auntie. A whirlwind of emotions and passions. I wanted something different. Something more. She felt that what she offered me should somehow be enough.

Then all her auxiliaries and clubs produced clamor and disarray in our daily life comingled with the constant intrusions from her "other" business.

Herbal medicines and potions—the remnants of her Louisiana roots and the only vestige of a heritage she'd given up long ago— were still alive and well in East Texas. Housed in the rear of the house and in Auntie's backyard botanical garden, she deemed herself a Voodoo herbalist, one in a clan of many, although those words were rarely spoken in anything other than whispers. Her surreptitious, and often scorned, trade hailed boisterous and anxious clientele, but through the years sustained a booming enterprise.

After my departure, I soon found that my Auntie Zanne could be a tempest all on her own and, oddly enough, it was what I admired most in her.

But it was the one thing that others feared.

I didn't envy Pogue one bit when Auntie came back into the kitchen and discovered Josephine Gail had been warped by his questioning.

"What have you done?" she said and gave Pogue a wallop across his back with a wooden spoon she grabbed off the sink.

"Wait, Babet!" he screeched, his rough exterior cracking in her presence. "I didn't do anything."

"Look at her!" Auntie said. "Good Lord!" She grabbed Pogue by the collar and pulled him out of the chair. She got behind him and with her palms in the middle of his back, bent at the knee, legs spread, she started to push. "You are out of here!"

"Babet, stop," he said, standing his ground. "I'm the sheriff. This is my job."

"Just cause a chicken's got wings, don't mean it can fly!" Auntie Zanne yelled.

"I have to do my job," he said.

"No, you don't! Not here," Auntie said then looked at me. "Don't just stand there. Come and help me."

"Auntie!" I said.

"Babet!" Pogue said.

"I thought you were going to watch him," Auntie said to me. "He is going to send her off the edge."

"I think she's already there," I said.

"My heavens!" Auntie said. "What kind of doctor are you? Is that how you let people treat your patients?"

"My patients are usually dead," I said.

"Well, it wouldn't have been long before he killed Josephine Gail." She gave Pogue a kick in the back of his knee. "Get going," she said. "You are out of here."

"I'm not finished," he said.

"Probably best if you don't ask her anymore questions," I said. "You were kind of rough with her, Pogue. That isn't even like you."

"I was nervous," he said and glanced at Josephine Gail. "I'm sorry. I was just trying to get answers."

"You were trying to kill her," Auntie said.

Pogue looked at me and I nodded.

"Alright," he said and wriggled his shoulders, tugging on his shirt to straighten it out. "I was a little harsh."

"A little?" Auntie screeched.

"I was wrong, okay?" he said remorsefully. "But at some point, Babet, I'll have to come back. I have to bring Doc Westin and I still have more people to talk to."

"Out!" Auntie said, teeth clenched and out of breath. She threw her wooden spoon at him.

"Bye Romie," Pogue said, then left.

"And I think I might just have to call the medical board on you!" Auntie Zanne said to me. She went over to Josephine Gail and sat in the chair in front of her. I had my fingers crossed that there weren't any objects close by for her to hurl at me.

Instead she took her friend's hand and rubbed it. Then Auntie leaned in to meet her forehead with Josephine Gail's. "You're gonna be okay, sweetie. I got you."

"You want me to put some water on?" I asked.

"That'll be nice of Romaine, huh?" She talked to Josephine Gail instead of me. "I think that'll be good for you, some more of my tea."

I filled up the teapot and put it on the stove.

"Before I turn you in to the board," she said, sitting back in her chair without looking at me, "I'ma need you to check her out. Her mind and body are fragile enough and she was in all that rain."

"Okay," I said.

"I'm going to keep her with us. Put her in one of those rooms." She nodded toward the back hallway off the kitchen where she usually saw her clients. "I'm going to make up the bed for her." She stroked Josephine Gail's hair. "And don't ask her any questions, either." Auntie put up a finger to warn me. "Check her out without a word."

"Okay," I said again.

I went over to Josephine Gail and sat in the seat that Auntie Zanne had just vacated and I took her hand. Holding it, I looked at her. I tried to let my face show all the compassion I had and the pain that I felt for her.

"It's going to be okay," I said. "I'm just going to get my medical bag and take a look at you."

I stood up and as I started to leave, she tugged on the hem of my top and pulled me down. "I didn't do it," she whispered to me. "It wasn't me."

Chapter Six

Everyone who'd been at the funeral home was a suspect according to Pogue.

In my guesstimation, that could be anyone in Roble.

All nine hundred and eighty-four of them.

And with Auntie's social reach, it could encompass all of East Texas.

But I believed Josephine Gail. I didn't think she had anything to do with it, other than finding the body. Auntie's house was always filled with people, traipsing through for one of her businesses or the other.

I played doctor to Josephine Gail without asking her anything that pertained to the murder, only questions that could have been found on any medical records form. I prescribed her something to help her sleep and was about to head to the drugstore to get it when Auntie dismissed it with the familiar wave of her hand and cooked her up another cup of brew instead. We ate dinner in silence, and even though Auntie seemed not to be speaking to me and never needed any help cleaning, I started on the dishes while she put up the leftover food.

My hands in soapy water, I heard a knock on the back door before it swung open.

"Babet," Rhett said stepping inside. "The guys just wanted to say goodnight."

"You all finished?" Auntie asked as two more people stepped through the door.

"Yep. For the night," he said.

"Hi Romaine," one of the men said, his face lighting up. "I didn't know Babet was bringing you back with her."

"She's here to stay," Auntie said.

"No, I'm not," I said and then smiled. "Good to see you, Spoon."

"You remember him, Romaine?" Auntie asked in spite of me just calling him by name. "He's Flannery's husband."

Dexter "Spoon" Poole was thin with a large, oblong head earning him his nickname. His skin was tanned and leathery-looking, he had strawberry blond hair and a scraggly beard. His wife, Flannery, was the closest thing that we had to a beauty queen in Roble. She had black hair and emerald green eyes. Even now in her late fifties, her beauty had endured as she aged and still gleaned envy and admiration. One of the women in Auntie's many clubs, Flannery, other than marrying Spoon, hadn't done much else.

I had always looked at her with wonderment. Why would someone so beautiful not want to leave to see what the world could offer her? Her not wanting to venture out and share what she had with more than her neighbors had fortified in me a desire to go.

"Is that my only claim to fame?" Spoon looked at Auntie Zanne. He had a scratchy voice and spoke in low tones. "That I married Flannery."

"That, I'd say, is a feat, Spoon," Auntie Zanne said. "She was the prettiest girl in East Texas. How you managed to snatch her up, I don't know. You sure I never fixed you a love potion?"

"Never did. It was all me. And my charm," he said with a grin.

"Of course I remember Spoon," I said. "And not just because he's Flannery's husband."

I said it, but I didn't mean it. Those were the only memories I could conjure of him, him being with her.

"So, what are you guys finished with?" I asked.

"We were rehearsing," Rhett said.

"Rehearsing?" I repeated.

"I'm Gus." A burly guy spoke up and stuck out his hand. "No one's going to introduce me to this pretty lady?" He had long hair, a round fat face, rosy cheeks and two chins.

"She's not just a pretty lady," Auntie said. "She's my niece. Don't you see the resemblance?" She came and put her five-foot three frame next to my five-foot eight one and produced a big grin. "Smile."

So I did.

"Spitting image," Rhett offered with a chuckle.

"Gus lives out on Josephine Gail's property," Auntie said. "He plays the Cajun fiddle, Romaine." I could see the little mischievous sparkle in her eyes. "He's pretty good," she said.

"Thanks, Babet. I try," Gus said.

"He made his fiddle," Rhett said. "I think that's pretty impressive."

"You did?" Auntie said. "I didn't know that. Might have to hire you to do some carpentry around here."

"Hey, what can I say," Gus said. "I'm good at working with my hands. Just give me a call."

"You playing your fiddle at the festival?" I asked.

"Nope," he said. "I save her just for me. Got a store-bought one for when I play gigs."

"Maybe you could make another one," Auntie said. "I might want to give one as a Christmas present come December."

"Auntie," I said, warning her. I could tell she was ready to spill the beans.

"So, what do you play, Spoon?" I asked.

"He's our drummer," Rhett offered.

"Oh. Okay," I said.

"You guys want something to eat?" Auntie said. "I was just putting it up. We've got plenty left. Romaine eats like a bird."

"If you don't mind," Gus said.

I could tell by his size he liked to eat.

"I'm always in for some of your cooking," Spoon added.

"Well, I'm going to head upstairs," I said. "Get out of your way."

"You're not in our way," Gus said. "We don't want to put you out."

"You're not," I said. "It's just been a long day."

"A *very* long day," Auntie agreed.

J.R. followed me up to my childhood bedroom. It had been a long week and I was dead tired. No pun intended. Throwing parties, moving, riding for nearly a whole day on a train, and coming to Roble to find a dead squatter in one of the viewing rooms that I ended up partially examining was enough to make me sleep through the next few days.

I found my room just as I had left it eighteen years ago. I hadn't minded it looking like it did when I was only visiting because I knew I wouldn't have to tolerate it long before I'd be back in my own grown up apartment. But with this visit having no definite end in sight, the room made me queasy. Posters of the Eiffel Tower, Arc de Triomphe, and Prince—places and people I'd hankered for then— now represented a long ago fulfilled reality. I glanced around the room.

It was a large bedroom, big windows, and a nice-sized sitting room attached. Everything in both rooms was some shade of purple, fluffy, and cheap. I had over the years become decidedly more upscale and, I'd like to think, classy. I didn't want to start backsliding.

I hoped to God it wasn't that I was looking down my nose at Auntie, her friends or her way of life. But it just wasn't for me. Not anymore.

That wasn't bad to say, was it?

The room had been dusted, my desk was neat, and the bed had fresh linens. It looked as if I had left this morning.

"Has Auntie been washing my clothes again?" I asked J.R. He tilted his head and let out a bark. "Figures," I said. "I haven't been here in two years, and for some reason she thinks she needs to keep everything clean and ready for me."

My auntie rewashed my clothes, folded them, put them in the dresser drawers, and then changed the bed sheets at least once a month. Every time I'd come home to visit, I would take some of my clothes and give them to Goodwill. Somehow, she'd still found enough of them to keep my drawers full.

I opened the dresser drawer and I could smell the Downy scent as it wafted out. I reached in and pulled out a pair of underwear I didn't recognize.

"J.R.," I turned to my dog, the black lacey thongs dangling from my finger, "does she go out and buy things to keep in here?"

He tilted his head the other way, his tongue hanging out.

He didn't have a clue what she was up to either.

I pushed the lacey bottoms back down in the drawer and plopped down on the bed. I pushed my bags that Rhett had brought up earlier out of the way.

Glancing around the room, I knew I couldn't stay. I wasn't this person anymore and I didn't want any semblance of that old life seeping into me while I slept.

"C'mon, J.R.," I said and sprang off the bed. "We're going to find somewhere else to sleep." I plucked a pair of pajamas out of the top drawer and pulled the comforter off the bed, causing my luggage to topple over. I balled the comforter up in my arms, snatched a pillow up and headed downstairs.

I was going to sleep on the main floor. Yes, there were dead bodies everywhere, but I didn't care. Unlike with Auntie Zanne, they kept quiet around me. Right now, I needed something that didn't scream out reminders of how badly my life was falling apart.

Yep, I'd feel more comfortable among the dearly departed. After all, the dead were my life–I grew up in a funeral home, I studied thanatology in school, had trained as a medical examiner to investigate it, and I had been christened by the Holy Roman Catholic Church in death by virtue of my name.

The actual translation of Romaine Gabriela Sadie Heloise

Wilder, the moniker given to me by my dear parents was in fact, "Dead Family Name – Dead Aunt – Dead Grandma – Dead Grandma – Wilder."

Death was my legacy.

Chapter Seven

No morning sun came streaming through the thick velvet burgundy drapes that hung on the windows of the funeral parlor. It didn't matter though. I couldn't sleep any longer.

I glanced at the time on my cell phone. Six thirty. A guttural groan gurgled out as I pulled one leg off the back of the couch where I must have thrown it in my night of fitful sleep. Untangling myself from the cover, I tried to sit up but fell right back down.

"*Ugh!*"

No. I didn't mind sleeping with dead people, but my body rebelled against sleeping on a sofa. Especially one that was shorter than I was. My body too spoiled for anything but my Tempur-Pedic Cloud Supreme memory foam mattress. I got up, supporting my aching back with my hand. I grabbed my cell phone and, stepping over J.R., moseyed into the kitchen. I could hear the water running and my auntie scrubbing away at something even at this early hour.

Eyes half open, "I need coffee," came from the back of my scratchy throat.

"I've got tea," she said. "I can brew you up a nice cup with a little something in it that'll make you attract men like flowers attract bees." I saw her grab a teapot through the slit of my droopy eyelids. "Find you a man down here that ain't married," she continued. "My plan is to put you on a steady diet of it, that way I'll kill two birds with one stone—get you to move back home with me permanently and get me a couple of grandkids."

I opened one eye and looked at her. She winked at me.

Even though she'd exchanged Mass for a two-hour sermon at the Baptist church, and speaking French for a Southern drawl, it didn't stop her from cooking up her "potions and brews." She swore by them, claiming she could cure whatever ailed a person, bring them true love, or drive away a cheating spouse. A horticulturist, she kept the tools of her trade in her backyard greenhouse. I never let her put any of that stuff in me, though. I bought everything I needed when I was ill at the town drugstore, and just let fate and flirting guide my love life.

"Maybe," I said, dragging my words out, "I'll just go down to the Momma Della's and get me a cup."

"I love Momma Della, but that coffee at her diner will make you sicker than a coon dog that tried to tangle with a rabid rabbit." She filled up the teapot at the sink and put it on the stove. "Plus, I was hoping you'd take a ride with me this morning. I may need that forensic eye of yours," Auntie Zanne said. "I've got an idea of who the murderer is."

"I've made my contribution," I said, and started rummaging through the cabinets with my one opened eye looking for a shot of caffeine. "And I don't think anything to do with that dead man is any of your business."

"Death *is* my business," she said. "And yours, too." She filled up a steeper with leaves she pulled from a canister and stuck it down in a cup.

"I'm done with it," I said.

"Okay," she said, drawing out the words. "I'll just have to go it alone, if you don't wanna help me."

I closed the cabinet door. "Nope. I don't wanna help you."

"Suit yourself," she said in a huff. "I'll pack my gun and go to Julep's by myself."

My other eye popped open. "My aunt, Julep?"

"One and the same."

"Julep Folsom?" I said in disbelief. I plopped down in a chair.

"How many Juleps do you know?" she said, setting the cup with the steeper in front of me.

"Pogue's mother?"

"Jesus, child. Yes. Your aunt, Julep. Pogue's momma, Julep. Julep Folsom. How many ways do I need to tell you?"

"And you're taking a gun?"

"I am."

"For what?"

"I may have to use it." She gave a firm nod. She leaned back on the counter and crossed her legs. "You never know what bag she might be coming out of. I may need it to protect myself." She put the teapot back on the stove.

"Protect yourself from what?"

"Your Aunt Julep has pulled that rifle of hers on me more than once, you know. Plus, now we know she's committed murder." Auntie Zanne pointed toward the backstairs. "She's a hardened criminal. I might have to stop her from making a run for it." She nodded the resolution.

Julep Folsom was my paternal aunt. She was my father's only sister, and the only sibling left. She had fought hard with my Auntie Zanne for custody of me after my parents died, and even though I had long since been past the age of maturity, they were still feuding.

But I knew she hadn't killed anyone.

Aunt Julep and Auntie Zanne hadn't always been the archrivals she was professing they were today. It was because of Auntie Zanne and her husband that my Aunt Julep and Uncle George moved to Roble to start a funeral home of their own in the first place. Auntie Zanne had helped them find the house she still used and got them both a funeral license. But things started to turn for them after my parents died. Aunt Julep didn't like that I'd ended up with Auntie Zanne, she wanted to raise me herself. I was, as she so often said, the only Wilder left. And then there were the funeral homes...

Auntie picked up the whistling teapot and poured the hot water in the cup she'd set in front of me. "Why would you think

Aunt Julep had anything to do with that man's death? She didn't have any reason to kill him."

"You don't know that," Auntie Zanne said, her eyes wide as saucers. She sat the teapot down and put her hands on her hips. "How in the world could you say that? You haven't been here in years."

I pushed the cup of "tea" she had fixed for me away and folded my arms on the table in front of me. "Two," I said.

"What?"

"I haven't been here in two years."

"Right. See. So you don't know if she had a reason to kill anyone or not. Especially since you don't know who he is. He might've been one of her unsatisfied customers that she snuffed out to keep quiet."

"Snuffed out?" I frowned at her choice of words.

"Her funeral home, Garden of the Dead, ain't doing so well over there," Auntie Zanne said.

"Garden Grove. You know her funeral home is called Garden Grove."

She waved her hand at me. "That woman is jealous of me and my booming business. Always has been. I get four or five bodies a week from all over East Texas. She's lucky if she bags four a month! She'd go to any length to put me out of business and keep that bad reputation she's got under wraps."

"And that's what gave you the idea that Aunt Julep killed that man?"

"I didn't come up with it on my own," she said and nodded. "That's what that man told me."

"That man? What man?" I frowned. "The dead man?"

"Yes." She snorted. "Whaddaya think? I been hearing voices in my head? I ain't crazy. You know they talk to me."

"The dead man told you that Aunt Julep killed him?"

"He was practically shouting it. Didn't you hear him?"

"Uh. No. Can't say that I did. What exactly did you hear him say, Auntie?"

"He said, 'I have formaldehyde in me!'" She made her voice sound as if she was yelling from the bottom of a well. "Surely if you didn't hear him say it, you had to have smelled it."

"I did smell it," I said.

"So. There you have it," she said.

"Have what?"

"Julep Folsom's Sickly Grove Funeral Home is the only funeral home for miles around that still uses formaldehyde. *Ipso facto,* she killed him."

"Garden Grove," I said. I didn't know why I continued to correct her, she'd been giving it her own name for years. "So, no one else around here uses formaldehyde in their embalming fluid?"

"You got cotton in your ears this morning, Sugarplum? Because you can't seem to hear a word I say." She walked over to the counter, picked up a folded newspaper, and threw it on the table in front of me. "Look at that newspaper article." Auntie Zanne jabbed the paper with her finger. "It says that they're arresting Josephine Gail for the murder of that man and that my funeral home is under investigation as a den of criminal activity and will be shut down indefinitely. That's exactly what Julep Folsom wanted to happen."

I read the article. It was a one-paragraph blurb that stated, "Josephine Gail Cox of Sabine County found an unidentified body at Ball Funeral Home yesterday. At this time, the cause of death is unknown."

I pointed to the article. "This doesn't say anything like what you just said."

"You better believe that when people read it, that's what they'll see. They'll think that my business is doing so well because I let murderers dispose of their bodies here. Your cousin, the sheriff, is going to put Josephine Gail in jail and run me out of business all to save his momma."

"I think you're getting all worked up over nothing, Auntie. I'm sure Pogue will get this figured out."

"Get what figured out?" An extremely tall, particularly thin woman walked into the kitchen. She was dressed in a plaid blouse that was buttoned all the way to the top and had a bolo tie tucked under the collar. The shirt was tucked tightly into a black pencil skirt. She wore flat black pumps that looked like they must have been a size eleven. "I've always been told that I don't have a head for figuring," she said. "So, I'm hoping y'all are not talking about me."

She sat down several bags in the kitchen chair and let out a sigh. "Morning," she said.

"Oh Lord, forgive me," Auntie Zanne said. "I forgot all about you coming in this morning." She turned the eye off under the pot she had on the stove.

"It's okay," she said. "I heard voices and just followed them back. I knew it had to be the living back here conversing."

"Yes," Auntie said. "This is where the living hang out." She smiled and walked over to the woman. "First. Welcome. And second. No, we weren't talking about you."

"Well, glad to hear it. And forgot about me? Ha! I'd like to see that happen. I don't think you could. I've been told I'm unforgettable," she said. "And you know why I'm unforgettable?" She didn't give us time to answer. "Because I'm different. My Aunt Bert said if you act different and think different from everyone else, you'll be unforgettable. So that's what I do." She turned and gave me an exaggerated wink, and a big smile that revealed large horse-like teeth.

It made me wince.

"Romaine, this is Floneva Floyd," Auntie Zanne said. "She's my new office manager slash receptionist."

"Floneva," I said. "That's an interesting name. Don't think I've ever heard that one before."

"Thank you," she said a big grin spreading across her face. "Don't believe I've ever heard of yours neither. Leastways on a girl."

I wasn't quite sure how to take that.

"And Floneva," Auntie continued her introduction, "this is my niece, Dr. Romaine Wilder."

"Doctor!" Floneva said. "Are you a real doctor?"

I guessed she meant as opposed to an imaginary one...

"Yes, I am," I said.

"Howdy!" She stuck out a big hand with very long fingers.

"Hello," I said and timidly extended my hand. I was nervous about her having a tight grip and crushing the bones in my hand with one squeeze.

"So where do you want me?" she asked Auntie Zanne.

"You are really early," my auntie said and glanced up at the wall clock.

"I always say if you lose an hour in the morning, you'll hunt for it all day."

Auntie and I looked at each other.

"Well, that answers that," Auntie Zanne said and bugged her eyes at me. "You'll be in that area up front where I showed you the other week. Come. I'll show you." Auntie grabbed a tea towel and wiped her hands.

Floneva signaled "stop" with her hand. "No need. My aunt said excelling in your job is a do-it-yourself project. I can find my own way." She patted her head of all-white hair. "You showed me once, you don't need to show me again."

"Was that your Aunt Bert who said that?" I asked, wondering if we were going to hear a lot about the woman.

"No. That was Aunt Geneva who said that. Aunt Bert's sister. She lived in Sunrise. I'd go there every summer to visit her. And she'd come to Hemphill to visit us." She gathered up her bags and headed out of the kitchen. "I am ready to greet the dead. Hello," she called out as she walked down the hallway. "I have arrived."

"Looks like Ball Funeral Home's dearly departed will have another person, other than you, to talk to," I said.

"She seemed much quieter at the interview," Auntie said thoughtfully. She turned the fire back on under her pot. "Not quite the character that appeared here today."

"Everyone has their strengths," I said. "Maybe her little quips might ameliorate the nervousness of people coming in."

"I'm not sure if that's one of her strengths. It makes her seem wacky. Not a good attribute for the receptionist of a funeral home. And Pogue's strengths don't include a sharp mind–something important for a sheriff to have."

Wow, I thought. She turned that conversation right back around.

"There's nothing wrong with Pogue's brain," I said.

"That boy ain't got the sense God gave a mule, bless his heart. He is all day stupid, and you know it."

Pogue, as a child, was a bit slow and he had such a huge head that it was easy for people to make fun. And to make matters worse, he'd fall over by just moving it away from center mass–all it took was a slight lean and he'd go tumbling. Auntie Zanne was always trying to get Aunt Julep to take him to a specialist in Houston because she swore it was filled with lead.

Pogue didn't do anything to discount Auntie's supposition, either. He'd do one dumb thing after another. And, she'd say, when you try to tell him right, he'd start crying. Auntie said he cried more than it rained in South America.

Pogue must've have gotten his head stuck between the spindles of the banister on the back steps inside our house ten times, and each time he'd drop those big old crocodile tears until somebody came to get him out.

"Why does he keep doing that?" Auntie Zanne would screech, her eyes big. "Is he thinking that maybe the space between there is getting wider? Because, I swear his head ain't getting no smaller!" She'd send him home and tell my Aunt Julep, "The only way we're gonna get him to stop putting that big ole noggin through holes in the banister is to cut it off!"

By the time Pogue got to high school, his body had caught up with his head, all his tears had dried up, and he was a changed person. He made valedictorian of his class and got a scholarship to college. But by then, Auntie Zanne had stopped paying attention to him. She didn't know the man he'd grown to be.

"No, I don't know it," I said. "And I think he can be a good sheriff and get this thing solved."

She waved a hand at me. "Oh phooey! Pogue can't find his way out of cardboard box. How is he gonna solve a murder?" she said. "And with his mother the number one suspect," Auntie Zanne continued, "he'll want to dump this whole thing on somebody else."

"Aunt Julep is not the number one suspect," I said.

"Yes, she is," Auntie said. "And I can't abide by him throwing Josephine Gail or my business under the bus. I won't sit around and watch that happen." She looked at me. "You should be worried about this, too. This place is your legacy. You are gonna inherit it one day. Carry on our family business."

"No thank you," I said. "I plan on retiring from the practice of medicine and ending up on a sandy beach hundreds of miles away from here."

"Morning, ladies." Pogue walked into the kitchen, pulling his hat off of his head.

"Well, look what the cat dragged in." Auntie crossed her arms across her torso. "Why are you darkening our doorstep so early in the morning?" Auntie asked, not even giving a second thought as to whether Pogue had heard her speaking ill about his mother. "You here to arrest somebody?"

"No, Babet I'm not," he said. "I'm here because it seems old Doc Westin woke up not feeling so good. He wants Romaine to do the autopsy on the John Doe."

Chapter Eight

"Oh, good," Auntie Zanne said as she clapped her hands together. "I want to know exactly what happened. We can get started as soon as I'm finished here." She pointed to the kitchen counter where she had a bundle of flowers, herbs and a mortar and pestle. "I've got a client. Little bitty thing, cute as a button. But she thinks her husband's cheating on her. If I were her, I'd get a new lock instead of some of my staying tea. He wouldn't be staying with me in my house or my bedroom. Then I've got two funerals this morning, and a club meeting, but I've got time -"

"I don't think Pogue meant for 'us' to do it," I said, interrupting the recital of her day's itinerary. I looked to Pogue to back me up. Standing tall in his uniform, freshly pressed and creased brown pants, his tan-colored short sleeve shirt, even if he felt he was on uneven footing heading a murder investigation, he looked the part.

"I didn't," Pogue said and pulled a chair out from under the kitchen table and sat down. "Just Romie." He leaned forward, resting his elbows on his knees and twisted his hat around in his hands. "She's the one with the medical degree."

After yesterday's debacle, I could see that it was getting harder for him to stand his ground with Auntie.

"Hogwash." Auntie Zanne waved her hand. "I'm the one with the funeral license. Somebody embalmed that man, and now, once she's done, he's going to have to be readied for burial properly. She," her finger pointing at me, "can't do that."

"And you can't perform an autopsy," Pogue said. "I've got a murder here that I need forensic information on."

"Like you know what to do with it," Auntie said.

"It's true." He closed his eyes and took in a breath. "I've never investigated a murder before. But I don't plan on messing this one up." He turned to me. "You think you can get it done today?"

I nodded. "I can. I should have something for you by mid-morning." I pulled out a chair, sat across from him and smiled.

"Before you get started on that autopsy..." Auntie Zanne said. Eyeing Pogue, she spoke to me. "I need to talk to you about the help I need on the festival. I've got a folder of stuff for you to go over and familiarize yourself with."

"Help from me?" I asked. "A folder full of stuff?"

"Yes, from you," she said. "Yes, a folder full of stuff. You promised before we left Chicago."

"I don't remember me promising anything," I said.

"Well, I do."

"Isn't it something that Floneva could do?" I said.

"Who?"

"Your new office manager slash receptionist," I said.

"Oh Lord, I forgot about her again. I probably should go and check on her." She seemed to be talking to herself, but then looked up at me. "She can't help me, though," she said, dismissing my suggestion.

"Why can't she help you?" I asked.

"You said it. She's new. Doesn't know a thing about what going on around here, or how I want the Crawfish Boil to be."

"Neither do I," I said.

"She'll get it all messed up."

"You're letting her run your funeral home without any instruction."

"Oh, hogwash. We're not even open yet. And you heard her, she wanted to go and talk to our dead guests. They can keep her busy until I can get to her." she said. "Don't you try and wiggle out of this. You promised."

"Can't what you need her for wait?" Pogue asked. "I need her now for the autopsy."

"That body isn't going anywhere," Auntie Zanne said.

"Yeah, but I need some answers so I can figure this thing out." Pogue stood up. "This is a murder investigation. I'd say that's bigger than a festival."

"I wouldn't say that," Auntie Zanne said. "And it seems to me that you think you have it figured out." She planted her hands on her hips.

"I never said I had anything figured out," Pogue said. "Josephine Gail is just a person of interest. She has information I need." He put his head down and muttered, "And if I could speak with her..."

"A person of interest," she clucked. "All she did was find a body. What?" She held up her arms. "You can't report a body now?"

Pogue looked exasperated. "Of course you can. And she's not the only one I need to talk to. I'll have to talk to Rhett." He swallowed, his mind churning. "And probably your new receptionist."

"Floneva?" Auntie asked. "About what?"

"About her whereabouts."

"Her 'whereabouts' was not here. I only hired her the week before I left, and this morning was her first day back here."

"You never know who might have information," Pogue said.

"Pshaw," Auntie said, dismissing his reasoning.

"Somebody's got to know how a body could get in here without anyone seeing it. I mean, how come only Josephine Gail noticed it? Lots of stuff I could ask."

"Stuff," she huffed. "The murderer snuck it in here. It should be easy to see he's quite the criminal. I mean look at him, he committed murder."

"You don't know it's a 'he,' Babet," Pogue said. "Could've been a woman."

"Don't I know it," she said and gave him a look.

"Look, Babet -"

"Watch your mouth," she said. "Don't say 'look' to me."

"I'm just saying, you know they say if a homicide isn't solved in the first forty-eight hours, it gets almost impossible to do."

"Pogue, that's TV. And it's already been forty-eight hours."

"How you figure?" he said, I could hear the defeat building up in his voice.

"We got those bodies from Hollarbach over a week ago," Auntie Zanne said.

"We don't know if it came in with the bodies, although I will go over and speak with them, too."

"Well, how else would it have gotten here?" Auntie threw a tea towel over her shoulder and leaned against the counter. "It couldn't have just walked through the doors."

"I'm not speculating that it did," Pogue said. "But I need answers to do this."

"Don't worry, Pogue," I said. I had let them go back and forth long enough. "I'll look into that for you. You'll have more to go on once I've done the autopsy."

"I could probably figure it out before he does," Auntie said.

"Don't go poking your nose in it," Pogue said. "This is my job."

She waved her hand at him, stood up straight and went back to stirring her pot on the stove. "I've got a list of things on my desk for you to do for me, Romaine," Auntie Zanne said over her shoulder getting back to festival business. "Won't take too long for you to do." She glanced over at Pogue. "And you can do them after you do that autopsy."

"See?" I said to Pogue. "Auntie understands priorities." I hoped she caught my sarcasm.

"And I need you to talk to Rhett," she said. "Afterwards, too."

"About what?" I asked.

"He's in charge of the zydeco band for the festival."

I eyed her. "And what do you think I'm going to do?"

"I don't know," she said and shrugged. "Whatever he asks you to do. He's my help and I need you to help him."

"All that medical training," Pogue said moving his head slowly from side to side. "And you end up being the assistant to the assistant to the chair of the Committee for the Annual Crawfish Boil and Music Festival."

Chapter Nine

A *rat-a-tat-tat* came from the back door. Pogue had just left out through the front, probably more nervous after his talk with my auntie than he had been when he walked in the door. None of it fazed her. She'd taken a cup of whatever she'd had boiling on the stove—the "staying" brew I'd thought she was making for her client and her husband— to Josephine Gail.

Maybe Auntie was thinking that her concoction would help Josephine Gail to stay out of jail.

There was a man standing there. I pushed on the screen to the back door and held it open with my hand, revealing a beautiful sunny morning. Clear blue skies, not a cloud to be found. I took in a whiff of air and thought perhaps, now that I was going to do that autopsy, maybe it would turn out to be a good day.

"Hi, Catfish," I said.

"Hi," he said, then I saw a twinkle spark in his almost hidden eyes. He pushed his hat up on his head. "Romie?"

"Yep," I said. I smoothed down my hair and ran my hand over my face. Did I look that different? "Are you telling me that you don't recognize me? It's only been a couple of years since you've seen me."

"Of course I do," he said and yanked on his green bucket hat, taking it off and scrunching it between his hands. He lowered his head, shuffled his feet and that old familiar grin spread across his face. "I just didn't know you were here." He peeked inside the door. "Babet didn't tell me."

Catfish's brown hair was cut close, neatly lined, and a stubbly five o'clock shadow made out his jawline, even though it was early morning. He had hazel eyes and caramel-colored skin. Not as rugged or crease-filled as one would think for a man who spent so much time outside.

Catfish owned property in the pinelands close to the Sabine River. He fished, hunted, and farmed. During the summer when I was twelve, after I first arrived in Roble, he appointed himself my guardian, even over Pogue. Not letting any of the kids tease me about being the uppity black girl who thought she was French.

When I first got to Roble, being sad was my go-to disposition, and with constantly being teased, it morphed into a stubborn streak. Catfish just seemed to understand me, and not hold any of it against me no matter what I did.

And stick by me he did. He'd walk me to school and back, take me on hikes in the forested land on the perimeter of his family's property, and he taught me how to wade through the shallow waters of the Sabine River to catch crawfish with my hands.

"I knew you'd see her when you brought over my crawfish." Auntie Zanne came walking back into the kitchen and over to the door. She pushed past me. "Do you have what I asked you for?" She poked her head outside the door.

"Yes, ma'am. I've got them right here," he said. "Three tubs of 'em, just like you asked for. Had my traps out all night catching 'em." A smile as bright as the sun popped up on his face. "Is Romaine baking her crawfish pies?"

"No," I said, and frowned.

"Yes," Auntie Zanne said at the same time. "And don't worry, she'll be sure to save a couple just for you."

That grin on his face widened, and he tucked his head even more. I peeked outside and saw clear plastic tubs of crawfish. Filled three quarters of the way with water, they were covered with blue lids with holes drilled in them.

"I don't know anything about me supposedly baking crawfish pies," I said.

"You make the best pies, Romaine," Catfish said. "Ain't never tasted none better."

"That's because you think 'ain't nothing better' than Romaine," Auntie quipped. She turned and headed back to the stove to check her brew. "C'mon in Catfish." She spoke over her shoulder. "I got breakfast. You hungry?"

"Yes, ma'am. Sure am. Just let me bring your catch," Catfish said.

"Leave 'em there till you eat," she said. "Then you can store 'em for me until Romaine can start on her pies."

"Yes, ma'am," he said, both he and my auntie seemingly ignoring me telling them I wasn't baking any pies.

"Sit," Auntie said and pointed to a kitchen chair, then looked at me. "You too."

He did as he was told. So did I.

I moved my cell phone over and folded my arms on the table.

"How about some eggs and grits?" she said.

"That'll be fine," Catfish said.

"Good," she said. "I've already got the grits cooking. They should be just about done."

"You got any bacon?" he asked.

"I do." She went to the fridge and grabbed what she needed. "And I've got just enough time to get the two of you something to eat, talk to Floneva about today's services, and check on Josephine Gail before I have to go to my Red Hat Society meeting at the Grandview over in Yellowpine."

"Something wrong with Josephine Gail?' Catfish asked.

"Red Hat meeting?" I interrupted. "They aren't really meetings, are they? They're just social gatherings."

"Yes," Auntie said as she laid the bacon into the cast-iron skillet. "I need the distraction. And social gatherings are how I keep up with all the skinny."

"Skinny?" I asked.

Catfish laughed. "She means gossip," he said.

"I know what she means," I said. "And I see that nothing has changed around here."

"I need to keep up with the goings on around here. It's an important part of my business."

"By 'it' you mean gossip?"

"It's information about the citizens in my community," she said.

"You don't live in Yellowpine," I said. "That's not your community."

"My community is all of East Texas." She spread out her arms to show the vastness of her reach.

Catfish started laughing.

"So, you're going out to keep up with the gossip about all of East Texas," I said, "and I'm supposed to stay here and make phone calls about the festival for you today?"

"You promised you'd help."

"You keep saying that, but I don't remember promising that."

"See how big-city living can corrupt your mind, Catfish?" Auntie Zanne said and cracked an egg into a bowl, then picked up another. "She can't remember anything."

"I'm sure she's not that forgetful," Catfish said. "And I'm sure she doesn't mind helping, either."

"You are a ray of sunshine, Catfish," Auntie Zanne said. "Always looking on the bright side of things. But even with your optimism, things aren't looking so good around here."

"What's going on?" he asked.

"Josephine Gail found a dead body that didn't belong here while I was in Chicago with Romaine." Auntie took a fork and flipped over the sizzling strips of meat. "The man had been murdered and dropped off."

"Oh, wow," he said.

"'Wow' doesn't begin to cover it," Auntie said.

"You didn't hear about it?" I asked.

"It happened yesterday," Auntie said. "Found out about it as soon as we got back."

"No. Didn't hear anything about it," Catfish said. "After rehearsal I was out catching crawfish for you. And I don't read the newspaper. Too much bad going on."

"It was a shocker," Auntie said.

"How did it happen?" he asked.

"We don't know," I said.

"But we've got ideas," Auntie Zanne said. She added some salt and pepper to the bowl and started beating the eggs. "Although what I think don't match what Pogue thinks."

"I don't have any thoughts," I said. "It's not my job. I find out the cause and manner of death and pass it on to law enforcement."

"That's what you did in Chicago," Auntie Zanne said.

"That's what I'm going to do here, too," I said.

"I can't remember there ever being a murder around these parts," Catfish said. "Plenty of accidents, but nothing intentional."

"Well, there's a first time for everything, and it's just Ball Funeral Home's luck that we are the ones all tangled up in the mess," Auntie said. She poured the eggs into a skillet she'd melted butter in. "And now we've got to try and get it untangled."

"Pogue will get it untangled," I said, correcting her. I turned to Catfish. "Auntie Zanne is supposed to stay out of it."

"Can you believe what she just said?" Auntie turned from the stove and spoke to Catfish. "How can I do that when Josephine Gail is involved?" she said. She grabbed some plates out of the cabinet. "She's my oldest and dearest friend." She put food on two of the plates. "And my business partner."

I wanted to object to the business partner part of her description because technically Josephine Gail wasn't a part of the funeral home ownership. But I didn't want to say anything bad about her "oldest and dearest" friend. It would just upset my auntie even more, and probably encourage her to dig that little upturned nose of hers in even deeper.

Auntie put the plates in front of us. "Eat up," she said.

"I'm sorry, Babet," Crawfish said, "about Josephine Gail

having to go through that trauma."

"Me too. And she's not taking it well at all. I've got to keep my eye on her, make sure she doesn't fall apart before this thing can get figured out." She made a third plate. "I doubt if she'll eat any of this," she muttered and headed down the hallway.

"You came back to a lot of excitement," Catfish said and shoveled in a mouthful of eggs.

"Anytime was a bad time to come back," I said.

"I'm happy to see you."

"Thank you," I said. "It's good to see you too."

"So, you working here in the funeral home now?" Catfish asked.

"No."

"You're not back to stay?" Catfish said. "If you don't mind me asking. Babet sure is acting like it."

"I don't mind you asking," I said. "I sure she wants me to, I'm not here to stay."

Auntie Zanne came back into the room. "Are you two still sitting here?" she asked.

I took a bite of my bacon. "We were eating the breakfast you made for us."

"Well, by the time you get through with it, it'll be lunchtime. Don't you have something to do?" she said and looked at me.

"I need Rhett," I said. "To help me with the body."

"Rhett's gone to gas up the car. We have two funerals this morning, and he has a family to pick up at nine."

"I can help you," Catfish said. "Whatever it is you're going to do. I know you said you weren't working at the funeral home."

"No, I'm not. I'm just helping my cousin out."

"Pogue?"

"Yes. Pogue."

"She's going to autopsy that body I told you about," Auntie Zanne said. "If she ever gets started."

"Like I said," Catfish said. He pushed his plate back. "I'll help you. I still help around here all the time." He turned toward Auntie

Zanne. "Babet knows she can call me anytime."

"You're not running for office, Catfish," Auntie Zanne said. "She doesn't need to know your credentials. And you should have done a better job helping out while I was gone. Maybe we wouldn't have an uninvited dead body to tend to."

"Auntie," I said. "You can't put that on Catfish."

"I'm just saying," she said.

"It's okay," Catfish said and let out an embarrassed chuckle. "She's right. I guess I could have come by more often. But I'm here now."

"Good. So now you've got help, Romaine," Auntie said.

"How about first I show Catfish where you want to store the crawfish," I said.

"How about if you get to your autopsy?" Auntie Zanne said.

"How about if I do both?"

"I'm going to have him put them in the pantry. Don't need a road map or a tour guide for that. They'll keep fine in there until you can bake the pies."

"I'm not baking pies," I said.

She swung open the pantry door. "In here," she said. "Make them easy access for Romaine."

"I'm not baking pies," I said.

"I'll get the crawfish," Catfish said.

"I'll get the door for you," I said. I swung open the screen and held it for him. When he squeezed by me, I leaned in and whispered, "I'm not baking pies."

He started laughing as he reached down for a tub and heaved it up, his muscles bulging as he lifted the water-filled receptacle brimming full with the little red mudbugs.

"Thank you," he said, that familiar smile on his face as he slid by me.

"No problem," I said. "I'll wait for you to get the other two."

"Auntie," I said as I stood at the back door waiting for Catfish. "Where's that old camera of yours?"

"Same place it's always been." She nodded her head. "Down in the Preparation Room. I still take pictures of all my clients."

"Good," I said as Catfish made his way for the second load. "I'd like to take pictures as part of the autopsy."

"If you ever get started." She turned and looked at me. "And make sure you talk to him," Auntie said. "It's important to speak to the dead."

"Thanks for reminding me," I said. I walked over from the door and grabbed my phone off the kitchen table. "I have an audio app." I waved the phone at her then stuck it in my back pocket. "I can use it to record. Then I'll type up the report for Pogue, so he'll have the info he needs to get started on his investigation."

Catfish came out of the pantry and went back for the third tub. I picked up our breakfast plates and put them in the sink, then went to hold the screen door open. After he got them in the pantry, we went back to the table and started to sit down.

"Bup, bup, bup, bup," Auntie said. "Don't sit down. You've got work to do." She moved her hands up, gesturing for us to stand.

"Okay. You ready, Catfish?"

A big grin spread across his face. "Whenever you are," he said.

"Well. C'mon. Let's go do this."

Chapter Ten

I ran upstairs, brushed my teeth, threw some clothes on and got the charger for my phone. Autopsies can take anywhere for two to four hours and I didn't need my battery running out in the middle of me trying to record my findings. Catfish waited for me, unwearyingly, at the bottom of the steps and smiled as I came back down like I was waltzing down the staircase in a prom gown and he was my date.

I smiled back.

Catfish's patience, even when we were as young as thirteen, had always been unwavering when it came to me. I remember he had to tell me several times while we were out fishing to be careful not to slip on the rocks.

"I know," I had said.

"Let me help you," he said and reached out to grab me.

"I got this. I can do it myself," I told him and eyed him letting him know not to do anything to help.

He stood patiently by and watched as I splashed about, crawfish slipping through my fingers, not getting a one and finally falling and bashing my knee on the sharp rocks.

I remember Catfish didn't say a word, knowing I was too embarrassed to want his help, and him not wanting to ever say, "I told you so." Instead, he waited until I composed myself and stood up. "I'll always be here for you, Romie," he had said. "Just say the word. I'll be there whenever you need me." Then he smiled and took me home so Auntie Zanne could bandage my knee.

As I reached the bottom of the steps, I grabbed his shirt and tugged him along behind me. We swung by Auntie's office where I picked up an inkpad, then we took the steps downstairs. Ornately carved oak banisters and curved staircase with an old-style tapestry runner was the entryway for grieving families to view their loved ones before the services. It was also the way to the Preparation Room.

Once there, I glanced around. I hadn't been down there in years and Auntie Zanne was right, her business was booming. And from the looks of things, she had invested wisely in upgrading her business.

There were six embalming stations, which I'm sure was overkill. Auntie was all Texas, though, so "go big" was how she did everything. The room was stainless steel, wood and granite. The floor and walls were white and there were bright, square-shaped, flush-mount ceiling lights. It reminded me of being back at the hospital.

"Which body you doing the autopsy on?" Catfish asked, looking around the room.

"He's in the cooler," I said. I stuck my phone in my capri pants pocket and pushed up my sleeves. "This way."

I opened the door to the cooler, and there he was, still dressed in his suit. Out of the casket, he'd been placed on one of the silver embalming tables, which was good for me.

"Let's pull him out and put him in station number six." I stood at the head and positioned myself to give the table on wheels a push.

"I got him," Catfish said and moved me out the way. "You get your camera."

"Okay," I said. I opened a few cabinets before I found the camera, and when I turned around, Catfish already had the table in position.

"Is this good?" he asked.

"That's perfect," I said. I held my phone and camera in my hand and realized I needed somewhere close by to keep them as I worked. I glanced around the room and spotted, next to one of the preparation tables, a metal stand with rollers filled with Auntie's embalming tools. I walked over and ran my fingers over the shiny instruments. Everything I needed was there. I placed the phone and camera on it and rolled it over to the table that held my John Doe.

He took a step back. "You need me to do anything else?" Catfish asked.

"Just one more thing. Can you help me get him undressed?" I asked. "Or are you squeamish about things like that?"

He vigorously shook his head and stepped forward. "I deal with squeamish all day long. Takes a lot for a fish to calm down after you pull them out of the water." He smiled at me. "Plus, you know I'd help you do whatever you'd want me to do."

"Same old Catfish," I said and smiled. "But before we do that, I want to get pictures of him."

"Like this?" he asked. "Fully dressed?"

"Yeah," I said. "Might be evidence of something."

"What?" He seemed amused.

"You never know," I said. "Something the investigators might need to see to link clues together. Better to have it then not."

"Investigators?" he said. "You mean, Pogue?"

"One and the same."

I snapped a few shots. Clothes. Hands. Head.

I'd already visually examined parts of the squatter for any trauma the first day we'd found him. But today was different. No one standing over me, and the answers to the mystery of this man were left for me to find.

I was excited to get to see the rest of him. "Okay, that should do it for now," I said and set the camera aside. "We've gotta get him undressed, but first," I pointed to the linen rack, "we'll need to dress for it."

I donned a poly laminated protection gown, with elastic cuffs, neck and waist tie, and handed one to Catfish. It had a repellent surface to keep us dry and stain-free. I slipped boot covers on and grabbed two full-face splash shields and showed Catfish how to fasten the adjustable Velcro strap.

"Too much rigor to sit him up. We need to roll him from side to side," I said. "Take his things off one side at a time."

"Okay," he said. "I'll follow your lead."

I pulled one arm out of the sleeve of the loosely fitted suit jacket. Catfish pulled him over and I tucked it under him and walked over to stand next to Catfish. "Now push him the other way."

I grabbed the jacket from underneath where I had tucked it and pulled it toward me. Then eased his other arm out. I folded it over and laid it on the counter.

Catfish swiped his hand across his nose. "What's that smell?"

"Yeah, it did just get stronger didn't it?" I said. "That's formaldehyde."

"Ain't that what they use in embalming fluid?"

"Sure is."

"I've been down here plenty of times when Babet still used formaldehyde," he said. "Never smelled this strong before."

"I guess it's just concentrated," I said. "That's one thing I need to find out about."

"Where would someone get formaldehyde from?" Catfish asked.

"If that isn't the million-dollar question," I said.

"So," he said licking his lips, a confused look on his face, "he was already done up to be buried?"

"Yeah. Looks that way."

"By who?"

"By the killer is my guess," I said. "Not by a funeral home."

"Unless someone at a funeral home is the killer," he said.

That was just what my auntie had been thinking. And she claimed she knew exactly which funeral home it was, too. But I didn't dare say that out loud.

"Now let's get this shirt off of him. We'll do it the same way we did the jacket," I said and walked back around the table. We repeated our actions, but as soon as I pulled his shirtsleeve out and Catfish pulled the body toward him, I saw what had killed him.

"Oh. Look at that," Catfish said looking over from the other side.

There was a slew of entry wounds across the Dead Guy's back.

"I'm going to need pictures of that," I said.

"That was a buckshot that hit him," Catfish said.

Buckshots were shotgun ammunition that housed large metal pellets in the shell. When a shotgun loaded with a buckshot is fired, the encased pellets spread out as they move toward their target.

"And look at this," Catfish said, holding the shirt we'd just taken off of Dead Guy in the air. "That looks like sap." Catfish pointed to a spot on the shirt, his nose so close it was almost inside the wound.

"Don't get so close," I said.

Geesh! I thought. Everyone around here wants to get their noses into everything.

He pulled back. "I wouldn't have," he said. "I know better."

I picked up a cotton-tipped stick from the stand with the instruments and walked around to where he stood. I swabbed the amber liquid he'd identified.

"It does look like the sap from the pines trees in Piney Woods, doesn't it?" I said and twirled the stick around in my hand.

"I'd bet my farm on it," he said.

I took the swab and put it in a plastic baggie I'd gotten from the counter. "What else do you see?" I asked, staring at the shirt. I had been hasty with him before. I knew better than to be like that with Catfish.

He smiled, knowing I was trying to make up. "I think I see some woodchips."

"Yeah. I think I see a few." I picked up tweezers and pulled the sliver of wood from the fibers of the shirt.

"Why would tree sap and wood be all over the back of this shirt?" he asked.

"Don't know, but I told you it was good to take pictures of the clothes." I grabbed the camera and took a few shots.

"You were right," he said.

I took the shirt and placed it in a brown paper bag. "Pogue can send this to the lab to be analyzed."

"Okay," Catfish said.

"How far back do you think the shooter was?" I asked Catfish's opinion, still trying to make up for being short with him.

"From the spread of the pellets, I'd say 'bout twenty feet or more." He walked over to the sink and washed his hands, shaking his head. "I think that meant this poor guy didn't see it coming."

"I think you're right," I said. "That's sad."

"It is," he said, flinging the water off of his hands before grabbing a paper towel. "But at least it didn't take much to find out what killed him."

"True," I said.

"So now you're done?" Catfish asked.

"No." I chuckled. "I still have more to do."

"Seems like an open and shut case to me," he said. "You've just found out what happened." He looked at me and winked. "But I know you know what's best, Romie."

"I know what's necessary," I said. "There's more to do if I want to be of any help figuring out whodunit. The murderer was trying to outsmart the police. There's no ID and he was put in a place where dead bodies are all over the place."

"Outsmart you? Impossible."

"Let's hope whoever it was isn't smarter than us," I said. "I just want Pogue to figure out who did it."

"I don't think there's anyone smarter than you, Romie."

"I think you're a little biased, Catfish."

"I am," he said and blushed. "Not ashamed for anyone to know it."

I stood up straight and took a moment before I spoke. "You gotta girl?" I asked. "Someone special you're seeing?"

"Nope. Gave my heart away a long time ago." He looked at me

with a spark in his eye.

"I don't know if that's such a good thing to do, Catfish. Others are not always as careful with it."

I made my notes about the wound on the back of the body, finished getting the body undressed, and told Catfish I could get the rest on my own. He left reluctantly, afraid I might need more help once he'd gone. But I knew I was fine.

I stretched the knot out of my back, adjusted the light and blinked hard a couple of times to clear my eyes.

This was familiar territory. I picked up Auntie's thirty-five-millimeter camera and took pictures while the body was in a prone position. I rolled his fingers over the inkpad I had grabbed from the office to use for identification purposes. The clothes might yield the decedent's DNA, but mostly it would be used to identify the culprit's. I'd use blood collected from the heart to do a profile on the victim.

A body on the table. Scalpel in hand, poised and ready. This was where I was used to being. Where I belonged. I ran my hand over his chest, cleared my throat and spoke into the mic on my phone: "Male. Caucasian. One hundred and seventy pounds. All tattoos, scars, and identifying marks will be documented photographically."

I bent over the body and instinctively began to cut in a thoracoabdominal Y-shaped incision...

Chapter Eleven

"I've got a report for you," I said to Pogue. He answered on the first ring. His anxiety was so obvious it seeped through the phone. "Seems like you were there waiting for it."

"Is it ready for me to pick up?" he said, not acknowledging my observation.

"Not yet," I said. I laid the phone on the desk and put it on speaker. "Thought I'd call you with preliminaries. Then I'll type it up for you."

"Preliminaries? What's that?"

I twirled the pen on the desk and breathed evenly, hoping to transfer my sense of calm to him. "Cause of death. Manner of death," I said.

I sat behind Auntie's expansive mahogany desk. Set in the middle of her office, there were two tufted brown leather chairs in front of it. I pushed the thick folder she'd left for me out of the way. I had festival business to take care of for her, but first I had to get the autopsy report together for Pogue. He was right–the murder investigation trumped Auntie's crawfish boil festival.

"Cause and manner." he repeated.

"Yep. Two different things."

"Okay," he said. I could hear the shakiness in his voice. His first murder and my auntie were a lot to deal with all at once.

"Gunshot wound to his back from a distance. One pellet

entered his heart. That was the cause."

I could hear him suck in a breath and hold it.

"Manner of death was murder," I said.

"Yeah." He let the breath out with a chuckle. "Of course it is. Can't shoot yourself in the back," he said. "Anything else you wanna tell me before you type it up?"

I shrugged. "It was kind of hard to place the time of death. I put in an estimation, but you'll have to couple that with your investigation to get a definite."

"Okay," he said. "A lot to do."

"Does your deputy have any experience with murder?"

"No. My deputy is just as green as I am. And he's on loan," he said.

"On loan?"

"Yeah. Just here to help for the week."

I didn't know what that was about, but I didn't ask.

"Doc Westin is the one with the know-how in stuff like this. Being a medical examiner for the tri-county, he's done dozens more murders than we've seen in Roble."

"We've never seen a murder in Roble," I said.

"I know. Just my luck he's sick." Pogue let out a nervous chuckle.

"I'm going to type up your report now, so you can get to it."

"That's the other thing, Romie. I didn't say anything before," he said, hesitating. "I had almost forgotten about it sparring and all with Babet."

"What?" I said.

"I've got this conference."

"What kind of conference?"

"National Sheriff's Association Conference," he said.

"Well, that's good," I said. "They may have break-out sessions on forensics or something that could help you learn about how to do this. And you'll meet other sheriffs. You could ask them questions."

"But what about that forty-eight-hour rule thing?"

"What do you mean?"

"The conference is in Reno."

"Nevada?" I said and chuckled.

"Yeah."

"For how long?"

"Four days," he said.

"Oh," I said. "Well you heard what Auntie Zanne said. That forty-eight-hour stuff is just on television."

"Yeah, I know she thinks she knows everything, but the show that's called *The First 48* is about real police officers and real crimes."

I didn't say anything. Maybe that really was a thing.

"Romie? You there?"

"Yep. Just thinking." I cleared my throat. "So maybe it is something to that. But there are cold case shows too. Murders being solved after years, sometimes decades."

"That's true," he said. "Although, I hope this murder investigation doesn't come to that. It would be quite embarrassing if I couldn't solve my first murder case."

"So, are you thinking about not going to your conference?"

"I don't know if I should. I mean it was paid for with county money, and it's pretty much mandatory because I'm a newly elected sheriff. Plus, I'm sure when the Board approved me going they didn't think that crime would magically stop while I was gone."

"I'm sure they didn't."

"So, do you think I should go?"

"Is your deputy going too?"

"No. He's the one holding down the fort."

"Oh," I said, understanding. "That's why he's on loan."

"Right. And like I say, I don't want him investigating it. He'll be leaving as soon as I get back."

"When are you supposed to leave?" I asked.

"Tonight," he said. "The conference starts tomorrow. I'll be back late Friday night. I think my flight gets in around eleven p.m. But I just don't know."

I laughed.

"Don't laugh, Romie. It's not funny."

I tried to stop laughing. How horrible, I thought, that his conference was scheduled right when there was a murder in Roble. And that meant leaving my Auntie Zanne, the notorious Nose-Poking Babet, running around loose trying to solve it while he was gone, and her main suspect was his mother.

"What are you laughing about?" he said.

"Nothing," I said, giggles still erupting. "You should go. I think you should go." I took in a breath to control myself. "The information and people you'll meet will be invaluable."

"So go?"

"Yes. Go."

"Even though you thought it was funny?"

"Even though I thought it was funny. Although I really didn't think the part about you going was funny. It'll be fine."

"So, what do I do about the report for now?"

"You can pick it up before you go, give it to your lab, and they'll call you with the results. Your phone goes with you, right?"

"Yeah."

"So they'll be able to reach you," I said. "Not that you can do anything from there. But at least you'll have something to work with when you get back."

"That's true," he said. "And nothing's going to happen to the body. It's not going anywhere."

"Actually, I'm releasing the body. I'm done with it."

"Who are you releasing it to?" he asked.

"Usually, it's the family. For now, I guess Ball Funeral Home & Crematoruim."

He let out a groan.

"Don't worry, Auntie Zanne will take good care of him."

"I guess that's okay, right? I mean it was already embalmed," he said. "You confirmed he was embalmed with formaldehyde?"

"Yeah. More or less. You'll have to send it out to a lab to confirm. But Auntie's nose seems to have it confirmed." I said. "But he wasn't properly embalmed."

"No?"

"No."

Living in a household that ran a funeral home, we both knew what that meant.

"So, you said it was hard to tell the time of death?"

"Yeah, but my guess would be three or four days. No longer than a week."

"So not too long before Josephine Gail called it in, huh?"

"That's my medical opinion," I said. I thought about how to phrase my next question. "Pogue. Is it true that Aunt Julep is still the only one that uses formaldehyde to embalm?"

He huffed. "I don't know," he said. "Honestly, I don't. You know how many funeral homes there are around here. I couldn't tell you who uses what."

"Put it this way," I said. "Does *she* use it?"

There was a long pause. "Yeah. She does. I think." He got quiet again. "But that doesn't mean anything, you know."

"I know," I said. "So who are you looking at then, other than Josephine Gail?" I asked. "I heard you say to Auntie Zanne you wanted to speak to other people."

"Yeah. Everyone in the funeral home," he said. "I'm thinking that's the best place to start. They had the perfect opportunity."

"How many people work here?" I asked.

"I don't know," he said. "You don't know?"

"You know I haven't been here much. She just hired someone."

"The new receptionist?" Pogue asked. "What's her name?"

"Floneva Floyd," I said.

"Should I talk to her?"

"I don't know," I said. "Now that I think about it, Auntie said she interviewed her and gave her a tour before she left. She would've known that the doors were always open and where all the rooms and dead bodies were after Auntie showed her around."

"And she knew Babet wouldn't be around."

"Yep. She had to know she'd be gone for two weeks."

"So I'll talk to her," Pogue said.

"Who else?" I asked.

"There's Rhett Remmiere," he said. "Babet hired him not too long ago and I don't know much about him."

"I don't either," I said thoughtfully. "He certainly isn't French."

"What?" Pogue asked. "Who said he was French?"

"No one said it," I said. "It was just the impression I got when Auntie Zanne introduced him to me."

"What do you think about him?" Pogue asked.

"Can't really say," I said. "Haven't had much interaction, but seems like he's loyal to Auntie Zanne even though I'm not quite sure what he does."

"Yeah, it seems to me he does a little bit of everything."

I hunched my shoulders. "That is what she needs around here. A jack of all trades."

"Being 'Jack' would have given him access," Pogue said. "So he could have easily been the one to do it."

"And I guess he's just learning the business," I said. "Might not be good enough to hide his inexperience."

"That was what I was thinking," Pogue said.

"Okay, so those are two people you can start with," I said. "Anyone else?"

"Catfish."

"Not Catfish," I said. I couldn't take that suggestion seriously.

"Why not Catfish?" Pogue said. "He was here. He knows the business."

"Why would Catfish do something like that?"

"We don't know the reason that anyone did it right now. That's why we can't rule out anyone that had access to the funeral home and the Preparation Room."

"Not Catfish," I said again shaking my head. "Now if someone was dead because they had bothered me, then I'd say maybe. But other than that, I can't imagine it." I grunted. "Moving on."

"Okay," he said, but I could tell he didn't like me dismissing his suggestion. "What about who was running the front office before Floneva? They would have still been there while Babet was away."

"I think that would've been Josephine Gail," I said.

"So we're back to her."

"Guess so," I said.

Pogue moaned.

"What?"

"This is just stupid speculation. This can't be the way to solve a murder. Sitting around and going through Ball Funeral Home & Crematorium's personnel directory."

"It's a start," I said. A start that I hoped he'd handle better than his talk with Josephine Gail.

"Look. I have to go," he said. I could hear the discontent in his voice. "You'll get me the report before I have to leave?"

"I will. I took fingerprints and a DNA sample for you, too."

"You did?"

"Yes. So run 'em. Send them to your crime lab. See if you can come up with a match. Get an ID on this guy."

"You know there's a lot of moving parts to this and it looks like I'ma have to do all of it long distance."

"Don't worry, you've got me. I'm here for you."

"Thanks, Romie. I do appreciate that. But with you comes Babet and she spells trouble."

I laughed. "That is true."

He hesitated before he spoke again. "I heard what she said about my mother this morning when I came in."

"I figured you had." I shook my head, although he couldn't see me. "But I know that Aunt Julep didn't do anything."

"You don't have to tell me she didn't do it," Pogue said. "Call and let me know when the report is ready. I'll come by and pick it up."

We ended the call.

I plugged my phone into the wall to charge and clicked on the computer. I had recorded my observations as I performed the autopsy, then included my thoughts as soon as I finished on what might have happened based on all the things I found. I wanted to type it up verbatim.

Now, my fingers poised over the home row of the keyboard, I thought again about what I had found out.

Our John Doe had never seen it coming and had died instantly. And with the body found somewhere other than where it happened, a lot of the regular clues were just not going to be there.

The DNA analysis of the clothes might help. But not much of anything else I'd found. With him being in that casket we didn't have the usual things to identify him. No wallet. No cellphone. No vehicle. He didn't even have on his own clothes. And the pine sap and wood chips I'd found on his shirt were everywhere, seeing that East Texas' backyard was the Piney Woods.

Pogue was right. The personnel of Ball Funeral Home was probably the best place for him to start. I just didn't like the idea of a murderer being right in my own home.

Chapter Twelve

"I. Need. You." My auntie had been whispering into the phone for a full thirty seconds and those were the first words I was able to make out.

"Did you say you need me?" I asked. "Are you alright?"

She'd gone to her Red Hat Society event. All decked out in a red, medium-brow floppy hat covered in organza and adorned with a silk bow, and a deep purple sheath dress that had a matching coat, her oversized tan tapestry purse clashing as usual.

The Red Hats were about having fun, something I felt she should have foregone seeing that we were in the middle of a murder investigation and her best friend, according to her, was the prime suspect. Plus, all she'd done since she'd bullied me into coming to Roble was complain about how overwhelmed she was with the festival and how much she needed my help.

I had been sitting in her office since I'd finished the autopsy. Then I made the phone calls she'd delegated to me. Delivery confirmation of the tents. Making sure the stage for the musicians would be up in time for the sound check. Calling the rental company to check the time the floor was being installed for the zydeco and Cajun dance contests.

Now she needed something more.

Thank goodness I had already pecked out the autopsy report on my auntie's dinosaur of a computer.

"I can't talk loud," she said. "Can you hear me?"

"Barely," I said.

"I need you to come here. To me."

"Did you say come to you?" I put a finger in my other ear and pressed the phone closer.

"Yesssss." Her whisper turned into a hiss.

"Why?"

"Can you just get here?" Her voice seemed desperate.

"Aren't you all the way at the Grandview?"

"Yessss," came another hiss. "Get Rhett to bring you," she said. "And get here quick." Then she abruptly hung up on me.

What a cliffhanger. She was so dramatic.

"What is she up to now?" I muttered and glanced at the time on my cell phone.

Eleven a.m.

I'd gotten a lot done and the day wasn't even half over, which only meant more time for Auntie Zanne to wrangle me into doing stuff.

I knew coming to Roble was a bad idea...

I blew out a breath and at the same time pushed off, propelling the swivel chair to where I sat back from the desk.

"Guess I have to go and find Rhett." I said and ambled out of the office and down the hallway. "So I can take a ride alone with the Definitely-Not-French-But-Possible-Murder-Suspect."

I remembered Auntie Zanne said he had to pick up a family at nine, but didn't know where he had taken them—a church, graveside service, or back to the funeral home—or whether he was back or not.

I decided to stop in the kitchen and make myself a sandwich to feed my rumbling belly. I'd look for him while I ate.

Head in refrigerator, Rhett found me.

"Plan on climbing in?" he asked.

He'd walked into the kitchen, startling me.

"Just looking for something to eat," I said. I stood up straight and turned to him.

Could he be a murderer? I gave him a good once-over. He was dressed in a button-down white shirt, probably the one he'd worn under a suit for the morning funeral. He had exchanged dress pants for the jeans I'd seen him in the first day I met him.

Well, one thing for sure, I couldn't tell if he was by the way he dressed.

"I was also looking for you," I said.

"In there?" He pointed to the fridge.

"My Auntie Zanne called. She wants you to bring me to her. She said it was important."

"Where is she?"

"The Grandview Motor Lodge," I said. "It's a motel out on Highway 87 in Yellowpine. Near Hemphill."

"I know where it is," he said.

"Okay. So, can you take me?" I asked.

"I can take you wherever you want to go," he said.

I narrowed my eyes and looked at him. "I just want to go to Yellowpine."

"And I'll be more than happy to take you there." He kept smiling.

"O-kaaay," I said, wondering why that grin was plastered on his face. "I'm just going to make a sandwich first. I'm starving." I pointed to the refrigerator.

"Take your time." He pulled out a chair and took a seat. "I'll wait until you're done."

"I can take it with me," I said.

"Or you can sit and eat it here," he said, smiling. He pointed to the chair across from him.

How creepy...

Chapter Thirteen

"You don't have to hold the door open for me," I said as I climbed in the car. Turkey sandwich in hand, I carried it wrapped in a paper towel.

Mr. Rhett Remmiere was creeping me out with all of his sudden niceness. I was beginning to wonder if he hadn't overheard me talking to Pogue and knew he was a suspect, because now he was all smiles and sweetness.

He'd sat and stared at me the whole time I fixed my to-go lunch, even offering to run out to Auntie Zanne's garden when I couldn't find any tomatoes in the refrigerator. And he stood by patiently, with that same smile planted, when I left Pogue's report with Floneva. I'd stuck it in a sealed envelope with instructions that she was not to open it or give it to anyone but the sheriff.

"I can tell you been out of the south for a while," Rhett said. "We open doors for ladies."

My brow creased. "Northerners open doors."

He didn't say anything to that, just shut the car door and headed over to the driver's side of the car.

"I was just saying," I said as he slipped into his seat. "I can do it."

"I wasn't saying that you couldn't," he said. "I was just being a gentleman. Like my mother taught me."

I didn't have anything to say to that. I didn't want to talk about anyone's mother.

"Thank you for taking me out to Auntie Zanne," I said.

"I don't mind at all," he said. "I'd do just about anything for Babet."

"She *is* a Roble darling," I said.

"Ahh. Did I notice a hint of sarcasm in your voice?" He glanced at me.

I lowered my eyes. "It's just that..." I glanced over at him, then shook my head. "Never mind."

"You're not a lot like her, are you?"

"What do you mean by that?" I asked, unsure how I should take his comment.

"Babet's a social butterfly. She's in the middle of everything. Always a part of the goings on."

"That she is," I agreed. "And always trying to drag me into it with her."

Although right now she was in the middle of nowhere.

Yellowpine was surrounded by the Sabine National Forest. When that fact popped into my head, it made me realize that it would have been a good place for our murder. Secluded. Small population. Lots of sap everywhere.

Is that why Rhett knew "exactly" where it was?

Out on an old state highway, close to the Louisiana border, Yellowpine was thirty miles from Roble. Thirty miles, I decided, would be the perfect time for me to start helping out my cousin by asking this guy a couple of questions.

I looked over at Rhett, still talking. What did he know about all of this? Why hadn't he said more after Pogue arrived? And why would Auntie want him to bring me to her? Hadn't she considered that he might be the one to have done the deed?

Rhett didn't look threatening. In fact, he was good looking. No glasses today. Maybe contacts? It was the first time I could get an unobstructed look at his light-colored eyes. They were striking, specks of gold that twinkled, something I hadn't noticed before, in the sunlight streaming through the windows.

Could those be the eyes of a murderer?

"Not like you," he was saying.

"What?" I asked. I hadn't been paying attention.

"You're nothing like your aunt."

"Oh. No," I said, surprised he was trying to assess me. "I'm not."

"No. You're more like a... I don't know," he said. He shrugged. "More like a *faire tapisserie*."

I arched an eyebrow. I was anything but a wallflower. Did he think it would sound better because he said it in French?

How could he say that? He hardly knew me.

Still, his comment made me feel self-conscious.

I smoothed down my hair. In all the heat and humidity of Texas it had started to curl up. No longer the straight tresses that I'd coveted in Chicago. It bothered me that I had no control over it.

No control over much of what I was going through as of late.

I ran my hand down the leg of the tan-colored pair of tapered, cotton, cut-at-the-ankle slacks that I'd thrown on. I had on a white, summer blouse and had stuck my feet in a pair of flat brown mules. Earlier, a lab coat had covered it, but still I thought I looked...I don't know—nothing like a wallflower.

I huffed.

"You okay?" he asked.

"Sure," I said. This wallflower is just fine.

"So, if you're going to live here," he said, "you're probably gonna need me to drive you around."

So you can insult me more?

"No. I won't," I said.

"No?" he said. "I wouldn't mind."

"I doubt I'll go out much," I said. "Only going out now because my auntie called. Plus, I won't be here that much longer."

"Here? As in Roble?"

"Yep. Roble."

"I thought you were going to live here."

"Oh no." I chuckled. "I'm not living here."

"Oh," he said. Confusion washed over his face.

"What?" I asked.

"It's just that I thought...I was told..."

"What? Did my auntie tell you I was staying? Because it seems like she's got the wrong impression."

He grinned. "Yeah. She did." He glanced at me, his smile re-emerging. "I was looking forward to getting to know you."

"My auntie only wishes I would stay," I said. "But Roble isn't the place for me."

"You like living the big life, huh?"

"It's just a different life, that's all. The one that I want. The one I worked so hard to get."

"I can understand that." He said it like he knew exactly how I was feeling.

"So you're just helping out while you're here?" he asked.

"Yes. And only reluctantly so."

"So. Good. I don't have to worry about you taking over my job," he said.

"Your job?"

"Yep. I'm the one she usually calls when she needs something."

I laughed. "Oh no, no need to worry. You can definitely keep your job. I don't want to go running around with her getting caught up in her harebrained antics."

"She does that?"

"Are you talking about Suzanne Babet Derbinay?"

"Yes," he said. "She's never asked me to do anything I thought to be harebrained."

"You must not have been around very long," I said. "Just consider yourself lucky."

This time he laughed. "She is rather eccentric with her greenhouse and all of her homemade remedies—"

"They're potions," I corrected. "And eccentric is not the word to use for that aspect of her."

"And she is in a lot of clubs," he continued.

"Now that does make her eccentric."

"I think she's cute," he said. "Especially at her age. She's got more spunk than I do."

"It's cute until she needs an accomplice. She'll wrestle you down and hogtie you until you give in."

"Has she done that to you?"

"Yes." I blew out a breath. "I'm almost sure that's why she wants me to come out to the Grandview now. She wants to include me in one of her nefarious plans."

"Ooh. Nefarious." He scrunched up his face like he had a bad taste in his mouth. "Should I turn around? Do you need me to take you back to safety?"

"You can't hide from her," I said. "She'll hunt you down. Make you do what she wants."

"No need to try and resist, huh?"

"I still try." I looked at him. "Call me crazy, because I know it won't work."

"I wondered how she got you to work the Information Booth at the festival. A big Chicago doctor and all."

I frowned. "I'm not working the Information Booth at the festival," I said.

He hiked up an eyebrow. "Babet told me you were."

"Oh Jesus!" I said and slapped a hand across my forehead. "I have to hurry and get back home."

"Home?" he asked. "I know you said you weren't staying, but isn't Roble still 'home' for you?"

"No. Definitely not." I shook my head. "I couldn't survive here."

"It's that bad?"

"Where are you from?" I asked.

"Houston."

"Then you know. Nothing like a big city. The night life. The amenities. The endless opportunities."

"Roble's not enough for you?"

"No, it's not." But as soon as I said the words, I knew it hadn't come out right. "Yes." I wanted him to understand what I meant.

"It is. It's just that I'm past all of this."

"All of what? The things here?"

"Yes."

That probably sounded bad, too.

How could I make him understand that by staying here, I would lose my identity? The only time I had felt like myself since I'd been back was when I was doing the autopsy. Now I was starting my mornings by having tubs of snapping crawfish brought over for me to bake pies without anyone asking me if I would, or if I even wanted to. Making phone calls to plan a festival that I had no intention of even going to and being called to come out on some stealth mission to aid my auntie and the ladies of the Red Hat Society to do who knows what.

Other than performing the autopsy, my life had taken such a turn. So much of a turn that I wondered if I could get it back on track. No more morning walks along the lakefront trail. No more taking in the comforting smell of the antiseptically clean hospital corridors, or my morning latte and scone. No more Dr. Alex Hale romancing me with candlelight and white wine. Holding me in his arms...

This new life, I was sure, was going to be detrimental to all I had held dear.

"You too big for it?" Rhett asked interrupting my thoughts.

"Maybe you should just stop asking me questions," I said. "I don't think my answers are coming out right."

He shrugged. "Just tell me what you mean."

"I mean that my life is back in Illinois. In Chicago. My job. My man. My friends. My life."

"You're seeing someone?"

I narrowed my eyes. "Why? What did Auntie Zanne say about that?"

He got quiet for a moment, and bit on his bottom lip. "I don't know if I should say."

"You started this."

"Yeah. I guess I did. She told me you were single." He glanced at me. "That you were needing someone to...I don't know...fill a void. Be with you."

I couldn't help but laugh. My auntie, the matchmaker, was a menace. I had learned not to be embarrassed about it years ago.

"That's funny?" he asked.

"No. It's just that she shouldn't have said that."

"Because it isn't true?"

I looked out of the window. Who knew what was true about my life anymore. I surely didn't.

Thought I'd better change the subject.

"She did tell me that I'm supposed to help you with the music," I said. "She said you were in charge of it."

"I am," he said. "Do you like music?"

"Who doesn't like music?" I asked.

"Now maybe it's me whose words aren't coming out right," he said. "I should have asked, what kind of music do you like?"

"The blues," I said. Here was a subject I didn't mind talking about.

"Wasn't your father a blues player?"

"How do you know that?" I asked.

"Babet told me."

"What? You and my auntie been sitting around having pow-wow sessions about me?"

"No. She likes to talk about you. I like to listen to her talk about you."

"Oh really?"

I thought I saw him blush. "Yes. Really."

"Yes. My father was into blues. I don't have too many memories of him without his Gibson Les Paul in his hands."

"Oh. You know about guitars?" he asked.

"I do," I said.

"A woman after my own heart."

I lifted an eyebrow. I wasn't going to ask what that meant.

"Well, I need help with the zydeco band," he said. "Remember you met a couple of the guys?"

"Spoon and Gus," I said. "So that's your band?"

"Not all of them and not really my band. I got some guys together just for the festival. Posted a couple of flyers. Asked around. So, I guess that makes me in charge of it."

"And what is it that you want me to do?" I asked.

"Well, I ran into a little snag, and Babet told me you could help me out."

"Doing what?" I asked, the radar on my Interfering-Suzanne-Meter ramping up.

"Baking pies."

"Pies?" I laughed. "What does that have to do with a band? Wait. What kind of pies?" I wasn't sure if she'd negotiated me to bake something other than those crawfish pies she'd been talking about.

"Crawfish pies."

I shook my head. "Okay. But why?"

"Well..." He hesitated. "I had to make a last-minute replacement."

"In the band?"

"Yeah."

"And?"

"And I want to tell the guys about the replacement at the sound check Thursday night. Over at the fairgrounds."

I leaned closer, indicating I was listening.

"Well, you know," he said. "I thought I'd make it a festive kind of evening, get everyone in a good mood by serving food and some beer. That usually calms people down."

"Beer doesn't always calm people."

He chuckled. "I guess that's true. Maybe I'll switch that idea out and get soft drinks instead."

"And my auntie volunteered me for the food part. Said I'd make crawfish pies?"

"Not so sure how the guys will take the new addition. They might get upset. Babet said that your crawfish pies are so good they could bring peace to the Middle East."

"She did?"

"She did." He glanced at me. "Are you really that good of a cook?"

I laughed. "People like my crawfish pies, it's true. But I don't think they'd do anything about forging peace anywhere. It never worked between me and my auntie."

Chapter Fourteen

Rhett Remmiere seemed to be trying to charm me. Acting all gentleman-like, professing an interest in me in a way that made me unsure if it was only platonic.

But I hadn't forgotten my promise to my cousin, Pogue. I wasn't going to let Rhett charm me out of remembering to help him out. And I'd certainly be remiss not to ask questions when I had one of his suspects right in my grasp. I had to find out what he knew about our John Doe.

I looked up and saw a mile marker. Only seven more miles to go. It was now or never.

"So, what do you know about that dead body turning up at the funeral home?" I asked.

"Whoa," he said looking over at me. "That was a one eighty in our little conversation."

"Is that a subject you want to avoid?" I asked.

"I didn't say that," he said. "It's just that we were talking about music, beer, and pies, not murder."

"You got an answer?" I asked.

He shrugged. "It's a mystery. Isn't that the general consensus?"

"A mystery that needs to be solved. Can you help piece any of the clues together?"

"I'd say the murderer was pretty clever. A funeral home." He shook his head. "Perfect place to hide a body."

"Do you consider yourself clever?" I asked.

I heard a small laugh come from the back of his throat. "You're not accusing me of anything are you?"

I didn't say anything.

"If I'd done it," he said, not sounding defensive at all, "I would have gotten rid of the body before Babet got back."

"Unless you didn't have time to," I said. "Maybe Josephine Gail found it before you could."

"Maybe," he said with a smirk. "But I had time to dress it all up and put it in a casket?" He shook his head. "Even if that happened, I wouldn't be ready to confess. I'd wait to see what you had against me." He took his eyes off the road again to look at me. "What do you have?"

I stared at him, unsure how to take this conversation we were having. "Nothing much yet," I said. "But we're working on it."

"Let me know when you get something," he said as we turned into the hotel. "Then we'll see about that confession."

A menagerie of red hats filled the parking lot of the Grandview Motor Lodge. A sea of poppies, bobbing and swaying atop a plethora of laughing and chattering women.

"I'll wait until you find her," Rhett said doing his own one-eighty, signaling it was time for me to get out of the car.

I stepped out and let my eyes wander. How was I ever going to find her? It seemed that the meeting was over, but there were still so many congregating around. Then I heard someone laying on the horn of a car. It made me jump, thinking I was in the way of a moving car, but nothing was coming past me.

Honk, honk! I saw a hand stick out of the window beckoning me over.

It wasn't Auntie Zanne's car, but who knows, she might be inside of it making a deal for me to bake more pies.

"Aunt Julep!" I said, peeking in the window when I got to the car. She was sitting on the passenger side. I reached in and hugged her, knocking her pillbox hat off its angle. "You a Red Hat Lady?"

"For fifteen years. Joined same time as Babet."

"I'm here looking for her," I said. "You're not driving, are you?"

"No. Got somebody drops me off and picks me up."

"Why are you sitting out here?" I asked. "It's too hot to sit in a car. I don't want you getting sick."

"It's running," she said. "Don't you hear it? We've got the air on."

"Oh, I do hear it," I said.

"I forgot my prize I won at the meeting," Aunt Julep said. "But if I do get a heat stroke, I know I'll be alright. I got my pretty niece, the doctor, in town now."

I didn't want to go through the whole conversation with her that I wasn't staying.

"So your driver went back it to get your prize?" I said instead.

"Yep."

"Did you win something good?"

"Don't know," she said and smiled. "Didn't open it yet. Was waiting until I got home."

"I'm so happy to see you," I said. "You know I was planning to come over. There was just was so much stuff going on at the house when I got there."

"I know," she said. "Murder." She scrunched her face. "I never thought I'd see it in Roble."

"Me either," I said.

"I told Pogue that whoever did it works in a funeral home."

"You think so?" I asked.

"Yes. I do. Most folks afraid of funeral homes. Don't go into one if they don't have to."

"Not even to hide a body?" I asked.

"Not even to hide a body," she said. "Looka there," she said and pointed out past the motel. "Why go in a funeral home when you got all them woods to dump it in?"

"Good point, Aunt Julep," I said. "Well I know my cousin will get it all figured out."

"He said you were going to help him."

"I'm going to try," I said.

"I hear Babet is trying to solve it, too."

"All Auntie Zanne is doing is getting in the way," I said.

"That's her specialty," Aunt Julep said. "But don't dismiss her. She's got a good head on her shoulders."

"A hard head," I said, which made Aunt Julep laugh. "You going to be okay here? I'm going to go find Auntie Zanne."

"Oh yeah, he'll be here in a minute. I just wanted to say hi."

"I love you, Aunt Julep," I said and leaned in the window to kiss her. "I'll be over to see you soon."

"You gonna come and sit a spell?"

"I sure am," I said. "We'll visit right proper like."

She beamed. "I'd like that."

Sheesh. Right proper like?

Two days in Texas and I was already butchering the English language.

The Grandview Motor Lodge, reminiscent of an Econo Lodge motel, was a three-story, u-shaped building with doors to the rooms on the outside. The railings on each floor were painted white, and in the center was a yellow-tiled swimming pool. The sidewalk was concrete and there were planters of alternatively pink and yellow rose trees.

It was a fairly large motel to be in Yellowpine, a small-town leftover from the timber boom of the late 1800s, early 1900s. The town hadn't even had a post office since the early 1950s, and I didn't think there could be more than a hundred people that lived there. The motel, as far as I could remember, was frequented by hikers, bicycle enthusiasts and the like, and evidently by the ladies of the Red Hat Society. Those few frequenters were probably the only reason it was still an up-and-running business.

I finally found Auntie where I'd started off—at Rhett's car.

"I thought you had to show me something that couldn't wait," I said after waiting for her for five minutes while she and Rhett spoke.

"I didn't say that," she said.

"You sounded desperate," I said.

"I don't know that desperate would be the right word. But pretty close to it, I guess," she said.

"So then, let's get to it."

"Okay," she said. She grabbed my arm and held on to it like she needed help walking. She turned back and waved to Rhett. "Isn't he just the sweetest man?"

I rolled my eyes. "I wouldn't know," I said.

"After riding all the way out here in the same car, you still don't know?"

"I don't know what you think you're up to," I said.

"Nothing," she said way too quickly. "I just thought you'd like to get to know him better."

"What I would like to know," I said, "is why you keep telling people that I'm going to bake crawfish pies?" I asked. "I'm not baking any pies. Especially enough to feed a band full of men."

"We've got a girl in the band, too."

"I'm not baking any pies," I said.

"Why don't you think about it?" she said, patting my arm. "Nobody makes pies better then you. Plus, you'll need the practice. I promised twenty pies to the crawfish booth, kiddo, and I want ours to be the best ones there."

"If I already make the best pies, why do I need practice?"

"I was thinking you might be a little rusty. I didn't remember seeing any stands up there in Chicago selling crawfish when you took me over to Navy Pier."

I rubbed my hand over my eye. "Why did you want me to come out here, Auntie?" I asked. No need to continue that conversation. She'd told everyone that I was baking pies. The only way I knew to get out of baking them was to find a place to hide where she couldn't find me, and I knew of no place like that.

She bumped herself against me "I need your forensic eye," she said.

"My forensic eye? Why? What's going on?"

"I think that I've found the crime scene."

"What crime scene?"

"Where Squatter Guy was killed," she said.

We took the steps to the second floor to a room halfway down the outside corridor. She swung open the door and made a big gesture of sniffing in the air.

"What do you smell?" she asked.

"Would the answer be 'nothing'?"

"No, it would not. Take another whiff." She did it for me. "Don't you smell it?"

"No, Auntie," I said. "I don't smell anything."

"Formaldehyde."

I breathed in again, making a production number of it like she had. Nothing. I stuck my head inside the door and tried it again.

I shrugged. "Maybe," I said, then gave it a second thought. "I don't know." I scrunched up my nose. "Maybe it's just still stuck in my nose from this morning."

"Oh heavens, darlin', you must be like that commercial says, 'nose blind' not to smell it."

She stepped inside the door and with her hands tried to usher the smell out to me.

"Uhmmm..." was all I had to offer.

"Well, if you can't use that nose, use your eyes," she said. "Do you see anything?"

"A motel room?"

"Other than that."

"No."

"No clues?"

"Clues of what, Auntie?"

"Murder."

"Murder..." I let my eyes drift around the room. "No blood," I said. "No sign of a struggle." I looked at her. "I don't see anything."

I stood at the doorway while Auntie Zanne waltzed around the room, stopping in different areas and looking to me and my "forensic eye," something I wasn't aware I even possessed, for answers. All I saw was a messy room I presumed belonging to a guest. And I wasn't even too sure it was okay for us to be in the room.

"Whose room is this?" I asked.

"Herman St. John."

"And who is he?"

"I think he's the squatter."

"The body at the funeral home?"

"How many other squatters do you know?" she asked. She pulled off her over-sized hat and started fanning herself with it, her usual high hair now deflated. "He rented the room about a week ago."

"How do you know that?" I asked. "I can't imagine how you could just happen upon this room and it just happened to be the room of the guy at the funeral home."

"I didn't just happen upon it. It's the universe settling in. Righting wrongs."

"I think it's about your nosy nature."

"Partly that, too," she said. "You know one of the members of my chapter of the Red Hat Society owns this place."

"And?"

"Raye Anne."

"Raye Anne. Who is Raye Anne?"

"Don't you remember her?

"No," I said. "I don't remember her."

"She owns this place. She's who I'm talking about. She gives me things that people leave."

"Is she giving you these things?"

"No. At least not yet. She gives her guests a certain amount of time to come back or call to claim their things."

"How long?"

"I don't know, but however long she gives, thirty days or so I'm guessing, the time hasn't passed yet on this stuff." She glanced over at me. "It's called abandoned property–all legal." She went back to walking the room. "She gives them to me so I can use them for people that don't have money to buy clothes for the deceased or to take to the clothing center where I spearhead the clothing drive."

She pulled open a drawer and shut it, then pulled open another one, bending over to look under the bed. I didn't say anything, and I didn't want to watch her snoop, so I stepped outside the door and looked over the banister at the pool.

Something black on the ground caught my eye. It was a black cigarette. I frowned. I thought smoking wasn't allowed outside of the rooms. I looked up and down the corridor. I didn't see any outside ashtrays. I bent down to get a closer look. It was unique. I didn't think I'd ever seen a cigarette that looked like that before.

"So anyway," she said and came over to the doorway. "Are you listening to me?"

I stood up. "You weren't saying anything," I said. "But I can hear you."

"Well we were on our way down to her storage closet," she pointed down the corridor, "and we passed this room," she said. "And it reminded her of the gentleman, that's what she called him– a gentleman–that had rented the room. It's hot. C'mon." She tugged at my arm and pulled me back to the doorway. Then she sat down on the bed and began fanning again.

"And?"

"And what?" she asked.

"And you were telling me how you got to see this room."

"Oh yeah. We were passing it..." She looked at me. "Did I say that part already?"

"Yes, you did."

"It's so hot. I can't keep up with my thoughts." She stood up and took off the thin coat that matched her dress. "Okay," she said. "So, we were passing the room and she just popped open the door. Then she said, 'This guest has been gone a couple of days. Maybe just off on a little side trip, but if he doesn't get back soon, his things will probably be going into the unclaimed pile soon."

"She's just going to give his stuff away?" I asked.

"Yes." She looked over at me. "All quite innocent," Auntie said.

"I told you that. She was just showing me the room, wanting me to see how people leave things and then disappear. But when she opened the door, that smell hit me in my face."

"And then you knew?"

"Yes. That's when I knew."

"The universe settling in?"

"That and the formaldehyde."

I took in another whiff of air. Still nothing.

"Why do you think there's a smell of formaldehyde in here?"

"Maybe they did the embalming in here?" she said.

"Where?" I said.

"Not on this bed, huh?" she said and bit her bottom lip. "It's not rumpled enough." She leaned in and smelled it.

There she went sticking her nose in things again. Literally.

"Well?"

"No more than what I smelled in the air," she said. "And the room doesn't look like anyone did any kind of procedure in here."

"No, it doesn't," I said. "And I don't think it's important." I didn't want to tell her how little formaldehyde had actually been inside the body. I had to be careful about sharing info about the case with her because she'd run off and try to solve it before Pogue could get to it.

Like now.

"Smelling it is important," she said. "It's a clue."

"Maybe not." I said. "So, is that what made you think of the dead stowaway?"

"Yeah, and your Aunt Julep."

"She didn't do it."

"It's never good to jump to conclusions, darlin'. Didn't they teach you that in medical school?" she said as she peeked around the backside of the television set. "The fact is formaldehyde may have been what killed him."

Did she forget I'd just completed the autopsy?

She was probably just trying to goad me into giving her some answers.

"You jumped to a conclusion the very first time you said Aunt Julep was the culprit."

"I based that statement on facts."

"And that's what makes you think this Herman St. John is the same person as our John Doe? Facts?"

"That and he hasn't been back in the room for a few days."

"How many days?" I asked.

"Why? What do you know?" she asked. She stood up and narrowed her eyes. "What did you find out in the autopsy?"

"Nothing I can share with you."

"What? Oh good heavens, Sugarplum. You have to tell me, we're partners."

"Partners in what?"

"Clearing Josephine Gail's name."

"I don't think you have to worry about that."

"Why? What did you find?"

"Here's a fact for you," I said. I figured cause of death was something I could share, and hopefully something that would stop her from her self-appointed investigation. "Dead Guy died from a shotgun wound to the back."

"Oh," she said and thought about that for a moment.

"And then he was embalmed?"

"That's about all I can tell you."

She waved her hand at me, dismissing my secrecy. I'm sure she figured she'd get something out of me eventually. "So. You notice something in here? A clue that goes along with what you found out during the autopsy?"

"Clue? No, I don't see anything. What do I notice?" I asked, sarcasm in my voice. "Other than the maid needs to come and clean this and that you," I swirled my finger at her, "are trespassing? I don't see anything."

A spark came into her eye. "The maid," she said, then wagged a finger at me. "That's a good idea, I'll talk to her when we're finished here."

"Talk about what?"

"Like why she hasn't cleaned the room. Or dumped the trash." She bent down and looked in it. "Oh. Look at this. Woodchips." She picked up the can and brought it toward me. "How do you think those got in here?"

I backed further outside the door. "I'm not looking," I said.

"And why would they be in the trashcan? I don't see any on the floor."

"I am not going to be complicit in your wrongdoings."

"Looking is not going to hurt."

"I don't know," I said. "It might."

"And it might be a clue," she said. She took the wastebasket back to where she'd found it next to the desk and set it down.

"What do you think is in here?" She pointed to a briefcase that was set atop the bed, the flap opened as if someone hadn't long ago gone into it.

"I think that it's none of our business."

"I think we should see what's in it," she said.

"I think that's illegal," I said.

She looked at me, and without moving her eyes, swept her hand across the bed, flipping the briefcase over the side and causing the contents to spill over onto the floor.

"Oh my," she said and placed her hand over her chest. "I'm just so clumsy." Auntie Zanne stooped down, picked up the few items from the floor, and placed them on the bed.

"Auntie Zanne." I shook my head and stepped back a foot farther. "Did you call me here to help you commit felonies?"

"Felonies? Oh heavens, Sugarplum," she said sitting down on the bed and spreading out the items. "What in the world do you mean?"

"This," I waggled a finger at her pile on the bed, "I'm sure is obstructing justice. You should have called Pogue instead of me."

"Why would I call Pogue?" she asked. "I don't know for sure who this stuff belongs to. And we're not trespassing, either. Did you forget I said Raye Anne let me in?"

"I'm sure they make jail cells big enough for all three of us."

"I think we need to study all of this stuff more." She shuffled through the items on the bed. "It might be a clue. Maybe we should take it with us."

My hand flew up to my eyes. I didn't want to see her in the act. "You can't take anything in here," I said. "It's evidence."

"How could it be evidence? Didn't you say that my conclusion that this is the squatter's room was very unlikely, and as faulty as my conclusion that it was your Aunt Julep that did it?"

I hadn't said that exactly, but even if the universe was settling in like she said, I did think it was highly improbable that this room belonged to the dead guy.

What were the chances?

But, either way, it was impossible that it was my Aunt Julep who was the killer.

"It doesn't matter, Auntie Zanne. You can't take anything. It's illegal."

"But it would be more like stealing then obstructing justice, right?"

"Oh, so you think stealing is okay?"

"Of course not, I was saying that it's not as bad as obstructing justice. Which, I'm not doing because we don't know who this guy is."

"And you're just stealing stuff from some random guy."

"Now you're understanding me, sugar."

"You need a good lawyer, Auntie."

"I keep one on retainer."

Chapter Fifteen

"There's Consuela," Auntie Zanne said. "She cleans all the rooms around here." She took off walking, mumbling as she went. "I need her."

"Need her for what?" I asked.

"I need to question her."

"Question her?" I almost had to trot to keep up with Auntie Zanne's short legs once she spotted the maid.

Consuela was a pudgy Hispanic woman, she had her black hair with stands of white pulled back into a bun. She had olive skin and brown eyes, a stocky build. There were beads of sweat popping up on her forehead and she wheeled her heavily stocked cart from door to door down the sidewalk.

"Maybe she saw Julep here," Auntie Zanne said.

"My Aunt Julep?"

"Really, Romaine that is getting very old."

"What?"

"You constantly asking which Julep I'm talking about. I'm going to tell you now, for the last time. I am investigating Julep Folsom. Your aunt. For the murder of my squatter."

"He's marked as John Doe."

"Fine. Squatter John Doe."

"Auntie, you know you can't make your killer fit the description of someone you want to be the murderer."

"It's Julep," my auntie said and nodded. "I just need to prove it."

I stopped and watched as she walked around the end of the U-shaped area. I had promised Pogue that I'd keep an eye on my auntie. But she was going off the deep end and it was she who'd taught me when things go bad, you don't go with them.

And then I thought, what could she hurt? If she went to Pogue with her crazy theory, he wouldn't go for it. He could just ignore her.

A smile spread across my face. I was just worried for nothing.

"Consuela," Auntie called out and waved to her as she carried an armful of linen into a room. "I want to talk to you."

"Hi, Mrs. Derbinay," she said with a heavy Spanish accent. "I have no time to talk. I very busy."

"I see you're busy," she said just as I arrived. She pointed to the pile of white sheets and towels Consuela was carrying and looked at me. "Help her out."

My eyes got big. "Help her?"

Consuela looked at me, then back at my aunt. "I don't need no help."

"Of course you don't," Auntie said, the whole time nodding at me to grab the load.

I pushed the handles of my purse onto my shoulder and tried to grab the bundle. Consuela wasn't letting go.

"Consuela," Auntie Zanne said, "I think one of the motel's guests has been murdered."

"Murdered?" she said and lost interest in the bundle. I stumbled once she let go of her grip. "I don't know nothing about it. I no murder no one."

"Of course not," Auntie said and then paused. She gave Consuela a questioning look, then shook her head. "I didn't mean *you* killed someone." Auntie tilted her head. "You didn't, did you? You can tell me, you know. If you have."

"No." Consuela raised an eyebrow. "I told you, it's not me."

Auntie seemed to consider that answer. I stood holding the

bundle of linen, too intrigued by this conversation to move.

"Well, do you know who it was?"

"Know who what?" Consuela asked.

"Who did kill someone?"

Consuela filled up her cheeks with air and blew it out as she flapped her arms and shook her head.

"Okay," Auntie said slowly. "But I was speaking of Room 207." Auntie pointed a thumb back to the room we'd just left. "Do you remember the person that was there?"

"Is he the one murdered?" she asked.

"Perhaps..." Auntie started to elaborate, but that seemed to make Consuela unhappy. She took the bundle from me and started into the room. "I tell you I know nothing about it."

Auntie looked at me then followed Consuela into the room.

"Did you notice any visitors coming to see him?" she said.

"Yes," Consuela said not stopping her work of stripping the bed. "I saw one person."

Auntie's eyes lit up. "A black woman. Short. Old."

She was describing my Aunt Julep. I knew exactly what she was up to.

"Auntie," I said.

She waved her hand at me, shooing me away, letting me know not to interfere. She wanted to get an answer to her question.

Consuela held onto the pillow she'd just taken the case from and thought about it.

"She was tanned, but I don't think she was black."

Auntie looked at me and gave a nod as if it were the answer she was looking for. "Julep is light," she said. "She could be mistaken for having tanned skin."

I rolled my eyes.

"What about her age? Did she look around my age?"

Consuela was flapping the sheet over the bed. She stopped mid-flap and looked at Auntie Zanne as the sheet floated down. "No. Not old like you."

"Was she short or tall?"

I guessed Auntie Zanne was going to continue asking Consuela questions until she got one that matched Aunt Julep's description. My auntie was a terrible investigator.

"I guess short," Consuela said and hunched a shoulder.

Auntie Zanne snapped her finger as if she just made the connection.

"And what did you see her do?" Auntie Zanne asked.

"Nothing," she said and shrugged. "I just see her go into the room with the man."

"Did she stay long?"

"Not the first time," she said.

"She came more than once?" Auntie asked.

"I saw two times," she said and nodded as if thinking. "Yes. It could have been more times."

"Would you recognize her if you saw her again?" Auntie asked.

"We have a lot of people that come here," she said. She grabbed the towels she'd brought in off of the chair and headed into the bathroom. She must have just left them on the counter because she came right back out. "But maybe."

That made me have a question. Nothing along the line of my auntie's crazy interrogation, trying to make the answers fit who she'd determined was the murderer.

"Consuela, may I ask you a question?" I asked.

"Sure. Why not?" she said. She grabbed a feather duster off her cart and came back in and went over to the dresser. "I have nothing better to do than stand around and talk to people. People not even staying in hotel." She fluttered the feathers over the dresser. "Ask me anything."

Her sarcasm wasn't lost on me, but I went on with my questioning. "When is the last time you saw the man that was staying in that room?"

She stopped dusting and thought about it. "I haven't seen him in a few days."

"Two? Three? How many days?" I asked.

"I think three days. Maybe four."

I nodded. If Auntie was right, which I was sure she wasn't, that would fit with the time of death.

Auntie glanced down at her watch. "I have to go," she said to Consuela. "But if you think of anything, call this number." She handed a small piece of paper to the maid and started toward the steps.

"Thanks for your time," I said and followed my aunt back to the parking lot.

"Did you find out anything?" I asked. "With your little interrogation?"

Consuela had gone into the room she'd been cleaning and shut the door, leaving us standing outside. She seemed quite pleased with shutting us out.

"No. I didn't," she said. "Did you?"

"No," I said.

"You know, I made a big deal out of Pogue not knowing what to do..." Auntie's voice trailed off.

"And now you don't know what to do?" I asked. "Now you see how hard it is to conduct a murder investigation."

"That's not what I was going to say."

"What were you going to say?"

"I was going to say...You know what, let's get out of here." She pointed toward the parking lot. "My car is parked over there."

She looped her arm around mine and we started down the steps.

"Auntie, don't' feel bad," I said. "It is hard figuring out who a murderer is even when you have been trained as a homicide investigator."

"What?"

"It's a lot, I'm just saying, to figure out. So don't let it bother you. You need evidence. Clues to lead you from Point A to B. Then to the murderer."

She didn't say anything else and was quiet as we walked through the parking lot. We made it over to Auntie's white Cadillac, the same make she used for the cars at the funeral home. She unlocked her door, then clicked the switch so I could open mine.

"What's hard is not having any cooperation," she said. "It would be easier to do this if I had some help." She looked at me. "That's what I was going to say about Pogue. That he was going to need help."

"I plan on helping Pogue," I said.

"Did you give him the autopsy report?" she asked.

"Yes, I did," I said.

"Good."

"Auntie, I had to give it to him. He's investigating the murder of the guy at your funeral home."

"I know. Didn't I say 'good?' You do what you have to do," she said. "And I'll do what I have to do to get information."

"That worries me," I said. "And then what are you going to do with the information once you've gotten it?" I asked.

"I'll let the sheriff know." She put her head down. "After I've solved it."

"Yeah, right," I said. "You're solving it?"

"You think I can't?"

"No. I don't," I said. "Evidently you think you can, giving Consuela your number, telling her to call you if she thought of anything."

"That's what people say when they're investigating a murder."

"Yeah, they do because they are able to know a lead when they see it, and they know how to follow it," I said. "You didn't get anything today with all your snooping and questioning. You just need to let Pogue do it. Give him any information you have or get."

"Heavens," she said.

"Oh, that's right," I said. "You said you couldn't trust Pogue."

"I never said I couldn't trust him." She glanced at me. "I said that he'd turn Josephine Gail in to save his mother."

"Isn't that the same thing?"

"No."

"Okay. So, are you planning on handing over to Pogue all the incriminating information you find?" I asked. "I presume about his mother?"

"No. I already told you I wasn't giving him anything until I solved it."

"Found the evidence against his mother?"

"Right."

"And how are you going to conduct this investigation? You'd need law enforcement to do things like run prints, match DNA, and follow leads. You can't do it without them. Without their technology."

"I have Rhett."

I frowned. "Your French-speaking funeral boy?"

She scrunched up her face. "What is a funeral boy?" She shook her head. "You better be nice to him."

"I'll be nice," I said. "I am nice. I was just saying who is he to help?"

"He's FBI. Used to be part of highly secret covert operations, he's certified in spying and everything. And now he's helping me look into this case."

"No, he's not," I said. "And I can't believe that man was ever a spy or anything close."

"Yes, he is." She sucked her tongue. "Well he used to be an FBI agent, and I probably shouldn't have mentioned his top-secret missions. But he still has a lot of connections. He told me that if the man was murdered somewhere outside of Roble and brought to my funeral home, it might not even be in Pogue's jurisdiction."

"Why would you want to do that to Pogue?"

"Do what?"

"You know he's trying to solve this murder."

"He's trying to make Josephine Gail out to be a murderer is what he's doing." She looked at me. "If only I could get him to drink some of my tea I could calm him down and talk to him about this. Right now he's so gung ho about solving it that he's not thinking straight."

I shook my head. I was thinking that I could say the same thing about her.

Maybe she should drink some tea...

"It's his job, Auntie Zanne," I said. "And he wants to do a good job."

"He's jumping to conclusions."

"He is not. He is just gathering information." She had a look of disbelief on her face.

"And," she said, "Rhett also told me that if I get him proof of someone else committing the murder, he'll make sure it gets to the right person."

I froze. I felt like my breathing had been blocked and someone was holding me down.

"What is wrong with you?" Auntie Zanne asked. "You look like you're lost."

I turned and looked at her. I felt sick–this conversation with her was making my stomach turn.

I was nervous that Rhett Remmiere, a man who followed my aunt around like a lovesick puppy, would kowtow to her and interfere in what Pogue was trying to do, especially now that he might be a suspect.

I scrunched up my eyes and stared at her. I wasn't sure if she was telling me the truth about her little fake-French friend. She did have a tendency to overdramatize and exaggerate. But I did know he'd do just about anything for her. And if she reported to him some information about Aunt Julep, I couldn't be so sure, if he did have some kind of relationship with the FBI, that he wouldn't pass it along to someone more important than a little ole County Sheriff like Pogue.

In the end, I knew it wouldn't amount to anything because Julep Folsom, my beloved aunt, hadn't murdered anyone. But in the interim, trying to straighten out all the wrong information disseminated, it sure could cause one heck of a hullabaloo.

Just the sort of thing my Auntie Zanne enjoyed being a part of.

"So, tell me this," I shifted in my seat and turned to face her, "if Aunt Julep killed him, why in the world would she bring him to your funeral home?"

"To make me look bad."

"And run the risk of getting caught? Murder is a very serious crime."

"Don't I know it, darlin'."

"Yes, you do," I said. "And so does Aunt Julep." I swallowed and held out my hands in an act of pleading. "She wouldn't take the chance of being found out. She could have put that guy in a pine box and put him in a potter's field somewhere and no one would have ever known."

"We don't have those anymore."

"Or even cremated him. She has a furnace, you know."

"Probably doesn't work." She turned up her nose. "Nothing works over that at the Broke Down Grove Funeral Parlor."

"Garden Grove," I said. "And she would have embalmed him properly."

She cut an eye at me. "He wasn't embalmed properly?" she asked.

"No. Not even close. Now doesn't that tell you it wasn't Aunt Julep?" I tried to reason with her. "She knows the Code of Ethical Conduct for the Care of the Decedent. Even if you think she could commit murder, you couldn't think that she'd violate a code of ethics."

She sucked in a breath.

"I can't let Josephine Gail go through this," she said, her voice wispy. "Have you seen her?" She turned and looked at me. I thought I might have even seen a tear in her eye. I didn't ever remember seeing my auntie cry. "The last time she was like this, she was administered shock treatments."

"Electroshock therapy?" My brows knitted together.

"It'll kill her if that happens again." She took her eyes off the road to look at me. "I'm investigating why my friend went into a deep depression just because she found a man in our funeral home."

"Is that the reason? Maybe it was something else."

"You're a doctor, Romaine," Auntie Zanne said. "People who

suffer from depression don't always know what's bothering them. Sometimes they feel lost and alone for no reason."

"I know that."

"And it doesn't matter what we say or what we do, they just can't snap out of it."

"I know that, too, Auntie."

"But what we can do is be supportive. Be a friend." She swallowed. "And I've always tried to be a friend to her. And this time, my way of being supportive is to see if perhaps my squatter is the reason she's feeling so bad and why. And the only way I can do that, help try to make her feel better, in my opinion, is to find out what happened."

I turned and gazed out of the window. Now I was starting to feel bad. Giving my auntie such a hard time. I probably could have been more supportive of her breaking the law and snooping around.

Wait...that didn't sound right.

Chapter Sixteen

I hadn't paid much attention to where we were going on the way back from the Grandview. I had stared out of the window for the better part of the trip, seemingly in my own world. Mostly because I didn't want Auntie to have the chance to pull me into any more of her craziness, so I avoided any talking with her.

But when I realized where she'd taken me, I wished I had taken notice and flung myself out of the car onto the asphalt road somewhere along the highway.

"I just want to have a look around," she said as she parked the car two houses down. "C'mon, Romaine. Get out of the car."

I didn't move.

I'd only been home a couple of days. Still, I should have gone to see my Aunt Julep by now. She was the only paternal relative, besides Pogue, that I was close to and had ever had any kind of relationship with. And now, here I was sitting in a parked car down from her place of business, and it appeared the reason was not to show familial love, but to sneak around on her property with her archrival, Suzanne Derbinay, to find out if my Aunt Julep committed murder or not.

How would that make my Aunt Julep feel if she knew that?

I hung my head in shame.

"If you don't c'mon," she said, "someone will see us."

I didn't know why she thought the speed of me agreeing to

trespass would somehow keep us out of sight, but my legs just wouldn't move any faster.

"Why are we doing this?" I said, raising my voice as I got out of the car so she'd hear me.

"You're too loud," she said. "You'll call attention to us." She turned to walk into the driveway of the Folsom family business.

The Garden Grove Funeral Home wasn't as large as The Ball Funeral Home & Crematorium in name or reputation. It wasn't as grand, nor did it do the same volume of business, but it was well maintained and welcoming. My Aunt Julep's place catered to mostly black families, while Auntie Zanne's only requirement was that the person was dead. Nothing else mattered.

The front yard to Aunt Julep's establishment was full of green grass and colorful annuals that were, as I remembered, changed out often. I hadn't visited in a while, but it looked exactly the same.

As I made my way to the driveway, I bent over, ducking below the windows on the front and side of the house so that I could try to go unnoticed. Auntie Zanne, however, marched with her head held high, that red hat flapping in the breeze, and her nose in the air like she had every right to be there.

"Auntie Zanne," I called after her. I was tiptoeing through the grass trying to avoid the sidewalk. I should have called her, "Auntie Zany," because this was a crazy idea.

And I was following right behind her.

"Can you please not do this?" I asked as she rounded the funeral home and went into the backyard.

"I'm not doing anything," she said. "I told you I just–Hey! Look at this." She beckoned me over. I bent over and ran past the remaining windows.

"What is it?"

She pointed to a shotgun laying on the steps. It was in the process of being broken down and cleaned. A white rag, cleaning oil, some swabs, and a box of ammunition were sitting near it.

"So?" I said and hunched my shoulders. "It probably just means someone is cleaning it and they'll be coming back soon." I turned and looked from side to side. "So, we should get out of here."

"Looks like she's trying to hide it back here," Auntie Zanne said. "Could be evidence."

"Doesn't look like Aunt Julep's hiding anything. Looks like someone is cleaning it, like I said. And I can't picture Aunt Julep being the one sitting out here doing it."

"Take a picture."

"What? No."

"Where's your phone?" she asked and started patting me down. I pushed her hands away. "You can take a picture with your phone. There's an app or something, just like you said you could use to record when you were doing the autopsy."

"I know. It's not an app. It's built into the phone." As if she knew more about a cellphone than I did. She didn't even own one. "But there is no reason to take a picture of that."

"It could be the murder weapon," she said.

"No, it couldn't," I said.

"How do you know?"

I pointed to the box of ammunition. "He wasn't killed with a slug."

"What?"

"There were pellet entry wounds all over his back."

"Oh," she said. She seemed deflated.

"What did you expect to find here?" I asked. "A smoking gun?"

"No," she said and flapped her arms, then pointed at the shotgun. "But I was hoping that maybe it was *the* gun." She huffed. "Not exactly sure what I'd find," she admitted. "I was just hoping."

"Hoping that it was my Aunt Julep and not your friend whodunit?"

"Exactly," she said.

"Oh brother," I said. "Can we go before she sees me?"

"You don't want her seeing you?"

"No. I don't. Not while I'm out here with you looking for clues that will make her a murderer."

"It won't be my fault if she is," Auntie Zanne said in a huff. She swiped the barrel of the shotgun that was laying free. She knocked it on the ground and started walking back to the car, cutting across the grass in a diagonal, not even worried even a little bit about trespassing through the neighbor's yard.

"You can't force the shoe to fit," I called to her. I bent down to pick up the barrel. "Don't you remember the story of Cinderella? No one could make the shoe fit their foot," I said as if she didn't know the fairytale. "Same thing with Aunt Julep."

"Can I help you?" A rather tall, wide black man stood on the porch. He stuck his hand out and wiggled his fingers. I looked down in my hands, I was still holding on to the barrel. "That," he said, "belongs to me."

I didn't know who he was, but I handed it to him, then hightailed it the heck out of there.

Chapter Seventeen

It was a tug of war with Auntie Zanne to get the keys from her after we got back to the car. I wasn't going to sit idly by and let her drag me to any more of her imagined crime scenes. And I was ready to get back to the house. Unfortunately, that wasn't what Roble's Social Queen Bee had planned.

"I need to make a stop," Auntie Zanne said, two blocks before our street.

"Where?" I asked. "You want to go plant evidence at Aunt Julep's house?"

"No," she said. She looked at me disapprovingly. "Aren't you snippy? I have to go and check-in at Angel's Grace."

Grace Community Center, nicknamed Angel's Grace, was Auntie's hub. It was the home of Roble's Belles, the high school booster club, her food and clothing drive operation, and the county's soup kitchen. And it was her hangout. It was the second place I'd look if I needed her and she wasn't at the funeral home.

I did a U-turn. "I don't want to go there and stay all day," I said.

"Day's more than half over. Couldn't stay all day even if I wanted to."

"You know what I mean."

"I won't stay but a minute," she said. "I just have to check out everybody."

By everybody, I knew she meant her first-tier gossip mill.

I put the blinker on to turn into the parking lot. "You think someone here might have seen my Aunt Julep carry the body in?"

"It's possible," she said, more seriously than I liked. "Pull over there." She pointed. "I have a reserved spot next to the door."

"Figures," I said. I parked and waited for her to get out.

"Come in," she said. "Everyone wants to see you."

"Did you tell them I was here to stay?" I asked.

"Of course not," she said, acting surprised. "I wouldn't say that to anyone."

"You've told that to everyone else." I turned the car off and got out.

"No I haven't," she said, waiting for me to come around the car.

"You told Catfish and Rhett."

"Oh," she said and looked at me sheepishly. "I just told them in case they wanted to make a move. They wouldn't feel like they were wasting their time."

"Make a move? Auntie!" I said. "I don't want anyone to make a move on me."

"Not yet, but once I can get some of my tea in you, you'll be singing a different tune."

"Hi!" Auntie was greeted at the door by her fellow Belles. Chester, the only male Belle, yanking it open before she could even grab the handle. Mark, Leonard and Flannery stood waiting with nervous smiles on their faces.

"Are you okay?" Mark and Leonard asked at the same time. They stood on either side of her and placed their hands on her arms.

Mark and Leonard were twins. Twin girls. They loved their father so much that after he died, when they were only seventeen, they changed their names to his. Typical to people in the south, he'd had two names and so they each took one. At least that was the story that Auntie Zanne told me. Of course, by the time I met them, they already had their current monikers.

Our next-door neighbors, they were in their mid-seventies, and their names were the only things different about them. They were identical in every other sense. Their mannerisms, dress, and ailments. I heard many a time about Auntie having to go over to take care of them both getting sick with the same thing at the same time. Although being members, along with Auntie Zanne, in the Distinguished Ladies' Society of Voodoo Herbalists, one would think they could heal themselves.

"Yes, I'm fine," Auntie Zanne said. "But I had to have Romaine drive me over. This is all a lot to take in."

I just shook my head at my auntie's exaggeration. She'd been driving most of the day.

"Romaine!" Mark exclaimed. I guess they had just noticed me. "It's so good to see you!" She came over and took my hand. "Look, Leonard, isn't she still just as beautiful as the day we first seen her?"

"Yes, she is," Leonard said.

"Thank you," I said.

The twins were always reminiscing. It seemed easier for them to remember what happened thirty years ago than what happened the day before. But even with their shaky memories, Auntie swore she couldn't run the center without them. Without any of them, including Chester and Flannery.

"So good to see you," Flannery said and came over. Squeezing past Mark and Leonard, she hugged me. "Spoon told me he'd just seen you."

"Yep. Over at the house. He's in the zydeco band," I said.

"He is," Flannery said with a smile. Just as pretty as the last time I'd seen her. "And I think him playing those drums makes him happier than me."

"I don't think that's possible," Auntie Zanne said. "But I came over to get information."

She had a need to be the center of attention.

"I need your help. But I want to keep all of this amongst ourselves," Auntie said.

"Of course," Mark said and took Auntie's hand and led her into the back kitchen. "Come on, let's get a seat."

Chester ran ahead and pulled a chair out from the table that sat in the corner. The room was all stainless steel and commercial grade. Auntie and her clan had served many a Thanksgiving and Christmas meal from there.

Auntie took a seat and put on a fake exhausted look. "I just don't know what's going on at my funeral home," she said. "I leave for two weeks and the whole thing goes to hell in a handbasket."

"It's terrible," Chester said, shaking his head.

Chester wore his Roble Belles-monogrammed shiny blue jacket with pride and participated in gossip just as much as the women.

"How do you think it happened?" Flannery asked.

"I don't know. All I do know is that Josephine Gail didn't do it."

"Of course she didn't," Mark and Leonard said at the same time.

"How could anyone think such a thing?" Leonard asked.

Auntie looked over at me. All I could think was that if she mentioned my Aunt Julep, I was going to scoop her up and stuff her inside the kitchen's commercial fridge till she cooled down.

"I don't know," Auntie said. "But you know she is the one that found the body."

"Well, what about your new girl?" Mark asked. "Did she see anything?"

"She just started," Auntie said.

Mark and Leonard looked at each other.

"What?" Auntie asked.

"Well..." Leonard started. "We saw her."

"Go into the funeral home," Mark added.

"While you were gone," Leonard finished their sentence.

"At first, we thought maybe she was set to begin working," Mark said. "But..."

"She never came back," Leonard said. "At least not until the day after you got back. You and Romaine." She smiled at me.

"That was the day she was supposed to start," Auntie Zanne said.

"Oh," they said.

"What do you think that means?" Chester asked. "Do you think she did it?"

"I don't know," Auntie said, shaking her head. She tugged on her bottom lip. "But I don't think so."

"What's her name?" Flannery asked.

"Floneva Floyd," Auntie answered.

"She's from Hemphill," I said. I looked at Auntie. "A hop, skip and jump from Yellowpine."

"She sure is," Auntie said, nodding.

"You better check her out," Chester said. "She seems like a good candidate."

"Who do you think, Babet?" Flannery asked.

"We've got a couple of leads we're following. But I don't think it was anyone around here," Auntie said. "Because wouldn't that just be awful?"

"Awful," the twins said in unison.

"Maybe Leonard and I should come over and view the body," Mark said.

"Good idea, Mark," Leonard said. "To see if we recognize him." She nodded. "You are going to have a viewing, aren't you?"

"What a good idea," Auntie Zanne said. "I hadn't thought of that."

"I don't think it's a good idea," I said, which made everyone looked at me disapprovingly.

"Oh look," Chester pointed out the mullioned front windows. "It's Coach Williams."

"The coach?" Auntie said, her attention diverted just that quickly. "I need to speak with him about summer practice." She looked at me. "You can get the car. I'll be right out."

"He coaches high school football," I said, guessing. Auntie wouldn't have called him "Coach" otherwise.

"Yes," Mark and Leonard said together.

"The leader of our Roble Belles," Flannery said.

"Amen," the four of them chimed.

Chapter Eighteen

We had finally made it home. Auntie still had enough energy to go and embalm our John Doe.

I sat on the back porch with J.R. and a glass of ice-cold lemonade. Sweat dripped down the side of it, lemon, mint, and ice packed into the glass. I laid my phone on the banister and put my feet up next to it.

"Long day, huh, J.R.?" I said.

He went over and laid down at the top of the steps.

"Exactly how I feel," I said.

I looked around and remembered how I used to hang out on the back porch. It was so calming and gave off such good vibes. The back of the house was so different from the front.

There were lots of live oak trees that covered every part of the property, in fact every inch of Roble, and why not. The town's name meant oak in Spanish.

There was no definition to Auntie Zanne's backyard. No rhyme or reason. Auntie's perennials grew tall and wild all over the yard. A plethora of colors, a bouquet of fragrance. Butterflies flitted and bees buzzed about.

The windows in the white-framed greenhouse sparkled. Auntie Zanne's place was a potted palace. There were rows of the annuals she grew for the front of the funeral home, and the plants and herbs she used for her teas and brews she made from recipes she claimed were hundreds of years old. But there was nothing old about her greenhouse. It was modern with ample room to expand and plenty of head room. There was a mist system, a heating system, and a wall for all of her coveted tools.

And to the rear of it, a rambling pebble stone walkway staggered its way down to a white gazebo that bordered a small pond, the verdant grass surrounding it was lush and vast.

The sun seemed to shine brighter in this part of the house. None of the gloom or the sadness that surrounded all that entered through the other side.

The front of the house was stately. A testament to its time and era, updated and preserved, it had found a new, useful purpose—one, my auntie taught me from the first day I arrived, that will never be outdated.

Ball Funeral Home & Crematorium was a haven of sorts for exuding the care and respect due not only to families at the low points in their lives—but to the dignity, transport, and shelter of the remains of the decedent. It was a beautiful facade to the public, a sanctuary to the grieving.

I took a sip of my lemonade and thought about my first day back in Roble. I closed my eyes.

Back in Roble...

I didn't want to say back *home*, even though Rhett had given me grief about that. I just needed to keep telling myself that being back was only temporary and not let myself forget that I was going to make a way back.

The day had been so crazy and busy that I'd almost forgotten how unhappy I was supposed to be. Crazy and busy was what I was used to, but this kind of busy had been different. It had felt good doing that autopsy. And the possibility to get more involved and help Pogue was intriguing. In my position in Chicago, I'd always just handed over my findings to the detective in charge and that ended my involvement. Law enforcement would ask me for the cause and manner of death, an approximate time, and perhaps a handful of questions, but that was as far as it ever went. I was never a part of putting the clues together. I ran my hand over my arm. I had goosebumps thinking about the opportunity.

I didn't know what I was going to do about Auntie Zanne, though.

For some reason she was dead set on my Aunt Julep being the murderer. And my little old auntie was a force to be reckoned with. She would be in the way, demanding to be heard, coming up with all of her own theories, and causing all kinds of confusion. Everyone in Roble respected her and listened to her. Pogue would have to fight against that to solve this murder. I guess I could run interference. Not a job I was looking forward to.

And one my auntie wouldn't make easy for me to do.

I could do so much to help if Auntie Zanne would let me and Pogue do this. Help Pogue make a name for himself and keep my Aunt Julep from being accused and Auntie Zanne dragging her name through the mud. We could help Josephine Gail, which seemed to be all Auntie Zanne wanted. Perhaps she didn't realize that it was what I wanted too.

I picked up the phone and googled the name of the man registered at Grandview Motor Lodge. I didn't find one thing about him. It was like he didn't exist.

Then I thought about Josephine Gail. I wondered if when she was feeling bad—deeply lost in her depression—did it feel like how I'd been feeling? I had always wondered if she was feeling the way I did when I lost my parents, or how I felt now that I had to come back to Roble.

Yeah. If I were completely honest with myself, I'd have to say that I knew exactly how Josephine Gail felt. The only difference was I didn't know how she could make it back after going down that road so many times. I'd only felt that way a time or two and right now I wondered if I could. It must be hard for her living in that world all the time.

I let out a long sigh.

But I needed to convince myself that I could make it back to normal—heck, to happy even—if I could just get back to my life. My apartment. My job. And to my Alex.

Well, he wasn't completely mine.

Still, a girl could hope.

He had promised me, and I believed him, that one day soon we'd be together. After we'd met and started dating, he was what seemed to complete the life I had been chasing when I left Roble. After finding him, I had everything I wanted.

But maybe now that I'd left, he'd forget about me. About his promises. I wondered did he even think about me. I'd been busy all day and it was just now that my thoughts had settled on him. Had his thoughts come around to me?

I looked at my phone.

I hadn't heard from him. Sure, he had stopped by before I left Chicago, and gave me a call to make sure I'd arrived safely once I got to Roble. But neither time were we able to talk.

I missed him terribly. I wondered if he missed me the same way.

Then my phone rang and startled me.

Maybe it was Alex.

I took my feet off the banister, sat up and picked up the phone, my heart pounding I mentally crossed my fingers. Wouldn't it just be such a coincidence if it were him?

I looked at the phone screen. The number that was shown wasn't a number I recognized, but it was from a Chicago area code. Maybe it could be...

I answered it, only to find it to be a telemarketer.

How did they even get my cell number?

Shoot.

I started to lay the phone back on the banister and thought, why not just call him? I didn't have to wait until Alex called me.

I put in the code to unlock my phone and clicked on the dialer icon. Then I just stared at the screen. I blew out a breath and punched in his number. Before it started to ring, my fingertip hovered over the END button. I needed to talk to him, so I hung on.

Two rings. No answer.

Pick up.

I glanced at my watch.

He should be home by now...

By the fourth ring, I was holding my breath and starting to feel sad and dejected. I didn't want to feel like that.

Maybe I should just hang up.

"Hello." His picking up caught me by surprise. I had been so busy debating whether I should hang up or not.

"Romaine? Baby," he said. "I'm so happy you called. I was just thinking about you. About how much I miss you."

I let out the breath I'd been holding.

Chapter Nineteen

That couch was going to be the death of me. Just the two nights was putting a strain on my back that eight hours standing doing autopsies hadn't made me feel. I felt as if I'd never be able to straighten my spine out again.

The house was quiet, and as I made my way into the kitchen. I didn't see Auntie Zanne anywhere. She might have been on a run. Picking up bodies wasn't a nine-to-five kind of job.

I heard my phone ring as soon as I walked into the room. I did a U-turn and went back to the Death Trap Couch where I had plugged it up the night before.

"Hello," I said as I headed back to the kitchen.

"We got an ID."

"Oh, hi, Pogue." I switched ears, pulled out a chair and sat at the kitchen table. "How's your trip going?"

"Good. You were right. I am learning a lot."

"See. I told you. Although I don't know how much you could've learned. You haven't been there twenty-four hours."

He laughed. "So, did you hear what I said?"

"You got an ID?"

"Yes. They just called me."

"On your John Doe?" I asked. It had just clicked what he meant.

"Yep," he said. "His fingerprints were in the database."

"That's good," I said. "Was it somebody local?" I hadn't felt like it was because if Auntie Zanne hadn't recognized the dead squatter, he couldn't have been from around these parts. She'd met so many people in her line of business and participating in all her auxiliaries and clubs, and she was not one to forget a face.

"They belonged to a Ragland Williamson. Last address they had for him is in Houston."

"Houston?" I asked. "Long way from here."

"Yeah. I know," he said.

"What was he doing here?"

"I don't know," Pogue said. "All I have on him so far is the name and an address. Not even sure if it's a current address. I'll have to look into it."

"Okay," I said. "That's good. That's a start."

"But Romie..." I could hear the nervousness seeping into his words. "After I do that, I don't know where I'd go from there."

He had assured Auntie Zanne that he knew what to do, but I knew my cousin. His mind at this point, with him being new on the job, probably wasn't as analytical as it needed to be for such a big undertaking.

"You'll figure your way through it," I said. I wanted to show my support. "Things will fall into place. And, don't forget, while you're in Reno, ask questions."

"Is that the way they do it in Chicago? They just wait until things fall into place? And ask other people questions?"

"They have a lot of experience." I stood up, reached for the teapot on the stove and filled it up with water at the sink. "You don't have to do what anyone else is doing," I said balancing the phone between my shoulder and ear. "But I would say, yes. That's the way they do it. Those detectives in Chicago were new at one time too. They had to learn, just like you do."

"Yeah, but they had someone helping them. Mentoring them. I don't."

"You've got me," I said. I turned up the flame under the teapot. "I'll help you. I already told you that."

"How?"

"I'm the acting medical examiner on this case."

"Yeah, I guess you are. Doc Westin has a bad case of the flu. He might be out for a week or so, and with his age, maybe even longer. So, basically I'ma deputize you as the deputy coroner."

"I've already done the autopsy."

"It'll be retroactive." He paused. "If there is such a thing. I don't know if I was supposed to fill out any paperwork."

"I'm sure it'll be fine. We can backdate if necessary."

"Good idea. So you're officially my deputy coroner. Okay?"

"Okay," I said resolutely. "See, I can help in that capacity and we can discuss any clues you find. I can help you check into anything that you need me to. Medical examiners can have good detective skills. Don't you remember that television show *Quincy, M.E.*?"

"No. And I thought we agreed television isn't a good analogy for us."

"Oh yeah, I forgot."

"And I want you to help me, I just don't know," he said and paused. "You have Babet nagging you, dragging you along with all of her craziness."

I thought about her in that motel room. And wanting to have a service so the whole town could view the body.

"Yeah, about that," I said. "Auntie is planning a funeral."

"A funeral!" he screeched. "Why?"

"To see if anyone recognizes the body."

"Oh Lord, Romie! Please. Please don't let her do that. That's gotta be tampering with evidence or abuse of a corpse or something."

"I'll try," I said.

"Don't try, Romaine. Do it."

I didn't say anything. I was thinking how I could stop Auntie Zanne from doing it. My thoughts were flitting around. I couldn't think of one way to stop her.

"Romaine! Are you there? Did you hang up?"

"Yeah. No. I was just thinking," I said.

"You're not helping her do this, are you?"

"No. Of course not."

"I know she can talk you into stuff."

"No, she can't," I said. "You know she's can't talk me into anything that I don't want to do, right?"

"There's two sides to that coin," he said. "And why does she want to do this? She already has it made up in her mind who the killer is."

"*Humph*," I mumbled. "She says the same thing about you."

Chapter Twenty

I hung up with Pogue and sat cross-legged in the chair.

His name was Ragland Williamson.

He wasn't a John Doe any more. He had a name. Lived in a big city. He'd had a life.

And what was he doing in little ole Sabine County?

The man who was registered at the motel, Herman St. John, wasn't the man that had been found in my auntie's funeral home. They were two different men and probably, like the owner of the Grandview said, the St. John guy had just gone off for a couple of days. Nothing fishy about that.

I wonder, should I tell her about her being wrong?

Not that I had believed Auntie Zanne. With her "universe settling in theory" making her able to find the one place that Dead Squatter Guy had been staying before he got to the funeral home. And her smelling formaldehyde, and trying to get me to smell it too...

Okay, I might have gotten a whiff of it.

Why would the smell of formaldehyde be in a motel room?

She had been right about one thing though. He hadn't been embalmed there. I shook my head. Dead Guy hadn't actually been embalmed at all. Whoever put that embalming fluid in him, on him, or wherever they put it, didn't know what they were doing. There was still blood in the arteries and veins and the organs inside the body cavity hadn't been touched.

I knew that when I watched her search that motel room. While she looked for clues that Aunt Julep had had something to do with it. Then I had let her drag me off to do reconnaissance on my Aunt Julep's funeral home.

I blew out a breath.

I can't let Pogue know I did that. But, in my defense, I thought, I didn't really have a choice. I was in her car, and if I wanted to get back to the house, I had to go with her.

Yeah, but you didn't have to get out of the car.

All of that didn't matter now because Auntie Zanne's guy wasn't the John Doe. And what I needed to worry about was making up to my Aunt Julep for going to her funeral home, snooping around and not even saying hello to her. Especially after I'd gotten caught.

The whistle went off on the teapot and I popped up out of the chair. I went to the cabinet and swung open both doors. The shelves were stacked with canisters and jars full of herbs, teas, and sundry other items, most of them from Auntie Zanne's greenhouse.

"I'm not touching anything in here," I said and closed both doors. "Darn it. I forgot. I meant to pick me up some coffee." I looked around the room. "Maybe there's some in the pantry."

"Howdy," Floneva said as she walked in the room.

I swirled around.

"Hi Floneva," I said. I'd been wanting to speak with her. She was one of Pogue's suspects. "Keeping busy?"

"Not much to do when everyone around is dead."

"True," I said. "So. What do you think about working in a funeral home?"

"Not my first rodeo," she said.

"No?" I asked. "You worked in a funeral home before?"

"Yep. I like mortuary science. I started to get my license, but I didn't do too well in school," she said. "My grandmother said just 'cause I don't mind being around dead people didn't mean I should try to be a mortician."

"Really now," I said. "So you went through the embalming classes and everything?"

"Yep. That was about the time I flunked out. Ain't ashamed to say it. Gotta know your own limitations my Aunt Bert used to say."

"So, did you stop by here before we got back?"

"Got back from where?" she asked.

"Chicago."

"Oh yeah. I left my sweater here when I came for the interview. Came back to pick it up."

"That's all you did while you were here?"

"Yep." She looked at me. First time I'd seen her without a goofy look. "I just came in to get my lunch out of the fridge," she said. "If you don't mind."

I waved my hand toward the refrigerator. "Go ahead."

She got her lunch and walked out without saying another word.

Suspicious, I thought.

Floneva knew how to embalm. And, it appears, not very well since she hadn't finished the classes. That was something Pogue needed to know.

And I'd be sure to tell Auntie Zanne. Maybe it would give her someone else to go after other than my Aunt Julep.

Poor Aunt Julep.

I slung open the pantry door to find coffee and saw the tubs of crawfish Catfish had left.

Auntie and her pies.

Ugh!

But then I got an idea.

I didn't have any plans on making pies for Rhett and his band of dissidents. I mean, what was the big deal in adding a different band member? That couldn't possibly cause a revolt. From what I remembered while living with my parents, musicians were all one big happy family.

I surveyed all the little mudbugs snapping their front claws and smiled. No need of letting all of Catfish's catch go to waste. I'd make a pot of crawfish étouffée for my Aunt Julep. She loved it, and it would be a peace offering. I'd use it to smooth over things, even though Aunt Julep didn't know I had anything to make up for.

I grabbed a bucket and tried to lift it. My back couldn't take it, and the muscular definition in my arms that I had worked hard to build wasn't enough to compensate. I bent over, tugged at the tub and, walking backwards, pulled it out into the kitchen. I stood up, put my hands at the lower part of my back and stretched. Then I took my foot and pushed the tub of crawfish over by the stove.

I found a big lobster pot, filled it three fourths full of water and filled it with spices I found in Auntie Zanne's cabinet. Just the ones I knew for sure were what they were marked. Thyme. Black peppercorns. Salt. A little cayenne pepper. I turned on the fire underneath to get it to boil.

I needed rice, tomatoes and the trinity of Creole cooking–onions, green peppers, and celery. I knew even though Auntie Zanne had gone all Texan on me, she wouldn't ever let her kitchen be without any of those things. I pulled open the refrigerator and there, under the glow of the interior light, sat a shiny pepper, fresh celery stalks, and a ruby red Better Boy tomato. I grabbed them, put them on the table and found a clove of garlic and a white onion in a small basket on the counter. Auntie Zanne kept enough garlic to deter a drove of vampires.

I rolled up my sleeve, and a smile spread across my face. The one thing I did better than death was cook.

Chapter Twenty-One

This was the second time I was going to visit one of my Aunt Julep's properties since I'd been back in Roble. First to the funeral home. Now to her house. Both times on a mission. This one a little kinder.

My peace offering, neatly wrapped, was still hot. My rice had come out perfectly: every grain separate. The crawfish étouffée was so aromatic and yummy smelling that it brought Floneva from the receptionist area to the kitchen while I was cooking. She told me the smell made her mouth water and could probably wake the dead.

"Don't be surprised," she had said, "if a couple of those bodies rise to come in here just for a bowl." I, of course, after such a compliment, couldn't deny her a heaping helping of it.

I took out a bowl for Auntie Zanne and Rhett, packed the rest and drove to Aunt Julep's with a smile on my face. I sang along with the radio, happy to be in the car alone. I had found the keys to one of the older model Cadillacs that Auntie only used when there was a need to accommodate more family members than could fit into the late model cars she owned. I knew she wouldn't mind if I borrowed it for the day.

The Garden Grove Funeral Home, unlike Auntie Zanne's, was housed separately from the living quarters. The Folsom's family home was much smaller and located a couple of blocks from their business. I pulled up in the driveway and took in my surroundings before I got out of the car. I could see the house was in need of repair, not as well cared for as the business property.

"I know Pogue isn't too busy being sheriff that he can't see to his momma's house," I muttered as I pushed opened the car door.

I went around to the passenger side and pulled out the two pots—I didn't want to mix the rice in until it was served. Still humming my tune, I went to the back door. But before I could even make it to the steps, I saw something that forced me to drop my little ditty and almost spill all of my morning's work. There, by Aunt Julep's trashcans, were four plastic, Air Force blue-colored jugs with FORMALDEHYDE printed across the front.

What in the world...

The first thing I thought about was Auntie Zanne. I was happy that she'd chosen to go to the funeral home to look for evidence rather than Aunt Julep's house. This would have definitely been her "smoking gun."

Had someone taken some of the contents of one of these jugs and used it on Dead Guy? Was it someone that worked at Aunt Julep's funeral home?

This wasn't good.

I made a mental note to tell Pogue about the danger of his mother having formaldehyde in her backyard, and to have the lab check it to see if they could match the lot to what had been used on Dead Guy.

Geesh.

I shook off my discovery and thoughts of murder and walked up the steps to the back door. Aunt Julep never locked her doors. Most people around Roble didn't. It was probably how Auntie Zanne had gotten a stowaway at her house. Even so, most people who didn't frequent a home often had enough manners to knock on the door before they entered.

I was raised to have good manners.

"Knock, knock," I said as I turned the knob, pushed open the door and stepped into the kitchen. "Aunt Julep? You here?"

"Who is it?" The voice was faint.

"It's me, Aunt Julep. Romaine."

"Ah! Romaine, baby," she called from the other room. "Here I come. Oh my goodness! You should have called, I could have fixed you something to eat."

I set the food down on the stove, my smile growing wider knowing I was going to surprise her.

"Oh, I should have," I said. "Because I'm starving."

She appeared in the doorway, her dentures showing evenly lined teeth.

"Come give me a hug, baby."

I went over and hugged her.

"I'm so glad you came by," she said.

"I told you I would," I said. "You doing okay?"

"Oh fair to middling." She patted my cheek, her smile widening. "C'mon. Sit down." She pointed to the kitchen table. "Tell me what's going on with you. We didn't have time to talk the other day." She grabbed my arm and leaned on me as we made our way to the table. "What you been up to since you been back?"

My Auntie Zanne was spry, but I couldn't see that in my Aunt Julep. Only two years older than my Auntie Zanne, her health was in no way as good.

Maybe all of the associations and societies Auntie Zanne was in kept her on her toes. Or maybe, as she'd probably say, it was all of her brews that kept her young. Whatever it was, she didn't look anything close to eighty-two, while aging had definitely taken a toll on my Aunt Julep.

Maybe I should swipe something from Auntie Zanne's cabinet to give to her...

Auntie Zanne could still probably walk a mile or two down a country road. But not Aunt Julep. It seemed she needed help making it across the room. She shuffled along, her shoulders and neck drooped. I knew she was diabetic. I had often helped her check her glucose and discussed her diet with her whenever I'd come to Roble, and the few times she'd made it to Chicago. As far as I knew, it was under control. She maintained her doctor appointments and so she always told me, kept up with all of her medicines.

But now, I'd been back a few days and hadn't checked in yet. I felt bad.

I'd also known a time or two when she'd gone to my Auntie Zanne for a brew when she "was feelin' poorly" as she put it. Yep. Perhaps it was time that she made a visit to see Auntie Zanne. I knew I always railed against her remedies, but for some, taking something that you believed in was almost as good as getting something prescribed by a doctor.

Seeing Aunt Julep in this shape really made me upset with my Auntie Zanne as well. How could she think that Aunt Julep, in the condition she was in, could hunt down someone through the woods and shoot them in the back? What could she have been thinking?

"What you got there?" Aunt Julep pointed to the covered pots I'd put on the stove. "I thought I smelled something when I came in here."

I stood up and walked over to the stove. I picked up one of the pots, took it to her, and opened it. "I made you some crawfish étouffée," I said.

"Oh!" she said and covered her mouth with her hands. "That looks so good." She looked up at me. "I was going to cook for you."

"I was happy to do it," I said and bent over to make my face even with her. "I like doing things for you."

"You so sweet," she said and cupped her hands around my face. "Thank you."

"I'll grab us some plates," I said, standing up. I sat the crawfish dish on the table, grabbed some dishes from the cabinet, silverware from the drawer, and the rice I'd left on the stove.

"You hungry?" I asked.

"Well, if I wasn't before," she said, "with all those good smells you've filled my kitchen up with, I am now."

I fixed our plates and we ate until our bellies were full and laughed until Aunt Julep started coughing.

"Let me get these dishes," I said after we finished up.

"No, I can get them," she said and started to push herself up from the kitchen chair.

"Really, I don't mind," I said and touched her arm. "Don't get up." I cleared the table and started some dishwater in the sink. "I like helping you."

"Thank you, baby," she said.

"Aunt Julep?" I said as I rubbed the soapy water over a plate. "I just saw a couple of plastic jugs out in your backyard. They were marked with the word 'Formaldehyde.' Is that what's in them?"

"Oh, that's just some spent embalming fluid mixture."

"Oh," I said. "I thought everyone around here switched from using that to save the environment or something." I didn't want her to think I thought anything bad of her.

"I needn't worry none about the environment," she said. "I'll be dead before it hurts me."

"Don't tell me you don't believe in global warming?"

"Child, it's been hot in Texas all my life. And I'm sure for many lifetimes before mine. I don't think it could get much hotter. It was one hundred and four degrees last week."

"Why are those jugs there?" I asked. "Why aren't they at the funeral home?"

"I thought they'd be safer here. No one's going in and out of here except Pogue and a couple of ladies from my church," she said. "Too many people at the funeral parlor."

"That was a good idea, I guess," I said. "But what are you going to do with them? You can't just store them here long term."

"I got a guy that comes out and gets rid of all the waste. They were just put there the other day. I'll give him a call."

"A guy, Aunt Julep?" I creased my brow. "You know all that hazardous waste is pretty dangerous. You gotta be careful."

"You know I know that. I can't afford a professional company no more. Business isn't as good as it used to be. Gotta do the best I can do with what I got," she said. "But I know he does right by it. Disposes of it properly."

"Are you sure?"

"I'm sure," she said. "And it's the last of it." She squinted her eyes at me. "I have changed over to the no-formaldehyde embalming fluid. You didn't know that?"

"No," I said, and I wanted to add that apparently neither did Auntie Zanne. "Pogue didn't tell me."

"Well, I would have thought Babet would have told you. She campaigned around here long enough for it."

"Did she now?"

"Yes she did. And there's no saying no to her. At least not for long." She ran her fingers along the edge of the table. "I just had to wait until I used up what I had. No money to waste like that. But I had to cancel the hazardous waste pickup."

"I didn't know that you were having hard times, Aunt Julep," I said. "Why didn't you call me?"

"Call you for what?"

I shrugged. "I don't know," I said. "Money."

"I don't need your money," she said. "It's what happens when you get old. You can't do all the things you used to do. And I get by fine. Just can't do no added extras, that's all."

I guessed that was true. I just gauged everything by Auntie Zanne's standards. I should have kept up with my Aunt Julep more.

"Have you been feeling alright?" I said, not wanting to keep harping on her finances.

"I'm no spring chicken," she said. "The years have caught up with me."

"So who is running the funeral home these days?" I asked.

"I got a boy just finished up with funeral school. And Mr. Pollack and his wife still work for me."

"Mr. Pollack," I said, trying to conjure up a face to go with the name. "I don't think I know him."

"Well, he sure knows you," she said. "Said he seen you yesterday over at the funeral home messing with his shotgun."

Chapter Twenty-Two

I stood at the doorway of my old room and groaned. J.R. ran behind me, jumped on the bed, off the other side and ran in and out of the open closet.

"What are you so excited about, boy?" I asked him. "It couldn't be this room." He cocked his head to one side and looked up at me.

I had spent nearly the entire day with Aunt Julep. She had wanted me to go over to the funeral home to see the improvements she made and so she could show me off to her employees. I had to come up with something quick to avoid returning to those premises. I didn't want to run into that Mr. Pollack again and have to explain to Aunt Julep why I'd been there snooping around and getting caught holding the barrel to his gun in my hands.

So I told her I'd do her hair and nails for her, then promised I'd come back and go with her to her doctor's appointment on Friday. I was sure that would light a fire under Auntie Zanne, seeing it was the first day of the festival and she wanted me there. But the festival didn't start open until seven p.m., giving working people time to get home. That would give me plenty of time to spend with Aunt Julep during the day. Saturday and Sunday were the long days and I had already planned on being there then for Auntie Zanne.

But now, back home, the downstairs was busy with folks and funerals and I needed a place to retreat. Looking around, it was easy to see that my bedroom just wasn't going to cut it.

Standing in the middle of the floor, I knew I wasn't ever going to be able to hang out or sleep in that room. Not the way it looked. Not with all of what it reminded me of.

And as for sleeping, I couldn't go back to that couch. My back was still sore from trying to sleep the last two nights with my head and legs hanging over the edge. It made me groggy in the mornings and seemed to zap my vigor during the day. I needed a good night's sleep.

I looked down at J.R., his tail wagging and tongue hanging out, it looked like he was the only one getting the proper rest. He was full of energy.

I blew air noisily out of my nose. I didn't know what I could have been thinking when I had Auntie Zanne paint the walls lavender. And all the frills—as I think back it had to have been her that forced me into it. How could I have ever liked anything so cheesy?

All I wanted while I was here, which I still had my fingers crossed wouldn't be long, was a place I could come and hide away. To relax. And to get enough restful sleep to make it through each day until I could go back to Chicago.

There were always people around downstairs. Or in any of the rooms off the hallway where Josephine Gail slept. Families coming in to make arrangements for their loved ones, the funerals, Auntie's club meetings and all of her "clients" coming in for her supernatural help. I really needed to be upstairs.

This room though, wasn't it.

"C'mon, J.R.," I said looking down at him. "Let's check out the other rooms up here. Maybe I can just move into one of them."

J.R. followed me as I walked down the hall and opened each door. There were six bedrooms on the second floor, some with beds, some converted to storage areas for Auntie's stuff. They looked different from what I remembered, yet none of them seemed right for me. Not as much light as in my room, or a lot less space.

I took deliberate steps to the last bedroom and opened the

door slowly. I tried to focus my eyes to peer inside.

It was exactly the same.

The door creaked as I pushed it all the way open. Other than the sliver of sunlight streaming through the opening in the heavy drapes, the room was dark. But there was no musty smell, or lingering telltale signs giving notice of it being unoccupied for years.

It had been the bedroom of my Auntie Zanne and her husband before I came. But after he died, she had never slept in the room again.

I walked over and ran my hand across the cool pillow on the bed. I looked around, focusing my eyes to make out things in the dim light. When I still lived in Roble, I had often-times heard Auntie Zanne go into the room at night. Once, I peeked through the door and saw her, just standing in the middle of the room, her arms wrapped around her chest like she was drawing in all her memories and holding onto them.

She had loved him so much, but, so I'd been told, only half as much as he loved her.

I went over and sat in an upholstered chair by the window and felt my eyes mist up. I didn't often mention it aloud, but I wanted a love like that, too. One like Auntie had. One like my parents. I had always hoped that was what I'd have with Alex.

Now, I wasn't so sure that I would.

He hadn't given me any hope to hang onto when I'd spoken to him the other night. Nothing more than the same things he'd said when I told him I was out of a job. Nope, he hadn't given me any indication of him coming to Roble to rescue me.

I didn't know why I counted on him. I was being silly. Silly in love with someone that couldn't possibly reciprocate. I swiped a tear that had somehow escaped and rolled down my check and sniffed back the others before they followed.

I could do it. I knew I could. I didn't need anyone to come and save me.

I stood up and walked to the door. I could go back and get a job in Chicago and start my life there. Again. All by myself. I'd done it before. Then I could take my time with Alex. I wouldn't feel so rushed about everything. So scared.

I walked out of the room, shut the door behind me and went back downstairs, J.R. hopping down the steps behind me. I grabbed a couple of large black trash bags and went back up to my room.

"If I am going to find a way out of this corner of the Piney Woods, I'm going to have to keep my head clear," I said. "And that means all this stuff has to go." I looked at J.R.

I was going to stay in my room, I decided, but I was going to fix it.

"We'll store all that craziness in the basement," I said and J.R. gave out a bark in agreement.

"I can do this," I said as I ripped Prince off the wall, the poster tearing down the middle. "Sorry," I told the Purple Artist as I stuffed him down in the bag. "Doesn't mean I don't still love you."

After him went all the other pictures, frilly purple pillows, and cheap room accents that Auntie Zanne had so carefully preserved for me, just like she did her bodies down in the Preparation Room. Only I wasn't done yet.

Chapter Twenty-Three

I got up early to Auntie Zanne shouting my name up the steps. I stretched and before I even swung my legs over the side of the bed, I knew I had rested better than I had any other night. Even sleeping on top of the mattress cover with bare walls, albeit still purple, was a definite improvement over the downstairs couch.

I sat up and looked around the room, satisfied that I'd made the right decision. Sure, I'd have to paint it and go shopping–buy furniture and accents that would suit me, but just the idea of that made me smile. That would give me the serenity I needed to plan my escape back to the real world. Things were looking up already.

"Romaine!" Auntie Zanne called again. "Will you get down here already? The day'll be over soon."

"Okay," I shouted back.

"Plan my escape from her," I mumbled as I padded across the floor and into the ensuite. "That's what I'm going to do."

I showered and went downstairs to the smell of bacon. "Good morning," she said. "Are you trying to sleep your life away?"

"It was the first time I got a good night's sleep." I pulled out a chair to sit and glanced at the clock on the wall. "It's not that late," I said.

"What's going on with you?" she said setting a plate down in front of me. "That silly room of yours making you anxious?"

Sometimes my auntie seemed to have a sixth sense about me.

Knowing when I was feeling bad even without me saying anything. Giving me encouragement and special treatment to make me feel better. Sometimes, though, she just feigned concern because she had something up her sleeve.

I watched as she poured me a glass of orange juice out of a pitcher in the refrigerator. "You think the room is silly?" I asked. I bit into a slice of bacon that was on the plate she given me alongside a sunny-side up egg, and toast cut on the diagonal.

"No. I love it. It reminds me of you," she said. "But it seems you're not too happy with it. Maybe you should do something about it before you resort to sleeping in a casket."

"I don't think it'll get that bad," I said eyeing her. "What do you think I should do about it?" I ran my toast through the gooey yellow yolk.

"I don't know." She shrugged. "Whatever you like."

"I was thinking about painting it. Doing some redecorating," I said. "What do you think about that?"

"I think it's a good idea. Can't have you troubled if you're going to be helping me around here. I need you have a clear head to plan the festival and solve this murder."

"I just want to paint the room," I said, not wanting to agree to helping with anything else.

"What color were you thinking about?" she asked.

"I was just thinking I'd keep it simple. Like white."

"Oh my heavens," she said. "Please don't do that. That room is too large. It'll look like a hospital."

"I like hospitals," I said and sipped on the juice.

*Ahhh...*Fresh squeezed.

"Yeah, but you don't want to live in one, do you?" she asked.

I sighed.

"How about if we go to the hardware store?" she said. "And you can see what you like."

"There's a plan," I said and crunched down the last of my bacon. "But I'm choosing the color."

"That's fine, Sugarplum. Whatever makes you happy. And I'll

ride with you. It'll be fun."

"Mmmhmm," I said getting more suspicious with every passing second of her niceness. "When do you wanna go?" I asked.

She smiled. "No time like the present," she said and grabbed her car keys from the wall caddy.

"Really?" I said. She acquiesced so easily and too quickly for me, she must've had something up her sleeve. But I downed the remainder of my juice and stood to put the glass and plate in the sink. "I'm ready."

"But first," she smiled at me. "We've got festival business."

"Oh, joy."

I knew she was up to something.

An hour later we were walking the fields at the San Augustine fairgrounds, home, at least for the last seventeen of its twenty-five-year history, to the Sabine County Annual Crawfish Boil and Music Festival.

We had left home after I helped her make a couple of phone calls and fielded questions from Floneva on protocol for going to the cemetery for graveside services. First thing Auntie Zanne wanted to do after we left home was check on the fairgrounds to make sure everything was ready for the vendors and musicians. I didn't know when we'd ever make it to the hardware store to get the paint she was so eager for me to have.

The grounds were spacious. There were acres of cleared land surrounded by a beautiful pine forest-lined exterior. There were paved walkways with benches scattered about, grassy areas and shade trees.

The city of San Augustine was considered large in our little neck of the woods—it had a whopping two thousand or so residents. Established before the Revolutionary War, people were getting lost in the pines around it as early as the mid-1500s. Birthplace to several colleges and the first churches in Texas of several denominations, it was the first stop to many entering Texas.

It had a good reputation and with it being the home to Mission Dolores, as a major local attraction, it was the first place Auntie

Zanne thought of as the new home for the festival once she became a member of the board of directors for the Tri-County Chamber of Commerce. It didn't seem to matter to her that the festival wasn't in the county it was named for.

"I was thinking of switching things up a bit," Auntie Zanne said as we walked into one of the covered shelters. "Maybe putting the bands and the dance floor closer to the entrance." She walked over and whirled around, her arms outstretched. "Here, I think. That'll make coming through the gates more fun. People will be out of the sun. The music will draw them in. Excitement and relaxation from the first step past the turnstiles." She turned to me. "What do you think?"

"It's your production," I said. "Do it up anyway you want."

"I feel so much better about getting this done now that I've identified our uninvited guest. I don't have to worry about that anymore," she said smiling. "Solving mysteries aren't as hard as Pogue made it out to be, you know? Look how I easily I did it."

"Auntie," I said, I paused between words and blew out a breath. I may as well let her know what I'd found out. She was getting too cocky for her own good. "The dead man Josephine Gail found at the funeral home was named Ragland Williamson."

"How do you know that?" she said, stopping and looking at me.

"I know because I took his fingerprints when I did the autopsy and Pogue ran them."

"Did he now?" she said and bit her bottom lip. I could tell she was thinking. "So, what? I didn't figure anything out?"

"Just thought you should know," I said. "That's all."

Her whole demeanor changed. "My, wasn't that smart of you, Sugarplum. Running his fingerprints." She sidled up next to me. "What else did you find out?"

"Not smart, Auntie. Taking fingerprints is just routine when you have a John Doe," I said. "Pogue found out that he was from Houston." I looked at her. "I'm telling you this because I wanted you to know that he isn't–wasn't–the guy that is registered at your friend's motor lodge. They're not the same person."

"Raye Anne."

"Raye Anne?" I shook my head to process. "Oh yeah. Yes. The guy registered at Raye Anne's place is named Herman St. John."

"So?" She turned and walked away from me.

"So that wasn't your squatter's name. They're not the same guy," I said. She squinted her eyes and ran her hand over her forehead. "I know you know what I'm saying, Auntie. Your universe settling in and righting wrongs," I made wavy motions with my hands, "by matching up the guy over at the Grandview with your squatter isn't what happened. And you finding that room with the smell of formaldehyde must have some other meaning."

"Is there anything else?" She turned and looked at me.

"Nothing I can share with you," I said in a sing-songy voice. "Now maybe you can just stick with festival business."

Chapter Twenty-Four

After I gave her my news, Auntie Zanne didn't have much to say. At least for a little while. She walked in circles under the covered shelter. A slow prance, taking measured steps, swinging her big tapestry purse back and forth, her head down. She looked over at me then slowly sauntered back my way. "I have something to share with you," she said. "But you have to promise not to tell Pogue. At least not yet."

"You're making me nervous," I said.

She took my arm and walked me out of the covered area and over to a park bench. We sat down and she took my hand, clutching it between the two of hers.

"Remember when we were at the motel?" she said.

"That day will probably be seared into my brain forever."

"Really?" she said and cocked her head. "Why?"

I shook my head slowly from side to side. "The sad attempt at you playing amateur sleuth. How could I forget?"

"Do you think it was a 'sad' attempt?" she asked. "I actually thought I did a good job at finding clues."

"By forcing Consuela's description of Mr. St. John's visitor to match Aunt Julep?"

"Oh," she said and waved her hand. "That was just my way of finding out if she was being truthful or not."

I rolled my eyes.

"So do you promise not to tell Pogue?"

"No."

"Romaine," she said. She scooted closer to me and batted her little eyes.

"Don't 'Romaine' me," I said. "Whatever it is you're getting ready to tell me, Auntie, you should think twice because I can't promise that I won't tell Pogue. It might be something that will help his case."

"Didn't you just tell me that Pogue's John Doe is not my motel man?"

"Yeesss." I drew the word out, speaking slowly.

She clasped my hand a little tighter and pulled it toward her. "So, what could be the harm in you not telling Pogue what I'm going to tell you?"

"Somehow, someway, I just know you've done something or are going to tell me something that will have some bearing on Pogue's case."

"Some. Some. Some," she said imitating me. She tugged on my hand. "And *some* bearing? Is that detective talk?"

I rolled my eyes.

"Oh for Pete's sake," she said and slapped my hand. "Whose side are you on anyways?" She pushed my hand away. "I declare." I opened my mouth to speak, but she didn't give me a chance. "Just say promise."

I didn't move or speak. I stared off past Auntie and started tapping my foot. If it were something I needed to tell Pogue, I'd never find out what it was if I didn't promise her I wouldn't tell. I glanced at her and narrowed my eyes.

What did she know?

"Fine," I said. "I promise."

Anything to learn what she knew.

"See," she said. "Was that so hard?"

"Are you going to tell me or what?"

"Yes, I'm going to tell you. Why else would I make you promise?"

I didn't say anything.

"Okay," she said. "You remember when we smelled formaldehyde in the motel room?"

"I remember you said you smelled it in there."

She glanced upward. "Okay, when I smelled it," she said.

"Yes. I remember."

"And you remember that you asked me why the smell was in there?"

"Mmmhmm," I said.

"Well, I think that the killer came there to remove any incriminating information. That's why that smell was in there."

"Removing information caused the room to smell like formaldehyde?"

"It was on him," she said and looked at me. "Or her."

"The smell of formaldehyde was on the killer?"

"Yes, when they came back to remove the information."

"What kind of information, Auntie?" I asked.

"About who he or she was, and why he or she needed to kill my squatter."

"Your squatter was not the guy at the motel," I said. "And can we just go with it being a 'he?'" I asked. "Just to make things easier?" She closed her eyes then opened them. "Auntie Zanne, have you seen Aunt Julep?"

This was a good a time as any to help Auntie dispel any of her nonsense that Aunt Julep had committed a murder.

"Of course I have," she said.

"Well then you should know that she isn't doing well."

"I know," she said and made her eyes big. "I'm not blind."

"Then how could you think that she did anything like murder someone?"

"Maybe she had Mr. Pollack do it with that shotgun, and she took care of the rest."

"You knew that shotgun belonged to Mr. Pollack?" I asked. "So why did you want me to take a picture of it?"

"You're not very good at investigating, are you?" she said. "You have to be on the lookout for anything that might have to do with the murder no matter how small or inconsequential it seems at the time."

There was no arguing with her. And the more I talked to her the more I felt like her accusing Julep Folsom was just a distraction. So I changed the subject.

"How did you arrive at this theory of yours?" I went back to what she'd been trying to tell me. "The idea that the killer came to the hotel room to scrub it of anything that might give him away."

"Because of this," she said and pulled a black portfolio out of her purse.

"What is this?" I asked and took the notepad from her.

"I found it in his briefcase."

"What briefcase?"

"The one that was on the bed in the motel room."

"The one you knocked over?"

"Yes." She folded her hands in her lap.

"Does this have something important in it?"

She put a big fish-eating grin on her face and batted her eyes. "Yes."

"Well, there goes your theory then," I said, hoping to douse that feeling of self-satisfaction she was coveting. "If you think your killer came into the room, reeking of formaldehyde no less, to get incriminating information, then he wouldn't have left this."

"He didn't see it." The grin was still there.

"It was on the bed."

"You'd make a bad detective," she said. "I found that briefcase under the bed."

"I saw it on the bed," I said.

"Did you see it when you first came in?"

"I..." I stopped and thought about it. I tilted my head and let my eyes drift off. "Maybe."

"You didn't," she said. "Really, Romaine. I put it there when you walked out of the room because you were too chicken to watch me canvassing the room. I found it and slung it onto the bed while your back was turned."

"You know, I'm not going to waste bail money on you, Auntie," I said. "Because when all your little deeds come to light, I'm sure you're going to be locked away for a very long time."

Chapter Twenty-Five

Auntie shot me a wicked smile. "I don't think I did anything wrong," she said.

"Except for stealing. Mr. St. John will be back to look for his things."

"Oh, poppycock," she said.

I looked at what was in her hand. "And why make such a production number out of it? Hiding your actions from me, and now showing me."

"Well, I didn't want you to think I was tossing the guy's room. Being a snoop."

"Auntie," I said, holding back a chuckle. She watched too many black and white movies. "Tossing his room? That's funny and that's exactly what you were doing."

"I mean at first..." she said, her voice trailing off. She turned to look at me out the corner of her eye. "I know. I know. I went in there to look. Even called you to come over so you could look with me. And, mind you, I did that because I was nervous about the whole thing."

"Right," I said.

"But after I actually found something-"

"The briefcase?"

"Yes," she said. "And the woodchips. I think that's a clue, too, you know. I found the nerve to do it. You know, to keep it up."

"To snoop." I said.

"Call it whatever you want, but it wasn't a thing I took lightly."

"You know I'm not believing any of this, right?" I said.

"Well, it's true," she said. "But you must admit, it turned out to be a good thing that I looked."

She took the portfolio back from me and opened it up.

"What is that stuff?" I asked as she pulled out a pile of papers.

"Evidence." She handed me a map from the pile. "But not any evidence that helps our cause. Except maybe this." She pulled the woodchips out of her purse. At some point after she took it, she'd apparently "bagged" it, I guessed to preserve it. It looked like one of the bags from her preparation room.

I tilted my head and looked at her bag of clues. I remembered that my John Doe had woodchips all over his shirt along with pine sap.

"Let me see that," I said and gestured for her to hand me the bag.

"What do you see?" she said and leaned in.

I blew out a breath. I guess it wouldn't hurt to share more of what I knew.

"I found woodchips on the decedent's shirt when I did the autopsy."

"Oh." She took in a breath. "My." She let it out.

I watched her process what I'd just told her.

"Don't get too excited," I said. "Because we are surrounded by woods." I looked around.

"It might just be something to get excited about," she said. She stared down at it for a moment, then taking it from me, put it back in her purse. "We'll just store it away for now. Maybe at some point it might help our cause."

"What exactly is our cause?" I said.

"*Tsk*," she sucked her tongue. "Proving Josephine Gail's innocence."

"Oh, yeah," I said.

"This, though. Right here. Is a big roadblock to us achieving our goal," she said and pointed to an area on the map that was circled in red.

"What is it?"

"That's Josephine Gail's land."

I poked my finger into the paper. "Right there? All of that?" I ran my finger around the circle. "Why is she living with you?"

"She lives with *us* because I need her, and she needs me."

"Why would the guy in the hotel room have a map of Josephine Gail's land?"

"Because he was here to investigate her land."

My eyes got big. "How do you know that?"

"I have my ways."

"What? The East Texas Rumor Mill? It's not always reliable, you know."

"My information is reliable." She reached inside the folder's pocket and pulled out a business card. "This came from a surveyor."

"A surveyor?" I looked at her. "Surveyors map land and do boundary disputes." I shrugged. "This land is already mapped out." I pointed to the map she had. "So Herman St. John is looking at some kind of boundary issues?"

"Didn't I just say that?" she said. "And correction, he *was* here determining boundaries."

"Because where is he now? Did he leave?"

"In a way," she said. I could tell she was hiding something.

I flipped over the card. "Whose number is this?" I said. There was a phone number handwritten on the back in black ink.

"I don't know. But it looks familiar," Auntie Zanne said. "I've been racking my brain trying to figure out why I know that number."

"Why don't you just call it?" I asked.

"Because if I know that number they may know my voice."

"If you recognize their voice, just hang up."

"It'll come to me," she said. "I don't make prank phone calls. Don't you have any sense of decency?"

"Oh my," I said, trying not to laugh. "Do *I* have a sense of decency? I don't think it's me we have to worry about."

"Watch it," she said.

"Maybe it's the surveyor's cell phone," I said. "Do you know this guy?" I flipped the card back over to the front. "Oh, maybe not because he's got a cell listed here."

"Right," she said. "Like I said, it'll come to me. And I found this, too." She pulled out another card.

"Jackson Wyncote, Esq." I said. "Who is he?"

"I think that he's the lawyer that Herman St. John worked for."

"Why would you think that?"

"Because," she said and licked her lips. "Josephine Gail told me he might be." She started talking fast, spilling out her words in one breath. "She also told me that the dead squatter at the funeral home was the same guy who talked to her about her land and told her that there was a dispute."

"Oh my goodness!" I said and jumped up from my seat. "You have to tell Pogue."

"No, I don't," she said, she yanked me back down to my seat. "And you promised that you wouldn't."

"No, I didn't," I said.

"Yes, you did," she said a little grin curling up at the corners of her lips. "And you can't go back on a promise."

"You tricked me," I said.

"Oh, Sugarplum, you're a grown woman. An educated woman. Surely you just don't fall for cons by little old women."

I narrowed my eyes at her.

"But wait," I said. "The body in the funeral home was Ragland Williamson. We got a positive ID from his fingerprints. How are they the same person?"

"He used an alias," Auntie said.

"An alias? Is that what you think?"

"How else are you going to explain it then?" she said. "I can't think of any other way."

"I don't know," I said.

"What other reason could there be for the dead body's fingerprints to come back to someone with a different name?"

I shook my head trying to separate all the thoughts that were swirling around in my head. I didn't even know what to say.

"Auntie..." I finally got my words together. "That means that Josephine Gail knew when she saw the dead guy at the funeral home who he was."

"Yes, she did."

"Why didn't she tell Pogue then?"

"She was in shock."

"Shock?" I said.

Then the words "acute stress reaction" rushed into my brain. I remembered Josephine Gail that first day I arrived. Standing out in the rain, soaking wet. She'd shown signs of lethargy. Her eyes had been glazed and she'd been unable to concentrate, even talk.

Acute stress reaction. A psychological shock that occurred in response to a traumatic event. Was her seeing the guy who was trying to take her land dead enough of a trauma to throw her into a mental stress episode?

Low blood pressure, confusion, feelings of guilt would have all been symptoms.

Add to that her history of depression.

I looked at Auntie Zanne. Right into her eyes. She'd stayed quiet while I processed the information she'd thrown at me.

"When did she tell you that she knew who John Doe was?" I asked.

"Just today. This morning."

"Is that true?" I asked.

"You're not calling me a liar, are you?" she asked. "That would be disrespectful, and not very nice."

"I didn't say that, Auntie."

"You better not," she said.

I took a moment before I even dared to utter my next thought aloud. "Did she do it?" I said, almost in a whisper. "Josephine Gail? Is she the one who killed him?"

"No," Auntie Zanne said. "Of course not. Would we be trying to prove her innocence if she'd killed him?"

"I'm not trying to prove her innocence," I said. "At least I hadn't been. At first, I was trying to prove that it wasn't my Aunt Julep." I frowned then lightly smacked my Auntie Zanne on the hand. "You knew all along it wasn't my Aunt Julep."

"I knew no such thing," she said. "And I still don't."

"How could you not know?"

"Because someone did it," she said. "And with us not knowing who it is, we can't rule anyone out."

"No one?" I asked.

"No one except Josephine Gail," she said. "Mark my words. It wasn't her."

Chapter Twenty-Six

We'd spent nearly an hour and a half walking the fairgrounds in ninety-degree weather and I knew it had been a bit much for Auntie Zanne. I decided to stop at her favorite air-conditioned diner, Momma Della's, so she could cool down. Everything at Momma Della's was either greasy or covered in gravy, including her, but the tea was sweet and ice cold.

Momma Della was big—she had big eyes, big lips, big hands and big breasts. She always looked like she was covered in enough grease to fry a chicken. Her smooth dark skin glistening as she barked out orders to everyone from behind the cash register where she was perched on a stool. She never moved from that spot.

"Morning, Miss Babet," she said when we walked in the door. "How you doing?"

"Hot," Auntie Zanne said. "Been walking the fairgrounds for the last two hours making sure it's ready for the Crawfish Boil and Music Festival."

"Well, I know you must be parched," Momma Della said. "It's hotter than a stolen tamale out there."

"It sure is." Auntie Zanne nodded in agreement.

"Heard about that trouble over at your place," Momma Della said. "I feel lower than a gopher hole about it." She swiped the sweat off her forehead with a white rag. "Is Josephine Gail alright?"

"Best as can be expected," Auntie said.

"Well if it's anything I can do, you just let me know," Momma Della said, then turned her attention to me. "And if this child ain't a sight for sore eyes," she said to me, a big grin on her face. "C'mon round here and give Momma Della a hug. Your auntie told me you was gonna come back here with her. I didn't believe she could do it."

I shot Auntie Zanne a look before I stepped behind the register and got wrapped up in a Della's bear hug.

"I'm not staying," I said. "Only here for a little bit."

"T'ain't what Babet says," Momma Della said. She threw back her head and let out a hearty laugh. "And I tend to believe whatsoever she says."

I glanced over at Auntie Zanne.

"We're busy as a church fan in July, but I always got a place for you 'n yours," Momma Della said. She pointed toward the back of the restaurant. "Go'on back and have a seat. I'll have two glasses of my good ole sweet tea brought round to ya."

The furniture in the diner was old, but scrubbed clean. The mauve-colored vinyl covering on the booths was split in places and had been repaired with duct tape. The Formica tabletops were dim, the fluorescent lights buzzed, the short swivel counter stools groaned if you turned them, and the wooden floor creaked as we walked over it. But the food was good, and people piled in for breakfast, lunch, and dinner.

Auntie loved the sweet tea but would tell everyone to steer clear of Momma Della's coffee. She'd say it was black as sludge and bitter as quinine. Although, I was fine with it. I'd drink it before I'd let her give me a cup of her "tea."

"Stop telling people I'm here to stay," I said as I slid into my seat.

"Okay," was all Auntie Zanne said, knowing that would shush me from saying anything else. I also knew that meant she wasn't going to stop.

We hadn't talked much since we'd left the fairgrounds and that was good. I had needed time to mull over what she had told me about her clues, and whether I was sticking to my promise about not telling Pogue. I was sure I could get one of my Chicago lawyer friends to argue, probably successfully, that I'd made that promise to Auntie Zanne under duress.

After the revelation–the information that Auntie Zanne got from Josephine Gail–I figured it was time to have a heart-to-heart with her.

We gulped down the ice-cold drinks and took a refill before we left and headed back to the Roble Hardware Store to look at paint. I drove.

Auntie Zanne sat with her hands folded and looked out of the window. I hadn't forgotten my way around Sabine County, something I wasn't too sure I was happy about.

We stopped at a stoplight, and suddenly Auntie Zanne acted as if she was having some kind of seizure. "Oh!" she groaned, her whole body jerked.

"What is wrong with you?" I said.

"That's it," she said and grabbed her chest.

I threw the gear into park "What's it?" I said frantically trying to find out what was wrong with her. I grabbed her arm. "Something hurts?"

She turned and looked at me. "No," she said and pulled her arm away. She opened out her purse and pulled out one of the business cards she'd shown me earlier. "The number." She pointed to the back of the surveyor's card and then to a bench that sat on the sidewalk. A painted advertisement on the front of it read: Realtor. Taralynn Williams. Service and Experience with Heart as Big as Texas.

I read the phone number on the card, then the one on the bench. "That's what you were having a seizure about?" I said.

"I knew I knew that number."

"Yeah, but you scared me half to death. I thought you were having a heart attack or something," I said. "I swear Auntie Zanne it's not that big a deal."

"It's a clue."

"Who is Taralynn Williams?" I asked. "You know her?"

The picture was of a strikingly pretty woman, her face belonging on a billboard for designer perfume or lipstick rather than a commercial business ad. She had shiny black hair and indigo blue eyes that even on the sidewalk bench sparkled.

"Of course I know her," Auntie Zanne said. "She's on several boards with me, including the Tri-County Chamber of Commerce. And her husband is Coach Williams."

"The man that came to Angel's Grace the other day?"

"Yes. Him."

The light turned green and I pulled off. Auntie turned to watch the face on the bench as we passed it for as far as her little neck would stretch. "What in the world does *she* have to do with all of this?" she said.

"I don't know," I said.

"I wish I'd known about this when I saw Coach."

"And what would you have asked him?" I said. "Did your wife kill the dead guy at my funeral parlor?"

She sucked her tongue. "No. Of course not." She batted her eyes a few times, I could see that she was thinking. "But I would have asked what she knew about him."

"It's quite possible that she didn't know anything," I said. I glanced at Auntie. "She is a realtor. This is about land. Maybe that was all the association she had with him."

"It has to be more than that," she said.

"Why does it have to be more than that?" I asked.

"Because you heard Consuela. She visited more than once."

"So?"

"So," Auntie repeated, mimicking me and bugging her eyes. "She would have met him at the property at least one of those times. Don't you think? Why keep coming back to the hotel? It doesn't make sense."

"We don't know that she didn't visit the property with him."

"Which makes her even more of a suspect," Auntie Zanne said. "If she did go there with him it would be the perfect place to kill him."

"I don't know," I said, uncertainty swirling in my words. "I think you're going about this all wrong."

"How so?"

"Because you keep zeroing in on one person. Getting a 'suspect' mixed up with someone just being a 'person of interest.'"

"A person of interest?" Auntie Zanne pursed her lips. "Now you're just repeating stuff Pogue said. Is that even a real thing?"

"Yes," I said. "It's a real thing."

"Well, I don't like it. If that were something I wanted to engage in, terming people just someone of 'interest,' which mind you, I don't, then everyone that ever talked to that man would be one."

"Then you have to narrow it down. But when you do, you have to include all the names you have even Josephine Gail."

"No," she said.

"Just to get the big picture, Auntie." I pulled into the parking lot of the hardware store.

"I can't even think like that," she said.

"You have to."

Auntie Zanne let out a huff. "Thinking like that could easily make someone conclude that she did it."

"No, it doesn't. Not necessarily. He was investigating her land," I said. "The investigation, by whoever initiated it wouldn't stop, right?"

"That's true," she said.

"So, I wouldn't think she'd think that killing him would stop anything, and probably would no one else."

"I wondered who hired him," she said. "They might know something that could help lead us to the murderer."

"That's a good question," I said. "Who hired him?"

"Wait," she said. "I should write some of this stuff down." She pulled a stenographer's notebook out of her purse. She flipped through the book and found a clean sheet.

"It couldn't be anyone from around here that hired him," she said.

"Why?" I asked.

"Because he used an alias."

"Right," I said.

"So maybe he was hiding from someone around here."

"Maybe so."

"Like Taralynn," she said.

"He did have her phone number," I said.

"Exactly."

"I shook my head. "I still think that he only had her number because of her occupation," I said. "But it is worth looking into I guess. Is she the type of person that would kill someone?"

"She is all fluff," Auntie Zanne said. "Designer wear. Manicured nails. A twang that any country-western singer would kill for."

I laughed. "So, she would probably be the target."

Auntie slipped the business card back in her purse, snapped the clasp closed and patted it. "Maybe so," she said. She looked at me. "How about we go and pick out some paint?"

Chapter Twenty-Seven

People started speaking to Auntie Zanne before we even made it into the store. The young sales clerk in the paint department gave her a hug, and someone passed her an envelope that I think was filled with money.

Who carries an envelope full of money on the off chance they might see her?

I felt as if I was out with the Godfather of Roble.

I looked at her and shook my head with incredulity. In all the years I'd been gone she hadn't changed. Maybe not the Godfather, but definitely a godmother, of the fairy variety and otherwise to so many people.

"How about this one?" Auntie said and showed me a swatch of a lavender paint nearly identical to what was currently on the walls.

"Wouldn't be any reason to change the color if I picked that one," I said.

"You used to like it," she said and frowned.

I cocked my head to the side and looked at her. "Don't you know that I don't like the same things anymore? I've changed."

"You're still the same to me," she said with an earnest smile.

"Then I'll have to try harder to show you that I'm different."

"I don't think that you could."

I blew out a breath. "How about we just look for something to cover the walls with. Something that's not purple." I saw her ready to speak, I knew she was going to tell me that lavender wasn't purple. "Or in the purple family."

"*Humph.*" Her one-word answer.

I turned back to the rack of colors, but before I could get a good look at the paint, Auntie grabbed my arm, firmly holding onto me at the elbow and gave me a yank.

"Whoa!" I said. "I'm trying to pick out a color."

"Didn't you just see who that was?" she said and dragged me out of the paint aisle and toward the front of the store.

"No," I said and pointed back toward the paint section. "I was looking at paint colors."

"Shhh! It's Taralynn's husband," she said in a hushed voice then pinched my arm.

"Owww!" I shrieked and snatched back my arm. "I don't know who he is."

"He was at Angel's Grace when we were there," she spoke in a strained whisper. "And keep your voice down."

"I barely saw him through the window," I said. "I don't know what he looks like."

"Shush!" She put her finger to her mouth. "We don't want everyone to know we're spying."

"You are dragging me through a store and pinching me," I said. "I think that alone will make people take notice. And why are we spying on him?"

"We need to find out why Taralynn would kill Ragland St. John."

"What? No, we don't," I said. "And his name was Ragland Williamson. St. John was his alias."

"We have to determine her motive."

"Well, I don't think stalking her husband in a hardware store will supply us with any clues as to why the dead man had his wife's phone number or what motive she had to kill him."

"Oh my," she said and stopped abruptly. I ran into the back of her. She turned and looked at me. "What are the odds of us seeing Coach Williams here when we just found out that it was his wife's number on that business card?"

"I don't know," I said. "I'm sure it probably isn't that high. We *are* in a town with only a few hundred people."

"It's the universe settling," she said. "Wrongs being righted."

I said the last part at the same time she did.

"Don't mock me," she said. She grasped the cuff of my sleeve and yanked. "Let me do the talking."

Chapter Twenty-Eight

"Coach" was a handsome, rugged Texan type. Sandy hair, baby blue eyes, clean-shaven. Wholesome looking. He had on a short-sleeved polo-like shirt with a Roble High School football emblem on it.

And standing with him at the counter was a beautiful young girl. I thought she couldn't be much older than thirteen or fourteen, and it was obvious to see she was related to the woman on the bench advertisement. She had her indigo eyes and dark hair. It was long, thick, and just as shiny as in the picture. Her skin was flawless, a feat I was sure for any teenager.

"Coach," Auntie Zanne said and walked up to him. "Fancy meeting you here."

"Hi Babet," he said. "It was an emergency of sorts."

"Throwing footballs in the house?" she asked.

"No." He laughed. "Our little gymnast was doing flips in the kitchen. Knocked the blender over. Thought we'd come pick up another one. You know Taralynn loves her smoothie shakes."

"Where is Taralynn?" Auntie Zanne asked and turned around to look for her. "She didn't come with you two?"

"She's at work," he said. "Amelia and I like to hang out together."

"My mother says he's a big kid," Amelia said. "She says because he was an only child and spoiled, he still hasn't grown up."

"You're an only child, too," he said and laughed.

"Hi, Amelia." Auntie Zanne's voice changed to speak to the child. "How are you?"

"Good."

"You getting ready for the festival?"

"Yes ma'am," she said.

"She's been practicing extra hard," Coach said.

"I've learned all the music Rhett gave me. I know it by heart."

"Good," Auntie Zanne said. "I knew you could do it."

A beaming smile spread across Amelia's face.

"Here," Auntie said and grabbed my arm, pulling me closer to her. "This is my niece. Her name is Romaine. She's a doctor."

Amelia's face lit up. "I want to be a doctor," she said.

"Really?" I said. "What kind of doctor?"

"I think I want to be a pediatrician," she said.

"She's an A student in science and math," her father said. He stuck out his hand. "I'm Chip Williams. Most just call me Coach."

"Nice to meet you," I said and shook his hand.

"And this is my daughter, Amelia. Not only is she the brightest student at Roble High, she's a gifted accordion player."

"And she's the newest member of Rhett's zydeco band," Auntie Zanne said.

"Is this who Rhett was talking about?" I asked. "Grown men not wanting a young girl to show them up?"

"Yes," Auntie said. "She plays a funky accordion. Might make them jealous."

Amelia blushed and I chuckled. "That's why he wanted crawfish pies for the sound check?" I asked.

Amelia's eyes got big. "You're making crawfish pies?" she said. "I love crawfish pies. I could eat them every day."

"I'd be happy to make them for you, Dr. Amelia."

"Thank you!" she said and bounced on her toes.

"I'm not worried about those guys," Coach said. "And I'm telling you, Babet. I will pull my baby girl if anyone gives her any problems."

"I'm not a baby, Daddy."

"You're my baby," he said. "My only baby and I'm going to always protect you. Even with my life."

"It's a sound check, Chip. Nothing to get so worked up about. And no one's going to give her problems," Auntie Zanne said. "I'll be there when she meets everyone."

"I'll be there, too," Coach Williams said. "You can count on it."

"We'll have extra pies for you," Auntie Zanne said. "Will Taralynn be there?"

Uh-oh. I knew where that was going...

"No," Coach said. "She can't make it. But I'll be there. The whole time."

"Is she out in Yellowpine?" she asked.

"Yellowpine? Taralynn?" He had a look of confusion on his face. "Why would she be out there? There's nothing out there. Why would you think she was out there?"

"She has an appointment to show a house," Amelia said. "She's coming to the show though."

"That'll be nice," I said. I wanted to try and cut in on the conversation before Auntie started asking crazy questions.

"Did you hear about the errant body at my funeral home?" she said.

Too late.

"Errant?" he said. "Oh." He nodded. "I did hear about that. Did they find out what happened?"

Auntie stood on tiptoe, leaned in and said, "He was murdered."

Coach looked at his daughter and then back at Auntie Zanne. "I don't want to talk about that in front of her," he said.

"I was just wondering if Taralynn knew him."

"The guy they found at your place?" Another confused look.

"Yes," Auntie Zanne said.

"Why would you think she knew him?" he asked. "Wasn't he unidentified?"

"Daddy," Amelia said, "I have to get to practice."

"Okay," he said then turned to Auntie Zanne. "We have to go.

We'll see you tomorrow night at the sound check."

"Well," I said after father and daughter walked away. "I don't think you found out anything with that line of questioning."

"Nothing other than he can't keep up with his wife," Auntie Zanne said.

Chapter Twenty-Nine

We headed home from the hardware store, six cans of paint loaded into the trunk, and I thought about what I'd had learned today–the dead guy had been staying at the Grandview Motel and left personal items; Josephine Gail knew the dead guy; and a woman that Auntie knew, Taralynn Williams, had gone to visit him several times. All of that information I knew had to be important to Pogue's investigation.

And I wonder how much more Josephine Gail knows...

I had heard Auntie go into Josephine Gail's room often after she became self-exiled. But from what I'd heard in my eavesdropping, it was Auntie Zanne who did the talking. Josephine Gail didn't ever seem to utter a word, just like that day Pogue questioned her. I had found out though that she had more to say to Auntie Zanne than I'd imagined.

Maybe I could get her to talk to me.

We pulled up in the driveway, I turned off the car but didn't move. I glanced over at Auntie Zanne.

"Are we getting out of the car?" she asked.

"I was thinking," I said hesitantly. "Maybe...after what you told me today...I should try and talk to Josephine Gail. Just to see what else she knows."

"I don't know that she knows any more than what I told you," she said. "But if she's up to it, might be for the best."

Well, that shocked me. I just knew I was going to have to put up a fight.

"Just let me make her some calming tea and we'll go and talk to her."

"I want to talk to her," I said. "Not I ask her questions and you answer."

"Okay," she said. "But only after I make the tea."

"You want to wait until after you've made tea?"

"What's wrong with that?" she asked.

I drew in a breath. I knew I should just quit while I was ahead. She wasn't fighting with me about the talk. I could give her the tea.

When we got into the house, Rhett was sitting at the kitchen table. He was eating a bowl of something he'd taken out of a pot that was sitting on the stove. From the smell of it, it was probably some of Auntie's conglomeration, as she called it. She'd throw the week's leftovers in a pot and serve it with rice. I'd learned long ago not to even take a whiff of the stuff.

I held my nose. "Don't you have a home?" I asked Rhett.

"There you go," Auntie said. "Of course he has a home."

"He's always here. Hanging out. Eating."

"I am not," he said and wiped his mouth with a napkin. "What? You don't like seeing me?"

I ignored that question.

"What're you doing day after tomorrow?" Auntie pulled up a chair next to Rhett.

"I thought you were making tea," I said. "Not sitting down to have a chitchat."

She waved her hand at me. "I am. I just need a word with Rhett."

I rolled my eyes.

"Haven't checked the schedule yet," Rhett said. "You got something special you want me to do?"

"I have to go to Houston-"

I cut my auntie off. "No, you don't." I knew what she was up to.

"Yes. I. Do." She sat up straight. "Actually, *we* do," she said.

"We have to pick up the trophies for the dance contest and...well..." She glanced over at me. I didn't know if she'd already told Rhett what she'd told me at the fairgrounds. "And we may make another stop that I might need your, uh, expertise for."

"What's going on?" he asked.

"Rhett," Auntie said, drawing his name out to show me she was directing her question to him, "we've found out a few things. I've just told Romaine, maybe I should run them by you, too."

"Auntie!" I said. "Don't share. Wait for Pogue."

"Rhett is going to help us."

"This is Pogue's investigation."

"And mine," she said. "Ours."

"You don't know how to investigate," I said.

"What is she doing wrong?" Rhett asked.

"She has a habit of deciding who the killer is and trying to make all the clues fit them," I said.

"No, I don't," she said.

Rhett looked at Auntie Zanne and smiled. "You can't do that, Babet," he said. "You need to look for a motive."

"That's what Pogue is doing," Auntie Zanne said. "With Josephine Gail."

"It's what you're doing, too," I said. "With Aunt Julep."

"Aunt Julep?" Rhett said.

"Julep Folsom," Auntie Zanne said.

"She's your aunt?" Rhett asked.

"Yep."

"That makes Pogue your...what? Cousin?"

"Yes," I said.

"Hah. I didn't know that," he said.

"You mean Auntie Zanne didn't tell you?" I said.

"No. I didn't," she said. "But that's not what this conversation is about. I need us to find out from Rhett what we need to do when we go to Houston."

"What he needs to do is teach you how to interrogate people," I said.

Rhett started laughing. "It's true," I said. "She badgers people."

"That's not true," she said.

"Who have you talked to so far?" Rhett asked.

"Consuela, the maid at the Grandview." Auntie Zanne pulled out one of the kitchen chairs and sat down. "Josephine Gail, of course, and Coach Chip Williams."

Rhett raised his eyebrows. "Why did you question the Coach?" he asked.

"Because Herman St. John had his wife's phone number in his room. On the back of a business card. But Coach Williams had his daughter with him, so we couldn't really talk. I may try again when he brings Amelia to the sound check."

"You should leave that man alone," I said. "Talk to his wife. She'd know why she was there."

"That's a good idea," Rhett said. "You need to find out why he was murdered."

"The motive," I said.

"Yes," he said.

"Well, I can't find out the motive anyone has if I don't talk to them," Auntie Zanne said, pouting.

"Talk to people, Babet. That's good," Rhett said, encouraging her. "You're on the right track," he said.

"But don't zoom in on one person and badger them," I said.

Auntie Zanne waved a hand at me and looked at Rhett. "I think I'm on the right track too," Auntie Zanne said. "I've got a lot of clues to follow."

"What other clues do you have?" he asked.

"Woodchips. A surveyor's name. An address in Houston. Someone that uses a buckshot rather than a slug." She looked at me and I nodded. "And the name of the man who came here and got killed maybe out in the woods of Yellowpine."

"You don't have his address in Houston," I said, going over her list in my head. "Pogue got an address when he ran his prints. But you don't know it. In fact, he's not even sure if it's a good address."

Everything else she listed, I agreed with.

"I've got an address for a Jackson Wyncote in Houston. I'm thinking it might be the lawyer he worked for," Auntie said directing her answer at Rhett.

"Oh," Rhett said and perked up. "You know his name? The dead guy? And where he worked?"

"Yep," Auntie said. "We know it."

Rhett's eyes got wide as Auntie relayed everything we'd found out about our dead squatter, and the info we'd gleaned on him, including how he was probably from Houston.

"So," Rhett said and leaned back in his chair. "That's why you're going down to Houston? To follow up on your leads?"

"I'm going to Houston on festival business," Auntie said and glanced at me. "But, yes, I thought I'd check out what I could about Mr. Williamson while I was there." She nodded. "That's why I would like for you to go with us. You know how to ask questions better than me or Romaine."

"Wish I could," Rhett said. "But you're doing a good job. You're on the right track. And it wouldn't be too farfetched that someone from Houston might have followed him down here."

"You think so?" she asked. "We talked about that, too."

"Sure, I think so," Rhett said. "Why would anyone here kill him?" He shrugged. "Especially in Yellowpine. What? The population there is like seventy-five or something, right? Seems unlikely he'd know someone there."

"So, you'll go with us?" Auntie Zanne asked.

"Uh," he said and looked at us sheepishly. "I don't know if I could."

"It's right down in your neck of the woods," Auntie said.

I tilted my head to the side. "Yeah. Didn't you say you were from Houston? Worked there too, right?"

"Of course he is," Auntie said. She got up, grabbed the teapot, went to the sink washed her hands and then filled it up. "That's why I thought he might be interested in riding down with us." She put the teapot on the stove and turned up the flame. "You could help us get around."

He turned up his mouth and shook his head. "I don't think I'll be able to go. But from what you've told me, Babet, I think you'll do fine."

"Told you I knew what I was doing," Auntie said to me. "I can't wait to get to Houston."

Rhett seemed to finish up his meal quickly after he refused to go to Houston, and Auntie Zanne got the tea ready for her friend.

I knocked on her door and opened it. Auntie went in first with the tea.

"Hi Josephine Gail," she said.

She turned and squinted at us as the light flooded into the room from the hallway. I stepped in behind Auntie and closed the door behind me.

"I have you some tea," Auntie said and looked at me. "And Romaine wants to talk to you."

Josephine Gail nodded, I could see a weak smile appear in the dim light.

Auntie sat on the bed next to her. I pulled up a chair and sat across from her.

Josephine Gail's yellowed, bad-dye-job hair was stringy. Her skin was dry and the bags under her eyes puffy and dark.

"C'mon, take a little," Auntie said and blew on a spoonful of tea. She put it to Josephine Gail's puckered lips and I heard her slurp it in.

"Auntie told me what you told her about the dead guy," I said and leaned in toward her. "I want to help. I don't want you to have worry about this."

"I'm okay," Josephine Gail said. She put a shaky hand up to her forehead and I knew that wasn't true.

"I'm glad you're feeling better," I said. She wanted me to think she was okay, so I went along with it. "Auntie told me that you saw Ragland—uhm, Herman St. John before he, uh, showed up here."

"Romaine," Auntie Zanne said. "Take it slow now."

"It's okay, Babet," Josephine Gail barely spoke above a whisper. "I don't mind."

"I'm going to ask you a couple questions. Okay?"

She nodded.

"When did you first see him? See Herman St. John?" I asked.

She cleared her throat. "Babet told me his real name is Ragland Williamson, Romaine. I don't why he thought he had to lie to me."

"Why did he want to see you?"

"It was about my land," she said. "Seems like somebody died or something and when they read the will, they thought he owned some of my land. I'm not giving up any of my land."

"No one wants you to give up any of your land," Auntie said.

I looked at Auntie. "So," I said turning back to Josephine Gail, "it was a boundary dispute?"

"The problem is," Josephine Gail said without me prompting her with a question, "it might be his land. I remember my father saying something about it years ago."

"Oh," I said.

"He said he'd kill someone before he gave up land we'd been working for more than a hundred years."

My eyes got big, my heart even started to race.

I wasn't sure if I wanted her to tell me any more. But she kept talking.

"I told that Ragland Williamson the same thing."

"Oh," was all I could muster up to say. I sat back in the chair and let out a groan.

"Any more questions?" Auntie Zanne asked.

I sat up and looked at the two of them. "Yes. I do have more." I said and took a breath. "What else was said when you first met him?" I looked at Auntie. "Other than you telling him what your father said."

She hunched a shoulder. "Just that he'd hired a surveyor and he was going out there to my land and he'd come back and talk to me afterwards."

"Did he come back?"

"No. Never did."

"Why didn't you tell this to Pogue?" I asked.

"She knew better than to tell Pogue," Auntie said.

"I thought she wanted to cooperate with him?" I said.

"You thought wrong," Auntie said. "But she's cooperating with you. That's good enough."

I wobbled my head, trying to clear it. Auntie Zanne's antics of counseling her friend to be evasive probably weren't going to help Josephine Gail in the long run, especially if Pogue ever got around to the filing charges against her. It was best he knew everything. I was going to have to tell him.

"Okay. Tell me about when you found him," I said.

"Here?" she asked and rubbed her fingers across her forehead.

"Yes. Here." I squinted my eyes. "You didn't find him anywhere else, did you?"

"No."

"Yeah. Okay. Then here. When you found him here."

"He was down in the crematory. Ready to go into the furnace. He would have gone in it too, if I hadn't have gone down there to retrieve something a family member of another decedent had stuck in their loved one's casket."

"One person in the family hadn't realized that the decedent and the casket weren't going into the ground," Auntie said.

"That's right," Josephine Gail said and nodded. "They called, so I went down to get it. That's when I noticed the other casket. The one with that Ragland guy in it."

"What made you notice it?" I asked.

"The casket was from the showroom," she answered.

"Oh," I said. I looked at Auntie Zanne. She nodded.

I knew that Auntie Zanne wouldn't have prepared a viewing of a person being cremated in one of her sample caskets. She had special ones she used for that. It seemed Josephine Gail knew it too. And, evidently, she was very familiar with the inventory.

"And that's when you called Pogue?"

She gave a curt nod. "After I realized who he was."

"You called Pogue?"

"You asked that question already," Auntie Zanne said. "And she told you yes. Seems like I'm not the only one that needs to brush up on their interrogation skills."

Chapter Thirty

I waited until the next day to bring the paint into the house and had to lug it up to my bedroom all by myself. Where were Rhett or Catfish when you needed them? I did check out the kitchen, but there was no sight of them. J.R. was always by my side, though, although he wasn't any help with getting those paint cans up steps.

Speaking with Josephine Gail with her sidekick, Suzanne Babet Derbinay present, had worn me out. I had gone straight to bed afterward.

After spending another night within my bare-walled room, the anticipation of redecorating had lifted my spirits tremendously. I had spent the morning picking up new linen, pictures for the wall, and ordering furniture for the sitting room. I got back to the house and went straight to my bedroom. I was ready to paint.

I stripped out of my going-out clothes, swapping them out for a pair of jeans and an over-sized shirt I'd found in Auntie's clothes closet from the inventory she kept for her clients. I pulled off my shoes and decided to stay barefoot. My southern habits were seeping back in one at a time.

I stood in the middle of the room, my hands resting on my hips and stared at the walls. The job was going to take longer than I thought. I had bought primer because I wasn't sure if those lavender walls could be fully covered by the Behr White Mocha I'd chosen. It was white, much to my auntie's chagrin, but not stark. It had a soothing brown undertone. Crisp and calming.

"Hello," came with a knock on my bedroom door.

I turned to find Rhett.

"I heard you were painting your room," he said.

"You heard right," I said.

"You want some help?" he asked.

I chuckled. "Would have been nice to have some when I lugged all this stuff up." I pointed to the paint cans, plastic tarp, brushes, and paint trays.

"I've got you some help downstairs."

My eyes questioned him. "Painters?"

"Unless you want to tackle this all by yourself?" He waved his hand around the room.

"How did anyone know I was painting today?" I said. "Oh wait," I said. "Auntie Zanne."

"She just doesn't want you smearing paint all over that pretty face."

"Yeah. Right," I said. "And people volunteered? Or is it just you she wrangled into helping me?"

"No. I said painters. With an 's.' Plural," he said. "They're all downstairs."

"That's not helping me any," I said. "The room I want painted is up here."

"Babet was feeding them. C'mon down. You'll see," he said. He tilted his head and poked out his lips. "*S'il vous plaît?*"

"That might work on Auntie Zanne," I said. "But it doesn't work with me."

"What?"

"That pitiful look." I wiggled a finger at his face. "And," I shook my head, "speaking French."

"Your Auntie Zanne told me that you love French."

"I do," I said. "But it's like you're using it to impress me."

"Ha! I don't think that I can impress you," he said. "You don't seem to like anything I do. And I speak French because I love the language. It would be nice to have someone to speak it with."

"You're not French."

"Did you think I didn't know that?"

"No. I didn't think that."

"I studied it. In school," he said. "And then for my job."

"And what job is that?" I asked. "Your secret one?"

"You don't give up, do you?" he said. "I told you, it's not a job I'm doing any more." He shook his head. "At least for now."

"For now?"

"Do you want to meet your painters or not?" he asked.

"Why are you so evasive when it comes to Houston and your job?" I asked. "It's like you don't want to tell me what it is you did."

He stared at me for a long, uncomfortable moment. He swallowed before he spoke. He seemed to try and arrange his words carefully. "It's just I don't like to talk about it much." he said.

"Well, if you didn't want it talked about it, you shouldn't have ever told my Auntie Zanne."

He narrowed his eyes. "I see. What did she tell you that keeps you so interested in it?"

"Yep." I gave a firm nod. "She spilled the beans. Ex-FBI. Possibly even a certified spy. That's the part that intrigued me."

"Certified?" he said and chuckled. "No such thing."

"Tell her that."

"So," he clapped his hands together, changing the subject, "do you want to meet your help or not."

I took the hint. I twisted from side-to-side, and let my eyes scan the room, taking in the space. "Lead the way," I said.

We went down to the kitchen and it was full of people sitting around the table. J.R. didn't seem to like the crowd. He gave out a bark and went over to his corner.

Auntie Zanne was in her usual spot standing at the stove and stirring in a pot.

"Hi Romie," Catfish said. He sat at the head of the table with Spoon and Gus, the other members of Rhett's zydeco band. And then there was Floneva. She was sitting in a chair pushed up by the wall, a grin on her face.

"Hi Catfish," I said and looked around the room. I stuck my hands in my jeans pocket. "Gus. Spoon." I nodded my hello. "Floneva. Catfish, what are you doing here?"

"He's part of your help," Rhett said.

"And a member of our zydeco band," Auntie Zanne said.

"Catfish," I said, surprised by him being there. "You're in the band?"

"Yep," he said and blushed.

"And what instrument do you play?" I asked. I'd never known him to be play anything.

"He plays the *frottoir*," Rhett said.

Leave it to him to use the French word.

"I didn't know you played the washboard," I said deliberately. Rhett was right, he didn't impress me, especially with his French. "I've never heard you play."

"I just learned it," he said and started grinning. "They needed one for the band."

"And I play the guitar," Rhett said. "Not that you've ever asked."

"I was getting around to it," I said and looked at him. "Although I wouldn't have guessed that."

"What? That I did something like your dad?"

"I'm sure you don't play anything like my daddy," I said. "He was the best."

"They were practicing," Auntie said. "Got in an early practice. Thought I'd fix them lunch."

"They are really good," Floneva chirped in. "I listened in. Best music I ever heard."

Now I saw why she was grinning. She was over the moon with the band.

"Then they agreed to paint your room," Rhett said.

"Oh really?" I said looking around the room. I wouldn't expect anything less from Catfish. But I hardly knew the other two. "Why?" I asked. "What did you tell them Auntie?"

"I didn't tell them anything," she said defensively. "And don't look a gift horse in the mouth, Sugarplum. You need the help."

"I'm not," I said. "I appreciate it."

"We don't mind," Gus said.

"I've never minded helping out Babet, or you," Spoon said. Babet's letting us practice here and I've been having a ball. Flannery said she ain't seen me this happy since my mare gave birth to twin foals. Real nice of Babet to let us come to her home—"

"Funeral home," Gus interjected. I guess he felt a correction was needed.

Spoon, Gus, and Rhett laughed. "Yes. Funeral home," Spoon said, "for us to use as a rehearsal hall these past three months so we could whip this rag-team of country musicians into shape."

"T'wasn't nothing," Auntie said, putting a twang in her voice and taking a bow. "Hospitality is just one of my many gracious southern attributes."

I shook my head. Auntie Zanne loved being the center of attention.

"Floneva," I said. "You in the band, too?" She was dressed in cowboy boots, her usual tight pencil skirt and a frilly white blouse. "I thought you were new around here."

"Told you, I'm from Hemphill. Just up the road."

"She's not in the band," Auntie said. "She's what you call a groupie."

That made Rhett and I both laugh. Floneva didn't seem to get the joke.

"So, I guess if the band is doing the painting that would exclude you, huh?" I said.

Floneva pushed her glasses up on her face. "I wish I had known," she said. "I would have been happy to help even though I'm not in the band. I'm just not dressed the part." She gestured down at her clothes. "I just came in to see the guys." I noticed her face went flush with that comment.

"Can you play an instrument?" Auntie Zanne asked.

"I thought about learning one," Floneva said. "But to do it, my grandmother told me, you have to play the right note at the right time, and I just couldn't seem to get those two things together."

"Everyone isn't musically inclined," Auntie Zanne said. "I'm sure you excelled at other things."

Floneva tilted her head back and blinked a few times. "Nope. Can't think of nothing."

I shook my head. "So, you guys aren't playing during the entire festival, are you? I asked. "That would be pretty tiring."

"No," Auntie said. "Didn't you read over that folder I gave you?"

My eyes drifted up toward the ceiling.

"If you had," she said, "you would've have seen that a couple local radio stations are scheduled, we have a professional band that's coming in, and a DJ."

"Professional?" Rhett said and chuckled. "What are we?"

"A band of backwood players," burly guy Gus said. "You heard Spoon. A ragtag team of musicians."

"Backwood players and well-fed painters," I said. "You guys got energy to paint after eating?"

"Sure they do," Auntie said. "Good thing too. You couldn't have painted that room by yourself."

"I was going to try," I said.

"You could've called me," Catfish said. "I would've come."

Auntie waved her hand. "We know that, Catfish."

Rhett poked me, and leaned in. "Looks like you've got an admirer."

I blew out a breath and walked over to the table, ignoring Rhett's comment. I didn't like people saying anything about Catfish.

"So, you guys don't mind? I mean really?" I asked. "I know you didn't think that you'd be roped into menial labor when you came over for your rehearsal."

"I'd do anything for crawfish pies," Gus said. "I go wild for anything crawfish."

I laughed. "You sound just like Amelia," I said.

"Who?" Spoon asked.

Auntie narrowed her eyes at me. "They are going to paint while you make pies," Auntie Zanne said. "So, if we're going to get it done, we need to get to it."

"Why would you promise them pies? I told you I wasn't baking any," I said. I glanced over at them. "Maybe I can just pay them?"

"Don't you start. You just said you were going to make them when we were in the hardware store," Auntie Zanne said. "Don't you remember?"

I remembered. Amelia. Little sweet Amelia.

"I do remember," I said.

"Finally! You remember something you said you were going to do," Auntie Zanne said. "So, you make the pies, and they'll paint."

"Okay, Auntie Zanne," I said, defeated. "But I don't know if I have everything I need."

"You do," she said. "I made a list and Rhett went to the store."

The two of them always seemed to be in cahoots in something about me.

"Well, before we get started," Gus said and stood up, "I need to get a smoke."

"I'm with you on that," Spoon said.

"Smoking?" I said, louder than I intended. "That's not good for you." I hadn't been around people that smoked in a long time. All of my friends in Chicago were health professionals. And those that weren't were health nuts. Smoking hadn't been a part of my social circle in years.

Everyone looked at me.

"She's a doctor," Auntie Zanne said as if she had to explain my comment. "People smoke, Sugarplum. Let them go do it and you get started on the pies."

Floneva stood up and raised one finger like she was in church. "If you fellows don't mind, I'll go out and take a smoke with you." She cut an eye my way then patted the side of her chest. "Got a couple tucked away."

"Oh no. You too, Floneva?" I said.

"Sorry," she said. "But I enjoy the littler buggers."

"Okay," I said. "Fine." I put my hands up, palms out. "But, maybe I should remind you three," I dragged my finger through the air at each of them. "Smoking kills."

Chapter Thirty-One

"I'm going to go up and get started," Catfish said after Gus, Spoon, and Floneva went out back to smoke.

"You want me to go up with you?" I asked him.

"No, I'm good," he said. "Where's the paint?"

"It's already up there," I said. "Paint, primer, rollers, brushes, everything you need."

"I'll go with you," Rhett said. "Get started. You," he turned to me, "can show Gus and Spoon up when they get back."

"Wait, before you go up, Rhett," Auntie Zanne said. "I want to talk to you."

"Well, I'll get started, too," I said. I looked under the cabinet for the lobster pot I'd used to cook the crawfish for Aunt Julep's étouffée. "I'm going to make enough to take tomorrow for Amelia."

"Who is Amelia?" Catfish asked.

"You just go up and get started painting if you want any of Romaine's pies," Auntie Zanne said.

"I'm going," he said.

"What do you need, Babet?" Rhett asked.

"I wanted to let you know that Romaine and me are going to Houston tomorrow. Wanted to see if you had any instructions for us."

"What?" I said. I stopped what I was doing and turned to Auntie. "Don't include me in that. I don't need instructions on anything."

"Too late," she said. "You're already included."

"I did try to talk her out of trying to investigate after she told me the other night she was going to Houston," Rhett said.

"I just bet you did," I said. I opened up the fridge and grabbed my vegetable trinity. I took them to the sink and rinsed them off.

"What is that supposed to mean?"

"We just talked about this upstairs," I said. "You know she told me how you told her you'd help her. Run any information she got past your friends in the FBI."

He held up his hands, his mouth dropping open. He looked at me then Babet.

I just left him standing there speechless and went into the pantry to get the rest of the ingredients I needed for my pies. When I came back he hadn't moved.

"Auntie Zanne," I said. "I'm going to need the stove. You have to move."

"Don't be hard on Rhett," she said, pulling her pot off and setting it on a dishcloth on the counter. She shot a glance over toward him. "He's helping us."

"I'm not being hard on him," I said. "I just said what you told me. And he's not helping me."

"Don't pay her any never mind," Auntie Zanne said.

Good. I didn't want to get involved with him and his secret FBI stuff anyway. I grabbed a cutting board and a knife and thought about what Pogue said. She did have a knack for dragging me along with her.

The back door swung open. "Hello," Gus said as he, Floneva, and Spoon walked through the door.

"You guys back?" Rhett asked.

"Yep," Spoon said. "All ready to paint."

"Okay. Good. I'll show you guys my room," I said.

"They don't need you to show them," Auntie Zanne said. "You're cooking. It's just at the top of the steps. They can find it. Plus, Catfish is up there." She looked at the three smokers. "Just call his name when you go up."

I knew Auntie Zanne did that because she wanted me to participate in the conversation she was having with Rhett.

"Well, I'm sorry you can't go," Auntie Zanne said, picking up the conversation back where she'd left off. "It would be great to have you."

I cast a look at Auntie Zanne. "You know somebody put that casket with Ragland Williamson in the crematory. Someone who knew everything about this place," I said. "Like someone that worked here." I raised an eyebrow. "Maybe Mr. Secretive," I pointed to Rhett, "is the one we should interrogate."

Rhett gestured a surrender and chuckled. "Still not ready to confess to this one. But when you get back from Houston, let me know what you found."

Chapter Thirty-Two

The further we got from Roble, the antsier Auntie Zanne got. By the time State Route 59 turned into I-69 after passing Cleveland, Texas, and she knew we were on the homestretch to Houston, I thought I was going to have to sit on her to keep her still.

"Can't you drive any faster, Romaine?" she asked me. "I don't want to miss him."

"Miss him?" I asked. "The lawyer?"

"Yes, the lawyer."

"Aren't you worried about picking up your trophies?" I said.

"They aren't going anywhere."

"And where do you presume your Mr. Lawyer is going?"

"I don't know," she said. "But I want to talk to him."

"What about if he's the murderer?" I asked.

She gasped and clapped her hands together. "Then my work will be done."

I shook my head. "Fearless," I said. She smiled.

She had made me get up at the crack of dawn. I was used to getting up early, but the rooster hadn't even crowed when we backed out of the driveway.

She was holding onto the lawyer's business card the whole drive down.

We found Jackson Wyncote, Esq. at his law office, which resembled more of a house. I, of all people, knew about converting residences into businesses. We opened the door and walked in.

"May I help you?" he said. He was sitting at a messy desk. A radio tuned in to a 1960s rock-n-roll station was playing in the background.

We explained to the middle-aged, gray-around-the-edges, bulging-bellied attorney that we were from the Ball Funeral Home & Crematorium. Auntie passed him a card. Then we told him most of what we knew about the passing of Ragland Williamson and the manner of his death.

"And he turned up at your funeral home?" was what he asked when we finished our truncated version of the story.

"Yes. He did." Auntie Zanne put on her I'm-All-Business persona. She straightened up her back and squared her shoulders, then she pushed her thumb my way. "She's the medical examiner that performed the autopsy."

"Oh," he said and nodded. "I can't believe it. I heard that he was doing better. Got a new job and everything."

"He was down there on a job, wasn't he?" Auntie Zanne asked.

"I don't know. If he was it wasn't for me. He hadn't been my investigator for maybe six months or more. I'd heard he was working for another lawyer. I didn't know for sure, though, because after the last job he did for me, for the most part, he fell apart. Too upset to work so he quit."

"What kind of case was it?" Auntie Zanne asked. "I only ask because we believe that perhaps someone here might have followed him there and killed him. Maybe someone from a case he worked on for you."

"Really?" he said. He looked down and started picking with his nails. "I hope that isn't true.

"That's a working theory," I said.

"Do you know why he was using an alias?" Auntie Zanne asked.

"An alias?" He scrunched up his nose. "I don't know why he would do that. I've never known him to do that," he muttered. He coughed into his hand. "No, I don't know. How do you know? I thought you were just the funeral home where he was found."

"We're working with the Sabine County Sheriff," I said. That wasn't too far off for me. I had told Pogue I'd help him.

"I can't really talk about cases, you know," the attorney said.

"Client-attorney privilege?" I asked.

"He was carrying your card in his briefcase," Auntie Zanne said. "At first we thought it was because he worked for you, but then we wondered why he'd only have one card. Maybe it was something *about* you?"

"I don't know why he had the card," he said. "But I'm sure it wasn't anything about me. Maybe just one he had left over."

"And maybe not," she said. "Anything you can tell us will help."

I didn't remember "us" ever concluding on a reason there was only one card, or even discussing it. But it did make sense.

"You know," he said, "he worked so many cases for me. He also had worked his own PI business, too. If it is someone from a previous case, it could be any of those."

"Well, what about the case that made him quit?" I said. "Is that information you can't share either?"

"Maybe not," he said. "That case is over, and all public record. Although, he couldn't go with that."

"This is a murder investigation now," Auntie Zanne said. "It's important to give any information you might have."

"I know," he said. "So, are you a part of the investigation?"

"The sheriff was called away. We're following leads."

Auntie Zanne's questions were so different than when she questioned Grandview's maid and the coach. She might actually get some information out of him.

He shook his head. "He was such a nice guy. Good investigator, too."

"How long had he worked for you?" I asked.

"Oh, about six or seven years."

"And had you heard from him recently?" I asked.

"No." He shook his head. "No. I hadn't." He studied us for a moment. "I had a case. A murder case. And I had him look for any information to help me defend my client, who swore he had been wrongly accused. And he felt he found he'd found something that would exonerate him."

"This is the last case he had with you?" I asked.

"Yes. He said he knew for sure that another man did it. But that man disappeared before Ray—we called him Ray—could get enough information even for me to try and build reasonable doubt."

"So the killer got away?"

Attorney Wyncote shrugged. "Not according to the law. My client was convicted. So in the eyes of the law he was guilty. The one who committed the murder."

"And that upset Ray?"

"Yeah, it did. Enough that he quit."

"What was the man's name that he thought committed the murder?"

He looked from me to Auntie Zanne and back to me. He seemed to contemplate what if anything he should share.

"When did he die?" he asked, evidently deciding against giving us any more information on that case.

"Dr. Wilder needs to pinpoint the exact time of death," Auntie Zane said and looked him directly in his eyes. "That's part of why we came to Houston. To find answers."

"We don't know how long he'd been in the funeral home," I added.

"How could you have extra dead bodies?" he said squinting his eyes.

"No. We don't have *extra* dead bodies." Auntie frowned, a sudden bubbling of discontent escaping from her. I knew she was holding back giving him a verbal lashing. She didn't like innuendos made about her business. "We have an obligation to each body we receive, and to the deceased's family. We take that obligation very seriously. Each and every deceased is in the best of care when they are with us, and have been for more than fifty years."

"The body was brought there when we were on vacation," I

said. "But it was discovered the first day we arrived back."

"But, even with him being uninvited, as it were," Auntie Zanne said, "we took care of everything. Although we didn't know who he was at the time."

Then he raised his head and hiked up an eyebrow. His whole demeanor changed. "Are you here for compensation?"

"No." Auntie Zanne said, clearly irritated.

"Is that why you embalmed him already? For money?" He lifted an eyebrow. "Because his wife may have wanted something different."

"We felt we couldn't wait. The medical examiner," Auntie pointed to me, "released the body to us. Plus, Mr. Wyncote, our services are the best in East Texas."

"I'm sure they are," he said. He let out a sigh. "Has his wife been notified?"

"No." I swallowed and discreetly crossed my fingers. I hoped that Auntie's little hissy fit hadn't made him tight-lipped. "He didn't have any identification on him, and we only learned his name by running his fingerprints. As we said, we found your business card, so, so far you are the only contact person we have." I looked at him. "We'd hope you would be willing to give us that information, so we'd have a place to send his body."

I was learning well from my Auntie Zanne.

Chapter Thirty-Three

I wanted to call Pogue and let him know what we were doing, but I would have had to lock Auntie in the trunk of the car. She would have been all over me like white on rice if she thought I was sharing what we'd learned so far with him. The only way I'd be able to speak with him was if she wasn't around.

Jackson Wyncote, Esq. had graciously given us the name and address of Ragland Williamson's widow. Her name was Kara, and I, in my role of stand-in medical examiner, was going to deliver the news.

I pitched the idea to Auntie that she could be my deputy. She threw that idea right out the window.

"Why would I want to be that?" she screeched. "I embalmed the body. I am the Funeral Director. Must I remind you that that's a very important role?"

She had me there.

"You'll have to use more tact and not get upset, though," I told Auntie as we pulled up to the house. "We were lucky to find her and get her information from that lawyer when we aren't even the police." I dipped my head and looked out the corner of my eye. "You know you have to use a little more tact along with your sympathy than you did with the lawyer if we're going to get any answers from her. She'll already be upset hearing our news."

"I don't need tact when I'm in Roble. All I need is this winning smile," she pointed to her mouth, "and my wit. People give me what I want."

"Well, this ain't Roble," I said. "And we can't solve this thing if you let people upset you and then get all snooty with them."

"What?" she huffed. "I didn't get snooty with that man."

"As soon as you thought he was saying something bad about your funeral business you got indignant with him," I said.

"I think I held my tongue quite well."

"Do you want to solve this thing?" I asked her.

"Yes. Of course."

"Then you can't try to get by on your smile and wit. And you're going to have to put a leash on that tongue."

"We'll see," she said.

"You don't have to wait to see. I'm telling you," I said.

"You just let me do the talking," she said. "After you give her the bad news. Just hand the baton over to me."

"I'm afraid your way might not get us anything." We were sitting in front of the little bungalow that Ragland Williamson had called home. "Don't say anything about how we paid the expense of burying him."

"I'm not," she said. "I didn't say it before, if you noticed. That man just assumed I did, and that was because he's a lawyer."

"What does being a lawyer have to do with anything?"

"You know they are all shysters. He probably thinks everyone is like him."

"That's not nice, Auntie." I opened the car door, and muttered, "But in your case that might be true."

"I heard that," she said.

We knocked on Ragland Williamson's door and it came open so quickly, you would have thought someone inside was expecting us.

That someone was his wife. Kara Williamson was petite with dark hair, and in typical Texan style, it was big. Her nails were painted red and she looked as if she was ready to step out of the door.

"Hello," Auntie said to the woman.

"May I help y'all?" she said.

"We're looking for the wife of Ragland Williamson."

She smiled politely. "That would be me," she said. "Kara Williamson. But he isn't here right now."

"Yes, we know," she said and put a solemn look on her face. "That's what we wanted to speak with you about. Could we come in?"

"Uh. Who are you?" she asked. She didn't seem suspicious, just cautious.

"I'm Dr. Romaine Wilder." I figured this was my cue to step in. "And this is my aunt, Suzanne Derbinay."

"Everyone calls me Babet," Auntie Zanne said, a faint friendly smile on her face. "We're from the Ball Funeral Home & Crematorium. In Roble."

Kara raised her eyebrows and straightened her shoulders like she was waiting for the catch.

"Is this about one of his cases?"

I hated to tell her while she was standing at the front door that her husband was dead. But with all her questions, I didn't think we make it inside if I didn't deliver the news.

"I'm sorry to inform you, Mrs. Williamson," I said in my most sincere and reserved voice, "that your husband, Ragland Williams, has died."

"Ray?" she said breathlessly. She leaned up against the frame of the door. "How could he be dead? He only went out on a job."

"He was murdered," Auntie said.

I guessed that was her using tact.

"Would it be okay if we came in?" I asked again.

"Oh," she said. I could tell she was trying to swallow back her tears. "Where are my manners?" She opened the door wider, a hospitable smile on her lips. Her eyes had lost their spark. "Please. Come on in."

"Thank you," I said and gave her one of Auntie Zanne's polite funeral home smiles.

"Have a seat," she said. "Would ya'll like something to drink?" Her voice was shaky. "I've got water, juice, soda." She seemed to be rambling. "I was just having a cup of tea." She pointed to a ceramic mug setting on the coffee table.

I guess she wasn't on her way out.

"No. We're fine," Auntie Zanne said. She went and stood by an armchair that sat across from the couch, but didn't sit down.

"Now," Kara said, wringing her trembling hands, "who are you again?"

"I'm a medical doctor," I said.

"She's the medical examiner." Auntie Zanne added to my description although I'd said that when we talked at the door. "She performed the autopsy on your husband." She put her hand over her chest. "And the city entrusted my funeral home with the care of your husband's body," Auntie said.

Kara's entire body seemed to be trembling, and I could see she was taking quick breaths like she was starting to hyperventilate, but I hadn't seen any tears. I knew that to many Southern women decorum was important. I thought perhaps she didn't want to break down in front of us. "Now, you say he's been buried?" She ran a shaky hand across her forehead. "How could that be?"

"No," I said and reached out and touched her arm. "He hasn't been buried."

Then I saw the tears. Her eyes were misty and she was squinting, it seemed to keep them from falling.

"We wanted to stop by, extend our condolences, and find out what you wanted to do with the remains," Auntie Zannne said.

"What I want to do?" Kara voice was so low it was almost inaudible.

"Yes," Auntie Zanne said. "Would you like for us to ship the body here for burial?"

"Oh. Right." She ran her hand over her face. "I do have to do that, don't I?" She nodded. "That would be good if you did that," she said. "I'll have to find...To get a..."

"It's alright," Auntie Zanne said. "We can help you with finding a plot."

"I'm sorry," she said. "This all seems so surreal."

"We understand," Auntie Zanne said.

"Now how did you say he died?"

"It appears to be a homicide," I said. Auntie's "murder" answer seemed too harsh.

Kara looked toward the door. "Is someone coming here to tell me that? I mean, to explain to me what happened?"

"That's why we're here," Auntie Zanne said. "To help with arrangements and explain as best we can. And," Auntie looked at her, "to see if you know anything about what happened."

She looked at me. "I-I don't know anything." She looked at Auntie. "How could I know? And we hadn't really prepared for anything like this." She lowered her head. "I don't know what to do about arrangements. I guess we just didn't think anything like this..." She looked up at us. "Anything like this would happen so soon."

"We certainly understand," Auntie said. "One can never adequately prepare for times like this. Especially when the passing is so unexpected."

Then the woman's tears came tumbling out. I looked around the room for a box of tissues, but Auntie beat me to it. She had a travel pack in her purse. I always had a box handy in my office, and she knew too to have them close by. It was the first time since we arrived that Kara had really shown any emotion.

"I can't do this," she said. "I can't even believe this is happening. That he's dead, let alone talking funeral arrangements."

"I know," I said. "It's hard to take in all at once." I put my arm around her.

"Where did it happen?" she said.

"Yellowpine," I said.

"In Yellowpine," she said, her words barely audible, and nodded. "I knew nothing good would come from him going there." She sniffed. "I didn't want him to go."

"It was just for business, wasn't it?" I asked. I knew I should've have just let her cry, without starting in with questions, but we needed to know. "He was an investigator for a lawyer, right?"

I didn't know that for sure. Jackson Wyncote had no idea why Ragland Williamson had gone to Roble, but I needed to get her talking.

"Yes," she said. "He was there on business."

"Do you know what kind?" Auntie asked.

We already had the answer to that question. I didn't want to wear out our welcome before we found out anything new.

"No. It was company business. You know, for the lawyer he worked for. But I knew he couldn't be that close to her and not try to contact her. I think he thought I didn't know where she was."

"Who?"

"His daughter." She flapped a hand. Her grief seemed to be taking a turn toward anger. "And her mother." She let out a hiccup with her last word. "To think they saw him last. Maybe even talked to him last. I am his wife." She covered her face with her hands.

"Did they live in Yellowpine?" Auntie Zanne asked.

"No!" The tears were spilling out now. She wiped her eyes, but the flood was more than one tissue could handle. I wiggled my fingers at Auntie for another one. "They lived in Roble," she said through her sobs.

"I know everyone in Roble," Auntie Zanne said, ignoring the woman having a breakdown. "What are their names?"

Kara blew out a breath. "His daughter is Amelia." She took the tissue from Auntie. "Do they know he's dead?"

"No," I said. "We only just found out who he was."

Auntie was blinking her eyes and biting on that bottom lip. I could tell she was thinking. "I only know one child in Roble named Amelia," she said. "And that's Coach Williams and Taralynn's daughter." She glanced over at me. "Someone must have had a child recently."

"I thought you'd know all about any child being born," I mumbled.

"No, that's her," Mrs. Williamson said, blowing her nose into the tissue.

"Who's her?" Auntie Zanne said, a confused look on her face.

"Taralynn. Amelia is Taralynn's child," Kara said.

Auntie sat down in the chair that had been offered to her earlier.

"Ray was her father," Kara said. "And I guess she got another one on me. He was with her in the end. Not me." She burst into another round of sobs.

"Ray was her father?" Auntie said, and I thought she was about to faint. She plopped down in the chair and stared off into space.

I felt odd man out, so I took a seat as well.

"You're talking about Taralynn Williams?" I asked.

"Yes. The woman he never stopped loving even after marrying me. The woman who got pregnant with his child and then broke his heart when she married his brother." She bit down on her lip. "Oh yeah, I know her."

Auntie sat forward, her eyes big. "Wait," she said. I saw her lips moving and her finger moving through the air like she was trying to add it all up. "So, Herman St. John -"

"That wasn't his name," I said.

"You know what I mean. He did know Taralynn. That's why he had her business card. But the other part, that couldn't be right," she said.

"Ah," I said and tried to hold my chuckle knowing it would have been inappropriate. "Something you didn't know."

"What's not right?" Mrs. Williamson asked.

"About Taralynn. She's married to Chip Williams. Our football coach. He couldn't have been your husband's brother."

"Charleston Williams?" Kara said. "That was Ray's brother."

"No," Auntie said.

"Excuse me?" Mrs. Williamson said.

"Coach Williams doesn't have any brothers or sisters."

"Well, he doesn't now because Ray is...he's..." Kara looked at me and I reached out and took her hand.

"They don't have the same last name," Auntie said.

"So?" Kara said sniffing.

"How could this be?" Auntie asked.

"Charleston changed his last name when he and Taralynn left Houston. I guess he thought that would help keep their secret."

"The dead guy and Coach Williams were brothers?" Auntie was mumbling to herself still stunned.

Kara and I stared at her.

"Auntie." I leaned toward her. "What is wrong with you? It's okay that you don't know everything that happens in East Texas."

"Coach Williams has always said," Auntie ignored me, "actually gone out of his way to let everyone know that he was an only child. That, he always told us, was the reason he had to find a wife that would spoil him because he was used to being the center of attention."

"Well, Auntie," I said, "looks like that wasn't true."

"It wasn't," Mrs. Williamson said and looked at me.

"He even said that's why he was such a good football coach. He had to have everything." Auntie shook her head. "Of course we just laughed, happy that he had that background and led our high school to victory time and time again."

"He did have to have everything," Widow Williamson said agreeing. "Including Taralynn and her child, and that just about killed Ray. Even after we got married, I knew he still grieved over that loss."

"And Taralynn would always nod her head, smile and say something about he was the other child in the house," Auntie said, still working out the news in her head.

"Is that what Taralynn said?" Mrs. Williamson said and turned up her nose. "I can't picture her being good to anyone."

"Oh yeah, she treats him good," Auntie said and then looked at Ragland Williamson's wife. "She spoils him and that girl of theirs."

"If by 'that girl' you mean Amelia, she was Ray's girl, not Charleston's or Chip's or whatever you call him." She swiped at her face with the tissue. "They formulated their lie a long time ago and made a pact to keep it," the wife said. "I think he only told me so he'd have someone to talk about his daughter with."

"She doesn't know about him?" Auntie said. "Amelia doesn't know Coach Williams isn't her father?"

"Not as far as I know," she said. "It's what Taralynn wanted and he would've have done anything to make sure she was happy. Even after all of these years."

"He did what she wanted him to do?" Auntie asked. "Even after he was married to you?"

"Yeah," she said and made a face like the thought of it left a bad taste in her mouth. "And I wasn't jealous of her, if that's what you're thinking."

"Of course not," Auntie said and gave me a look. "I wasn't thinking that. But if you don't mind me asking, what kind of things did she ask him to do?"

"Keep that secret. Let the lie about his brother being Amelia's father go. And the lie about his feelings for her."

"Why did they concoct that lie in the first place?" Auntie asked.

"Ray was in college when Taralynn got pregnant and wanted to finish school. I guess she couldn't wait. Her reputation was too important. Charleston has just finished school. I don't know how or why they did it, but the two of them got married and told everyone it was Charleston's child. She made her choice, and I guess Ray's brother didn't care about the lies or keeping it all secret."

We needed to switch gears. Although now we had another suspect with Coach Williams, a Roble scandal wasn't going to give us all the answers we needed.

"When was the last time you spoke to your husband?"

"I don't know. A couple of days ago," she said.

"A couple? Like two?" I said. That couldn't be true, I thought. We'd found him at the funeral home more than two days ago.

She hung her head and shook it slowly. "Maybe a week."

"Which is it?" Auntie asked.

"I was mad at him." Kara broke out in sobs again. "I didn't want him to go down there and I wasn't speaking to him. He'd tried to call me a couple of times, but I wouldn't answer. Then I just figured he'd stopped trying. I never thought he had stopped because he was dead."

"Do you know anyone named Herman St. John?" I asked.

"That's the name he used while he was down there."

"Why?" Auntie asked.

"I don't know." She dabbed at her nose with the rumpled tissue. "Probably so his brother wouldn't know he was down there. Probably so he could see her," she closed her eyes, "and no one would know."

"Had he used an alias before?" Auntie asked.

"No," she said.

"We spoke to Jackson Wyncote this morning—"

"You did?" she cut in before Auntie finished her sentence.

"Yes. He told us that your husband might be working for another lawyer now."

"He was. Mr. Wyncote was his old boss. When you talked to him, did he know anything?"

"Know anything?" I said. "Uhm. No. Not about the murder. But that's how we got your name and address. Your husband didn't have any ID on him when he was found."

"Where was he found?" she asked.

"In a casket in my funeral home," Auntie said.

"What?" she said. She sat back in her chair. "I don't understand."

"We don't either," I said. "But it looks like after he was killed, the person put him in a casket."

"Oh, my Lord." She covered her eyes with both her hands. "How did he die?" she asked without moving her hands.

"He was shot. In the back," I said.

"The back? Oh no!" she moaned and bent forward burying her head in her lap.

Auntie and I looked at each other. "Do something!" Auntie mouthed.

"What?" I mouthed back. Auntie hunched her shoulders. She was no help.

I tentatively stuck out my hand, then drew it back and looked at Auntie Zanne. She nodded at me. I stuck my hand back out and laid it gently on her back and gave her a rub.

"It's okay," I said. Auntie nodded at me again, I guess saying I was doing the right thing. "I know this hurts, but we're here to help."

"You're here to help?" Kara bounced up and screeched. "Where are the police? Why is a doctor and an old lady here telling me this?"

Auntie made a face at me like Kara's outburst was my fault. "Say something!" she mouthed again.

I didn't know what to say. I didn't want to say because the Roble sheriff was out of town.

"Mrs. Williamson, we're here because we have the remains and we couldn't tell you about them without telling you what happened. We only found out who he was, and we didn't want to leave his body...uh...unclaimed."

She looked at me and swiped the back of her hand across her nose. I reached over to Auntie for another tissue. She tried to hand me one, but I waved it away and pointed to the whole pack.

"Who killed him?" she asked.

"We don't know," I said and gave her the pack of tissues.

"Was it Taralynn?" she asked.

"We don't know," I said.

She sniffed and seemed to be thinking.

"It could have been someone here," I suggested. "Someone following him. Maybe someone from an old case he worked on?"

"Are you sure Mr. Wyncote didn't have some kind of idea?" Kara seemed interested in this conversation. "Ray used to work murder cases for him. Mr. Wyncote represented all kinds of dangerous people."

"He did mention one case," I said. Auntie hadn't said more than a couple words since she found out about our dead man's love child. "The last case your husband worked for him."

"Oh yeah." She nodded. "I remember. That case really

bothered Ray." She blew her nose into a tissue.

"Why?" I asked.

"Because he knew that the guy Mr. Jackson was representing was innocent. He told me that his boss finally got a decent guy for a client, and he couldn't do anything to help."

"Mr. Jackson told us his client got convicted."

"Yeah, he did. But Ray swore he knew who the real killer was. Is that who killed Ray?" she asked.

"We don't know," I said. I'd been telling her the whole time no one knew who the killer was, but that didn't seem to sink in.

"Did your husband ever tell you that person's name?" I asked.

"No. He only told me that he was from Stowell."

Chapter Thirty-Four

"Well, isn't Roble full of secrets," I said as we drove I-69 back home after picking up the trophies. "And lies."

I could see Auntie Zanne draw in a breath, but she didn't use it to speak. She sat quietly, her hand patting her leg to some inaudible beat.

We didn't stay much longer with widow Kara Williamson. Auntie had finally recovered, and we were able to make arrangements for the remains. I got all my questions answered, but nothing I found out trumped the information we learned about the sordid pasts of Ray, Coach Williams, and Taralynn.

"Josephine Gail knowing all that land might not be hers. Admitting that she knew who John Doe was when she called Pogue." I glanced over at Auntie Zanne. "That beautiful child, Amelia, is right in the middle of a real-life soap opera. Two brothers in love with the same woman. One of them fathering a child and allowing the other one to raise her. Both of them lying about it. It's all so unbelievable."

I flicked on the blinker, looked out my side mirror and changed lanes. "You see," I nodded, "that's why I don't like small towns."

"Every town is full of secrets," Auntie said. "And everybody lies. Seemed to me that it took you a while to find out about the personal life of that doctor of yours."

That was a punch in the gut...

"I don't mean to hurt your feelings, darlin', but life will deal you lots of bumps and sudden turns," she said. She stared straight out of the window, never turning to look at me. "If you don't have your radar on all the time, which is impossible to do, you gonna hit some hard roads more than once or twice in your life."

This time I didn't say anything.

"I just don't know what we learned that would help solve this case," Auntie Zanne said, then she turned and looked at me. "There's a lot of people with motives though."

"Pogue'll be home tomorrow night, I said. "Late. But back on the job early Saturday morning. We can tell him what we know."

"Isn't it remarkable how Ragland Williamson's wife looks so much like Taralynn?" she said, ignoring what I said about Pogue. "Like he was trying to replace her."

"I noticed that. From the bench picture, it would be easy to think they were related. Maybe even sisters."

"I know," Auntie said. "And what about Coach Williams always saying he's an only child? Making a big production number of it." She hunched her shoulders. "Why? Why would he do that?"

"I guess to keep his secrets."

"How would those secrets make Amelia feel?" I asked. "I would have hated not knowing my father."

"I would have hated that my husband was still in love with another woman," Auntie Zanne said.

"And that maybe he only chose to marry me because I looked like her." I said.

"You know what that sounds like to me?" Auntie Zanne said.

"What?"

"Motive."

"I think so too, Auntie," I said. "Jealousy is something that would make people do things they'd never do."

"It's possible," she said. "Kara, the poor wife, knew where he was. The name he was using. She could have done it and gone back home. Nobody the wiser."

I nodded. "I know who else had a motive."

"Who?" she asked.

"Chip and/or Taralynn."

Auntie nodded. "Without a doubt," she said. "Both of them had secrets to hide."

"And fifteen years' worth of lies to keep buried," I said.

Auntie gave a snicker. "Who wouldn't kill for that?"

We stayed quiet most of the way back, both of us lost in thought. I had a million questions in my head. Had we already met the killer? Had my Auntie Zanne's questioning caused concern and were we now in danger? Was he, or she, in Roble, or had they come from Houston? In our last phone conversation, I had tried to reassure Pogue about all the chips falling in place and not to worry. But now I was thinking I might just end up eating my words.

I looked over at Auntie Zanne from time to time. She seemed to be resting her eyes, or as she liked to say, her eyelids. And it wasn't until we got close to Nacogdoches that I heard a peep out of her.

"I want to pick up Rhett and the three of us deliver the pay to our musicians."

"What?" I frowned. "Why?" I said. "No. I was thinking about going to the mall and picking up some things for my room. I need bed linen. A clock. Some music."

"You'll get music tonight," she said. "How did you plan on going shopping when we've got a sound check tonight?"

"Uhm," I said, "because I wasn't planning on going to the sound check."

"You promised you'd bring pies to Amelia. Did you forget that, too? Because you're always forgetting something."

I glanced at the clock in the dashboard. It was a little after two. It'd be two thirty before we made it to Roble.

"What time is sound check?" I asked.

"Seven thirty."

"*Ugh!*"

"Be nice."

"And why does Rhett have to go?" I asked.

"Because he knows where everyone lives."

"There is a thing called GPS, Auntie. You can find anyone's address."

"I didn't say that he knew their addresses, I said he knew where they lived. They live out in the woods, no addresses out there."

"Oh," I said. "Couldn't you find city musicians?"

"Amelia lives in the city," she said. "Is that good enough for you?"

"I guess," I said. "And why is it I have to go?"

"Because you're my helper," she said and gave me a polite funeral home smile.

Chapter Thirty-Five

"Hey ya'll," Gus called out to us.

Auntie and I waved from the car as Rhett parked. Gus walked over toward us.

"Ain't quit," he chuckled and waved his cigarette smoke away. "I put it out as soon as I saw you coming."

"Is that what you were doing sitting out on the porch?" I asked.

"I always smoke outside."

Gus was our first stop. Seemed like he and Spoon lived one way from Roble, and Catfish the other. We decided to make Catfish our last stop because he was closer to home.

"Did you come out here to bring me more crawfish pies?" Gus asked. He was such a big guy, not fat, just large, and I could picture him eating a pound or two of the mudbugs all by himself.

I laughed. "No," I said. "Haven't you had enough?" I asked.

"Oh, no way," he said. "I told you I can't get enough. I used to work on a crawfish farm over in Winnie."

"Winnie?" I said.

"Uh-huh." He nodded. "Winnie, Texas. I grew up in a small town right next door to it. And when I was a kid, I used to go there and hang out, just hoping they'd offer me some. And when I got old enough to work, let me tell you, I couldn't wait to get that job. They didn't hire many folks, but they remembered me. We'd work only about three months out the year, but we'd catch so many that the pay for that little time kept us going the other nine."

"I'll bring more to the festival," I said smiling.

"Good. 'Cause let me tell you, even my momma don't bake crawfish pies as good as you."

I laughed and took a bow. "Thank you, kind sir. I'll be sure to bake extra for you."

"Well then what y'all doing out here?" he asked.

"We just stopped to bring your pay for being in the band." Rhett took out an envelope from his back pocket. "Didn't want you going on strike before the sound check tonight. Or worse yet, before the show Saturday night."

"Oh okay." Gus wiped his hands on his pants before he took the envelope from Rhett. "'Not to worry, though. I'll be there."

"You know, I think this is my friend's property," Auntie Zanne said.

"You talking about Josephine Cox?" he asked.

"Josephine Gail Cox," Auntie corrected.

"You've probably seen her around the funeral home no doubt," Rhett said. "When we were there practicing."

"Yeah. Of course. You know, I know her. I rent from her."

Auntie bit her lip. I could tell she was trying to figure out something. She turned around like she was trying to get her bearings.

"Did you see someone come out here looking at her land?" she asked Gus.

"Like who?"

"Like anybody. I know she told me she was trying to sell it."

"Uh. Can't say that I saw anyone," Gus said and scratched his head. "When would that have been?"

"About a week ago," she said.

"No. Don't think so." He shook his head. "You gotta come past my place to get into the property. For the most part, it's the only paved road here," Gus said. "I would've probably seen them." He turned toward the house. "I could ask Spoon," he said and turned back. "Him and his rifle out here hunting most every day."

"Oh, maybe I'll ask him when we stop and leave him his pay," Auntie Zanne said. "Josephine Gail hasn't been feeling too well and I want to make sure she doesn't miss a good deal if one comes around."

Why my auntie felt she had to lie to Gus was a mystery to me. But that was Auntie Zanne.

"Okay," Gus said. "I hope the next owners will be as nice as she is. I just like to be left alone out here. You know, to myself. I wouldn't want anybody always out here nagging at me."

"I can understand that," Auntie Zanne said. "We'll see you in a little bit."

We pulled out, headed to see Spoon and give him his paycheck.

"Remind me, Rhett," Auntie said, "and you can look it up, Romaine, to look into that crawfish farm in Winnie that Gus was talking about. We might can get them from there for next year's Boil."

"And put Catfish out of a job?" I said. "I don't think so."

"Oh, are you going to be the chairperson for the festival next year?" she asked.

"T-ha!" I said. "No."

"Then just do as I ask. Please." She turned around in her seat and looked at me in the back seat. "Look them up. You can do it on your phone, you know."

There she goes again. Trying to dazzle me with her cellphone tech knowledge.

I whipped out my phone and pulled up Google without an ounce of help from her.

Chapter Thirty-Six

I think the crawfish are multiplying in the pantry...

We'd finally got back to the house and I set out to make pies. I only wanted to make enough to keep my promise to Amelia, until Auntie reminded me that I'd told Gus I'd make him some too. I just let his flattery give me more work.

But the pies didn't take long. Five minutes to boil the crawfish, and with Auntie, Rhett, and Floneva taking out the tail meat for me while I cut up and sautéed the vegetables, we were on our way to the sound check early with a basket of pies. Floneva even went with us.

It would be fun, I thought as we drove out. My pies, Rhett's beer, and the music. Even if it was for the sound check, I couldn't wait to hear it.

And lo and behold, there was nary an objection to Amelia. I think even as grown men, those other players were stunned by her beauty. Chip's charisma didn't hurt either. Used to dealing with reporters, fans, mothers, and the like during football season, he was very personable. Auntie said he was mean, and maybe to his players he was, but around his daughter, he was a sweetheart. Maybe that was what drew him to Taralynn.

I wondered what the whole story was with the pregnancy by the one brother and subsequent marriage to the other. I watched Roble's football coach hanging out and laughing with the other fellows in the band.

While the musicians and Floneva, who seemed to have muscled her way into being an honorary band member, went out for one of their many cigarette breaks, Taralynn Williams came in and announced she was relieving her husband and would be staying and taking Amelia home afterwards. I saw my Auntie's eyes light up as soon as Taralynn walked into the covered area. I knew what she was thinking–this was her chance to interrogate.

Only problem–she didn't know the difference between interrogation and bullying.

Once the sound check was over and they played a set or two to help Amelia get acclimated, the guys sat around and drank beer that they got out the back of Spoon's truck.

Taralynn helped Amelia pack up her accordion. Once they'd finished and were on their way out, Auntie approached her. The thought of what she might say made my stomach turn.

"Taralynn," Auntie said. "Can we talk to you for a moment?"

"We?" she said.

"My niece and I."

Guess I won't be getting out of this one.

"Sure," she said and put her arm around her daughter. "What do you need?"

"Can we talk to you alone?" Auntie Zanne nodded toward Amelia.

"Oh. Okay," Taralynn said and looked at us. "Amelia, honey," she said and moved Amelia's hair out of her face. "I need to speak with Miss Babet. Can you wait in the car for me?"

"Sure, Mom," she said.

"Goodnight, Miss Babet," Amelia said. "Goodnight, Romaine. Thank you for the crawfish pies."

"You're welcome," I said. "See you tomorrow."

"Okay," she said. "See you tomorrow."

"Did you know a Ragland Williamson?" Auntie didn't waste any time. As soon as she thought Amelia was out of earshot, she dove right in.

"Who?" Taralynn said, trying not to show any expression. She shook her head. "No. I don't believe I do."

"Well, he knew you. He had your phone number."

"A lot of people have my phone number, Babet. Goodness, it's pasted on just about every bench in Roble."

"Maybe this will help jog your memory. He's dead."

I heard her voice catch in the back of her throat. "Who's dead?" she said, her voice cracking.

"Ragland Williamson."

"Dead?"

"Yes, Taralynn. He's dead," I said.

She covered her face with her hands and I could see a shiver rip through her body. She tightened up her muscles and let out a moan then turned away from us, seemingly to hide her emerging flood of emotions.

"He was murdered," Auntie Zanne said, not even a hint of sympathy in voice.

"I can't believe it," Taralynn said, her back still to us. "I just saw him—" She turned to us, her eyes big, and slapped a hand over her mouth, to let me know that wasn't a piece of information she wanted to share. "I-I mean..." The words stumbled out of her mouth and then she started sobbing.

"We know about your visits to see him," Auntie Zanne said. "And we know about your daughter."

"Amelia?" She sniffed back tears, her shoulders loosened. "What about her?"

"We know who her father is."

"What are you talking about?" Taralynn said. She swiped her hand over her face and licked her lips. "You've known Chip for as long as we've been here."

"Chip's not her father," Auntie Zanne said. "At least not her biological father."

"You don't know what you're talking about," Taralynn said. She turned and looked back toward the covered shelter. I was sure she didn't want any of what was to come to be overheard. "And why would you say something like that, Babet? You shouldn't go messing around in people's family business."

"Long buried secrets always seem to come to the light," Auntie Zanne said. "No matter how hard you try to cover them up."

"How is it that you even know anything about our secrets? About my daughter?"

"Kara told us."

"Who?"

"Ray Williamson's wife."

She sniffed back tears, and a look of surprise crossed her face. "He was married?"

"He didn't tell you that?" Auntie Zanne asked.

The tears came tumbling from her eyes again. "No." She started digging in her purse and pulled out a tissue. "He didn't tell me." She flapped the tissue in the air. "Not that I cared. That was over a long time ago." She eyed Auntie Zanne. "And nobody should have told you anything about any of it."

"They didn't just tell me, they told her too," Auntie Zanne pointed at me.

She would drag me into it.

I started to speak up in my defense, but I didn't get a chance. "What are you, a family of nosy nellies?" Taralynn asked. "Chip told me you were some big-city doctor." She raised her head, looking down her nose at me. "Looks like you wouldn't partake in small-town gossip."

"It ain't gossip if it's the truth," Auntie Zanne said.

"Well, nothing would come to 'light' as you put it, if people like the two of you didn't go around snooping."

"Your family's business is the reason that a man is dead."

"What?" she said, then shook her head as a realization sunk in. "Chip didn't even know that I'd gone to see Ray. He had no idea."

"Chip?" Auntie said.

"Chip didn't kill anyone!" Taralynn shouted the words, and then jerked her head around to ensure no one heard her. "And you can just take all your suppositions and accusations somewhere else.

I don't want to hear them."

"It never crossed my mind that it was Coach Williams who did the killing," Auntie Zanne said. "I thought you killed him. You're the one that was seen going up to the hotel."

"Me? What? Why would you think I killed Ray?" She looked puzzled. "Who saw me go up there?"

"Why did you go up there?"

"What?"

"Why did you go to the Grandview all those times? What was going on with the two of you?"

"Nothing was going on." She had gotten indignant now, and I was sure that Auntie's brand of wit wasn't going to get us very far. "And," Taralynn continued, "it's none of your business why I went over to that motel." She closed her eyes and shook her head. "But for your information, I went all of two times. He called me. Said he wanted me to help him."

"Help him with what?" Auntie Zanne said. "Was it about Amelia? Was he trying to see her?"

"No. He asked about her, yes. But we'd gone down that road a long time ago. He was okay with everything."

"He was okay with his estranged brother raising his daughter? The only child he ever had?"

"Yes!" Her voice got louder and went up an octave. "He left us." She lowered her head. "Me. He left me. He decided to go away. I did what I had to do. He realized when he got back that I didn't have any other choice. And he was okay with it."

"But now he wanted to change all of that, didn't he?"

"No." She frowned. "He didn't. Why do you keep trying to make it into something it's not?"

"He wanted to meet with you?" Auntie Zanne asked, not backing down. "Isn't that what you said?"

"Yes. That's what I said."

"About what?" Auntie Zanne asked.

"About some land. He wanted me to help him do a title search."

"Couldn't he have done that himself? He worked for a lawyer. Aren't they trained in that?"

"Well, his boss wasn't here. He was in Houston and I was here. I sell real estate, Babet. That doesn't just include houses you know."

"So, he lured you out there on the pretense of helping him with finding out who owned some land after you hadn't spoken to him in fifteen years?"

She lowered her head. "He didn't *lure* me. I had heard from him from time to time over the years," she said.

"Was it about seeing Amelia?" She brought up that theory again. "When he contacted you? Is that what he wanted?"

"No. I already told you no. That isn't what he wanted. He asked about her, yes. He wanted to know how she was doing," she said. "But Ray wasn't trying to hurt our family. Who have you told about this? If this gets back to my daughter, I swear, Babet..."

"What? You'll kill me?" Auntie Zanne asked.

Taralynn ran her hand over her face. "I can't believe this is happening and now...Now people know."

"Romaine is the medical examiner and her cousin is the law around here. You know Pogue Folsom. It's their job to know. And besides me," Auntie Zanne seemed remorseful, "no one else knows."

There she went including me again. I opened my mouth to speak, to try to defend myself.

"What kind of doctor are you?" Taralynn looked at me accusingly. "Aren't you supposed to keep information confidential?"

"I –"

"Not when it's a murder investigation going on," Auntie Zanne answered for me.

"I didn't kill Ray," Taralynn said. "He was the father of my child. And I don't have it in me to do anything like that anyway. It's not just I wouldn't, it's I couldn't."

She looked at the both of us. I didn't have anything to say, and I was thinking that Auntie Zanne had said too much. Then she walked away.

"Do you see how she immediately thought that it was Coach Williams that killed him?" Auntie Zanne asked me once we got into the Cadillac.

"Yeah, she did seem to think that when we said Ray Williamson had been murdered."

She pulled her seat belt across her and snapped it into the lock. "I've seen the coach at those football games," Auntie Zanne said. "He's as mean as a grizzly who's been awakened mid-winter."

"It could be he's just zealous about the game," I said. "You know high school football is next to God in East Texas. He's just fanatical."

"Maniacal might be a better word," she said. "And you remember how Chip said that he'd kill anyone that tried to do anything to his daughter?"

"He didn't say it quite like that, Auntie Zanne," I said.

"He made me believe he wouldn't take it lightly."

"Yeah," I said agreeing. "I got that impression, too. Lightly don't equal murder. And you know, that's how daddies feel about their little girls. It's not unusual."

"Considering that we've got a dead man on our hands who was the child's real father and had come to Sabine County to get her back, it is unusual."

"Auntie!" I said. "He did not come to get her back. He came down here for a job. There you go making up facts again."

"Then why did he call Taralynn?"

"She told you," I said. "To help with the land investigation he was working on."

"To help do what?" She reached in her purse. "He had spoken to a surveyor to help him, remember?" she said and pulled out the business card.

"That is true," I said. "But he needed her for a title search."

"Surveyor could have done that," she said.

"I don't think so," I said. "Surveyors mark boundaries. For boundary disputes. And that's what was going on, wasn't it?"

"You know it was," Auntie Zanne said.

"If Ray Williamson was going to meet a surveyor, he would have met him out at the property."

"I know."

"Out in the Piney Woods."

"Yes. I know."

"Then maybe," I said. "That's how he got sap and woodchips in his wound."

"You think Coach Williams followed him out there and shot him?"

"I think maybe whoever shot him, and I don't know if it was Chip, may have followed him out there and ambushed him."

"We need to find out where hot-tempered Charleston Williams was that day. Was he anywhere near Piney Woods?"

"Pogue will be back tonight. We need to let him do that."

"I think that we should call that surveyor," Auntie Zanne said. "He's local. We need to know what happened on Josephine Gail's land when he went to meet Ragland Williamson. What he saw." She looked at me. "Maybe he saw the killer."

Chapter Thirty-Seven

"The zydeco dance contest doesn't start for another half an hour," I told the couple that walked up to the information booth. "It's the first round today so you'd better hurry and get signed up if you want to compete."

"Thank you," they said in unison.

My auntie had roped me into staffing the booth. "Just for a couple of hours for the first night," she had said. "Then I've got it covered."

I think she just wanted me to do it to prove that she could get me to. I figured why not use my expensive education on directing people to the crawfish race.

The Festival had turned out grand. Lights were strung along the center walkway and booths lined the edges. Attendees could stroll their way through unique items, handcrafted and novelty, as artists, craftsman and vendors displayed their wares. Stuffed with official crawfish and football memorabilia, the two pseudo gods of the fair.

I had gone to the doctor's with Aunt Julep as promised. It appeared I had nothing out of the ordinary to worry about when it came to her health. Considering her age, weight and Type II diabetes, according to her doctor, she was doing okay. Her doctor was generous with his information about her and seemed quite caring. He reminded me of Alex and his gentle bedside manner.

It was just that she was getting old, and while getting that way is the same for everyone, not everyone grows old the same way. But whatever had made her shuffle around the kitchen that day I was there feeding her étouffée had since departed, because now all she talked about was getting to the festival and dancing to the zydeco music. I made another promise and told her I'd pick her up for the Saturday night show.

I guess how that old saying goes, "You're as old as you feel at any given moment." And this moment my Aunt Julep felt as if she could dance.

"Hi." I turned to the next face.

"Hi," I said back to the man in front of me. "How can I help you?"

"I don't know if you can help me. It's so many people here this year. I can't ever remember the first night being so busy." He looked around.

"The chairwoman this year was extra enthusiastic, to put it lightly," I said.

"I see," he said. "I'm looking for a Suzanne Derbinay? I stopped by her funeral home—um, the Ball Funeral Home and they told me I could find her here."

"Yes, she is here," I said. "I'm her niece, Romaine. Romaine Wilder."

"Yes, she mentioned you in her message, and the police. I'm Warren George. She said she wanted to speak to me about something. Sounded kind of urgent, especially after she mentioned it was a police matter."

"Ah, yes. The surveyor," I said and smiled.

"Yes." he asked. "I was on my way home, thought I'd stop by here speak to her, see what she wanted, and then walk around a bit.

"We had a question about some land you were called to do a survey on out here."

"*We?*"

"Well, we, she and I, are working with the police. The sheriff, I mean." I gave him a smile. "Pogue Folsom. He's a one-man operation and I am a medical examiner. So we're pitching in."

"Oh. So, then I can talk to you?"

"Yes. Just a couple of questions, if you don't mind."

"No. I don't."

"About the land you were surveying."

"Over by Yellowpine?" he said.

"Yes," I said.

"I don't know how much I can tell you. The guy never showed up."

"You were to meet him in his motel room?"

"No. Out on the property."

"Oh," I said. "The property where there was a land dispute?"

"That would be the one," he said.

"And he didn't show up there?"

"No. He didn't. I was a few minutes late. Tried to call him on his cell phone but got no answer. I waited around, spoke to a guy that lived out there and he hadn't seen him either."

"You spoke to someone out there?"

"Yeah, I guess he lived out there. Not sure. He came walking up to me and told me I was on private property."

"What did you say to him?" I asked.

"Told him I had permission and I was meeting someone out there."

"What was he doing?" I asked.

"Uh, he told me he was doing some woodworking, he had woodchips all over him. Said he was taking a cigarette break because he couldn't smoke around the varnish he used for his work."

"Did you smell any formaldehyde on this guy?"

"Uhm." He squinted his eyes and moved his head from side to side. "I couldn't tell you. Don't know what that smells like." His eyes went up and to the right like he was thinking. "He might have smelled like varnish," he said. "Or, I could think that because he told me that was what he was working with."

"Do you remember anything that stood out?" I asked.

"I remembered that he was smoking black cigarettes."

"Black cigarettes?" I said.

"Yeah. You know, rolled in black paper," the surveyor said. "I noticed it because I've never seen anything like it before."

"I have," I said.

Chapter Thirty-Eight

Once my Friday night duties at the Information booth were over, and without finding Auntie Zanne, I got in the car I'd been using and headed back to the house.

I knew Auntie Zanne would kill me once she found out I'd spoken to the surveyor, and then she would kill me again when I told her I saw that clue outside of the hotel room and hadn't told her about it.

A black cigarette.

I saw it when I was trying not to watch Auntie Zanne do her little illegal search of Herman St. John a.k.a. Ragland Williamson's room. And with it being outside the room, it was fair game. No problem with me picking it up.

Add that to the woodchips that were in the trashcan at that hotel and in the wound of my John Doe, it made me have goosebumps. I ran my hand over my arm.

But I didn't know that at the time, so I couldn't be too upset with myself. I did feel bad, though, and I knew why. The day Auntie Zanne told me that Josephine Gail knew the dead guy, she'd also said: "You have to be on the lookout for anything that might have to do with the murder no matter how small or inconsequential it seems at the time."

I hadn't done that.

She also said that the killer came to the room to find any

incriminating evidence, and now I see before he went in, he put out his cigarette.

I needed to get that cigarette.

I drove right past the exit for Roble and headed out to Yellowpine. I'd seen it on Monday and today was Friday. Would it still be there?

I drove as fast as I could down the unlit backroads of East Texas, and my heart skipped a beat when the Grandview came into sight. I leapt out the car and jogged back to the place I'd seen that black cigarette.

It was gone.

I could have kicked myself. If I had retrieved it when I was there the first time, Pogue could have ran a DNA test on it. Case closed.

"*Ugh!*" I stomped a foot.

Still, just to be thorough, I walked up and down the motel's sidewalk corridor of the second floor. Then I did the floor below it to make sure it hadn't fallen over before I left the motel.

Nothing.

I was going to have to tell Pogue. And I was going to have to tell Auntie, and that was something I dreaded doing the entire time I drove back to the house.

I checked the kitchen clock when I got into the house. It was only nine o'clock. Should I wait until after Pogue got back and call him tonight, then tell Auntie in the morning? Or should I tell her when she got home?

But while I was still standing in the middle of the kitchen, my mouth open in indecision, scratching my head, Auntie Zanne walked in the door.

"Whatch'ya doing, darlin'?"

"Nothing," I said and turned to walk toward the back door. "I was just going up to bed." I turned around and walked back the other way to get out of the kitchen and to the stairs.

"You lost?"

"No ma'am," I said.

Then she gave me one of her looks.

"What's going on with you, Romaine?"

Shoot.

Which was more important to me, I thought, my aunt hating me because I didn't give her information when it became available, or Pogue getting the information first?

There wasn't anything Pogue could do with the information I had gleaned tonight. So, with fear as my primary motivation, I opted to preserve my relationship with the woman who raised me.

Chapter Thirty-Nine

It was genius for Auntie Zanne to have decided, as a convenience, to move the music and dance floor closer to the front entrance. The rollicking blend of rhythm and blues with the funky, melodic music native to Louisiana's French Creole, drew participants and spectators with travel modes ranging from strollers to canes and walkers.

The 25th Annual Sabine County Crawfish Boil and Music Festival turned out to be a success, and it was with a smile and a tapping of my foot the next night that I sat enjoying the best part of it as I waited for my Aunt Julep. I had wheedled us one of the tables underneath the covered arena and was listening to the smooth beats which provided charity to my anxiousness.

Pogue was Aunt Julep's ride to the festival and there was some apprehension on my part in seeing him. Yes, thankfully, he was back in town, but I was bracing myself for our first encounter. I knew I'd have to fill him in on everything Auntie and I had found out, especially about the information I'd gotten from the surveyor. I just didn't know how happy he'd be about it. Fingers crossed, I hoped that he wouldn't jump all over me about withholding the information for as long as I had. It was a good thing his mother was going to be around, it might lessen the blow.

At least that was how I hoped it would go.

Auntie Zanne had been ecstatic about the new clue. She just

knew that's how *we*–I reminded her it would be *Pogue*–would catch the killer. She said, and I agreed, there couldn't be that many people around who smoked black cigarettes. I told her that even though I was just as excited about the clue, it might not be as important as we thought.

"Nonsense," is what she had to offer to that remark.

And even with my comment, I diligently ogled the guests and musicians who straggled in to see if any of them smoked tobacco wrapped in black paper.

Coach Chip Williams was the first person associated with the murder to arrive.

He was also *my* number one suspect.

Was it a jealous rage that made him shoot his brother in the back?

Right then, escorting his daughter, Amelia, who seemed ecstatic about playing, he was all smiles and seemed to share in her happiness. But, it may have been that it was because he was a doting father that he killed Ray. Never wanting Amelia to find out that his blood connection to her wasn't as close as she'd been led to believe.

As I watched them, I wondered if Taralynn was going to make an appearance. My second choice for a killer. She not only had a motive, but going to visit Ray Williamson at the motel several times gave her opportunity.

Yep. People will go to any length to keep their secrets.

The only thing I didn't know, was whether either one of them smoked.

And then came Floneva. She floated in–head high, horse teeth bared, the heels of her cowboy boots clicking across the makeshift floor–she looked like a Wild West Show participant. I had changed my mind on the designation I'd given her of honorary band member. I was beginning to think she was more like a roadie or groupie. The band wasn't due to go on for another forty-five minutes, and here she was already hanging out in their tent. Although I changed my opinion of her relationship to the band, I hadn't changed my mind about her being a possible suspect. And she did smoke cigarettes.

Who knows? Maybe even black ones.

Plus, Miss Floneva Floyd was from Hemphill, which was right next door to the hotel where Ray Williamson had stayed, and adjacent to Josephine Gail's land. So she knew the area. And, the twins, Mark and Leonard, had seen her going into the funeral home while Auntie Zanne was gone. Had she been scoping it out, and then later returned to make an after-hours visit to depose of a body? I didn't have a motive for her, but she was suspicious just the same.

The DJ spun tunes while the other members of the band filtered in and readied for their set from their tent. Gus. Spoon. Catfish. The sway of the music almost lulled me into a blissful stupor, thoughts of the murder held at bay, but the sight of Rhett Remmiere nudged me back to consciousness. He sauntered my way, a big grin plastered across his face. It seemed like every time I saw him, he acted more familiar with me and, I don't know...happy.

I wasn't happy at all about seeing him...

I didn't think that he smoked, but he seemed to have a furtive air about him all the same, and I knew he had something up his sleeve.

Something, perhaps, like murder.

"What are you grinning about?" I asked when he got close to me.

"I'm happy."

I arched an eyebrow. "About what?"

"To be here. To play my guitar." He tilted his head to the side. "To see you."

I sucked my tongue. "I'm still waiting to get that confession out of you," I said.

"Maybe after the set," he said and nodded. "I'm usually feeling pretty cooperative about most things after I've played my guitar."

"I can't wait," I said dully.

"You're going to stay and watch us play?" he asked.

"I wouldn't be able to go back to my Auntie Zanne's house tonight if I didn't," I said.

He chuckled. "She is quite proud of us."

"That she is," I said.

"So, what are you doing? Just sitting here?" he asked. "Babet didn't have any work for you?"

"I've finished my shift," I said. "She is gracious enough to allow me a break every now and then."

He didn't say anything. Just stared at me and smiled, which made me uncomfortable.

"Okay," I said. "Guess you better get ready for the show."

"Guess I better," he said but didn't move.

"Bye," I said and threw up a hand in a wave to try to get him to move along.

"Talk to you later," he said and finally turned and walked away.

Geesh. Auntie Zanne really knows how to pick the people she lets into her life. Wacky, I think, is the main criteria.

After Rhett left, I watched the entryway for Pogue and Aunt Julep. They didn't arrive until the DJ had taken leave and the band was just setting up on stage.

I waved them over. "Hey, Aunt Julep," I said after she arrived, a beaming smile on my face when I saw her shuffle over on Pogue's arm. "I saved you a seat."

"Oh, I don't plan on sitting down too much," she said, letting a shaky hand loose from Pogue's arm, and easing down into her seat. "I'ma be dancing all night."

Pogue and I exchanged an amused look.

"Oh look," Aunt Julep said. "There's the guy that picks up my embalming fluid. I'm going to put him down on my dance card."

I turned to look, but people had packed the place. The chairs around the tables were full and the perimeter of the dance floor was standing room only. So I wasn't able to see who she was pointing to.

"Well, I'm sure he'll be honored to dance with you," I said. "You point him out to me when you're ready and I'll go and grab him. And be sure to save me a dance, too. I think my zydeco dancing might be a little rusty. You can help me out."

"Will do," she said, a big old grin on her face.

"Romaine!" Auntie Zanne called as she strolled over to the table. I turned to greet her and she smacked me in the back which made me flinch. I didn't know if she might pinch me again.

"Yes!" I said, nervousness coming out in my voice.

"I found it." She bent forward and spoke to me in a strained whisper.

"Found what?" I took to whispering too.

She started to answer, but it was then that she seemed to notice Pogue and Aunt Julep.

"Julep," she said standing straight up and putting on a smile. "You're looking good. You dancing the zydeco tonight?"

"Yes, I am," Aunt Julep said proudly.

"Well, you were always the best I'd ever seen." Auntie Zanne smiled as she walked over to Aunt Julep. She touched Aunt Julep on the arm and placed her cheek next to hers.

She's so phony, I thought. One minute accusing Aunt Julep of murder, the next, she's her best friend.

Auntie Zanne stood up. "Do you mind, Julep? I need to steal Pogue from you."

"Oh sure," Aunt Julep said. "Romaine got us these seats. I'll be fine."

"Good. Because I need her too," Auntie Zanne said.

I glanced over at Pogue. I hadn't the faintest idea what Auntie Zanne was up to. Last I knew, she was barely speaking to Pogue.

"C'mon you two," Auntie said waving her hand at us. "Before the killer gets away."

"What?" Pogue said and got up. "What killer? Don't tell me somebody else has been killed."

"They might be if you don't hurry," she said.

She got behind us, and with a palm in each of our backs, she pushed us out of the shelter and to the back of the covered area near the musicians' tent. "Look," she said and pointed.

Cigarette butts were scattered all over the grounds. And at least a half-dozen of them were black.

"Oh. Wow." I said.

"What?" Pogue said. "What are we looking at?"

"He doesn't know?" Auntie said.

"I don't know what?" Pogue looked at me then Auntie. "What am I supposed to know?"

I shook my head. "He doesn't know." I made a flinching face. "I didn't have time to tell him yet."

"Tell. Me. What?" He spoke from between clenched teeth.

"Tell him," Auntie said and slung a finger toward him. "And hurry up."

I tried to do a quick recap of what had happened over the last four days while he was out of town, but he wasn't happy with that.

"Details," he said. "And don't leave anything out."

I backtracked and told him every detail. I recited it like I had done the autopsy report, not leaving out anything no matter how insignificant in case he saw something I hadn't. But, by the time I'd finished my little spiel, reciting all the clues to him, I had somehow figured out who the killer was myself.

Chapter Forty

Pogue was walking in circles by the time I finished telling him about my and Auntie's exploits while he was away at his conference, and about who I now thought the killer was.

His hands dug deep inside his pockets and the creases on his forehead were double-folded. He kept snorting and shaking his head, a low moan ruffling his lips with each release. He stopped abruptly near one of the black cigarette butts, stooped, and without touching it, stared at it.

"I need to get an evidence bag," he said, seemingly to no one, then stood and took another lap around the small circle he'd etched into the dirt.

"Nobody touch that," he said when he finally stood still. "I'm going to my car to get my gun and handcuffs." He looked at me. "I think I need to make an arrest. They're in there, right?"

"Yes," I said. "With no idea we've figured it out."

"No idea that *you've* figured it out," he said. Pogue gave me a look before he left. One that told me I shouldn't have done so much without him, or at least without letting him know.

When he got back, after what seemed like a good fifteen minutes, the three of us went to the tent that Auntie had had erected for the musicians to use before and during sets. All the zydeco players were there. And so too were Taralynn and Coach Williams watching over their daughter, Amelia, and the band's roadie, Floneva.

"Hey," Rhett said, looking at me as I came in with that same stupid big smile on his face. "It's almost time to show you what we've got."

"Before y'all go on," Auntie Zanne said, "we have some law business to take care of."

"Law business?" Rhett stepped back and looked around. "What is it, Babet?" Rhett asked.

"Pogue will tell you."

Pogue stood, feet shoulder length apart, and looked around the little tent. He moved in front of the flap—the only way out—then he looked at me. "You figured it out, Romie," he said. "You tell it."

"You sure?" I said.

He nodded. "I'm sure," he said.

"Figured out what?" Rhett asked.

"We've figured out who left that body in Auntie Zanne's funeral home," I said. I looked at Taralynn. "Before I say anything, though, I think that Amelia shouldn't be in the room."

"I agree," Coach Williams said. "We'll take her out."

"You stay, Coach," Pogue said. He stepped to the side. "Let Taralynn take her." He nodded at her, giving her permission to leave.

Everyone turned and looked at Coach Williams.

After Amelia and Taralynn left, I turned and looked at the people that were left. "I just said the other day that smoking wasn't good for you," I did a *tsk, tsk, tsk.* "And in this case, it sealed the fate of the killer."

"Who is it?" Rhett asked.

"It's Gus," I said. No pomp. No circumstance. I just spilled it.

"What?" Gus said, his voice going up a couple octaves. "What are you talking about?"

"You killed Ragland Williamson because you thought that he'd come after you for a murder up in Houston."

"Who?" Coach Williams asked, jerking around to face me. "Who did you just say was killed?"

"Your brother," Auntie Zanne said. She hadn't said anything else, but I'm sure she was happy to let him know she knew all about his secrets and lies.

"My brother is dead?" he said, disbelief on his face. "I don't believe it. How could you know about my brother?" He eyes were turning red and I could see them burning with tears.

"We know who he is—was," Auntie said. "And he's dead. Gus killed him."

"No!" Coach Williams said.

"Yes, Coach. He is," Pogue said.

"Just ask Gus," I said.

"You know those crawfish pies you make," Gus said between clenched teeth, "ain't good enough for me to sit 'round here and listen to you accuse me of murder."

"You mean of two murders," Auntie said.

"There was a black cigarette out there behind the shelter," I said and pointed that way. "We have an eyewitness that will say he saw you smoking a black cigarette."

"What does that matter?" Gus queried. "Everyone here saw me. We all smoked together. It don't mean nothing."

"Is that what you smoke?" Coach Williams asked. He went and stood by Pogue. I think he realized that Pogue asked him to stay in case he needed help apprehending Gus.

"Yeah. So what if it is? Like I said, that means nothing," Gus said.

"The surveyor who went out to meet Ray saw you smoking them."

"And you left one at the hotel," Auntie Zanne said. "We can match the DNA on all of those."

Auntie Zanne knew we didn't have the one from the hotel, but I guess she needed to be dramatic, even if it meant she had to lie.

"What hotel?" Gus wasn't letting his guard down.

"Don't play dumb," Auntie Zanne said.

"Is that all you got?" Gus said, a chuckle erupting from his throat. "You'll never prove anything with that."

"You've been dumping the formaldehyde from my mother's funeral home for her," Pogue said. "I'll bet it's the same kind that Romaine found during the autopsy." Pogue swung around and looked at me. "Can you check that?"

"Oh, you mean from the samples I collected?" I asked, acting like Auntie. I hadn't collected any samples from the back of my Aunt Julep's funeral home. But I was sure a lab could pull something off Ray Williamson's clothes.

Gus narrowed his eyes. "Your mother is Julep Folsom?"

"That she is," Pogue said.

"And that lab report will be able to match the formaldehyde in that man's body," Auntie Zanne said, "to the formaldehyde that Julep Folsom uses at the Garden Grove Funeral Home."

I turned and looked at my auntie. I think this was the first time she ever said the name of Aunt Julep's funeral home correctly.

"Is that possible?" Gus asked. "There's a test that can match the type of formaldehyde from two different things?"

"Yes, there is," I said and turned to Pogue. "Science is amazing. And, I'm sure that info is in the toxicology report I already requested." I looked at Gus. "That makes two things that can unequivocally tie you to the murder."

"Anyone could have taken that formaldehyde," Gus said. The burly little murderer was grasping at straws. "She left it in the backyard."

"True, Gus," I said. "But there is one more thing."

"What?" he asked.

"Ray Williamson was looking for a man from Stowell for a murder he was investigating. He felt like the wrong man had gotten convicted."

"So?" Gus said.

"So, he had evidence that you were the one that killed him." I smiled as the lie tumbled out. We didn't know of any such proof. "You told us the little town you grew up in was right next to the town of Winnie. So, I googled Winnie to see what was close by and it came up with a link that read 'people also search for...' That helped me figure this out."

"And what did people also search for?" Auntie Zanne said, helping me deliver my one-two punch.

"Well, Auntie, it said that people that searched for info on Winnie also looked for info on a town called Stowell."

"And why would that be?" she asked. Neither one of us took our eyes off of Gus as we volleyed back and forth.

"Because the two towns are just a three-minute drive apart."

"Well, don't that beat all," Auntie Zanne said. "Right next door, just like Gus said."

"Aren't you from Stowell?" I asked Gus.

"He didn't have anything on me," Gus said, not answering my question. "Because if he had he would have used it. He just kept harassing me."

"Or maybe he did have something, but he couldn't find you because you'd moved to the Piney Woods. No address. No job," Auntie Zanne said.

"If he didn't have anything on you," Coach Chip Williams said, "why would you kill him?"

"Yeah," Pogue said. "Why would you kill him?"

"And leave his body at Babet's place?" the Coach said. "I just don't understand."

"You knew," Auntie said to Gus, "because I had invited you into my home, that I'd be gone. So, you put that body there. What happened? Someone heard you before you had time to put it in the furnace?"

"He was going to put my brother's body in your furnace?" Coach Williams screeched.

"Did you really think that Josephine Gail wouldn't notice it?" Auntie Zanne asked.

"She's a scatter brain," Gus said. "She doesn't even know where her land starts and where it ends."

"Looks like she knows more than you," Auntie Zanne said. "She knew that body didn't belong at my funeral home."

"It's ironic, Gus, that you panicked when you saw Ragland

Williamson, because Josephine Gail Cox was the reason that he was there," I said. "Not you."

"What are you talking about?" he said.

"What did you think? That he'd come looking for you?' I asked.

"I wasn't going back with him," Gus said. "He knew the truth. That meant he knew what I was capable of. He should have left well enough alone. Somebody had gone down for that murder. I didn't care to make anything right."

"He didn't come for you," I said. "Not to drag you in. Your secret, at least at the time you shot him, was safe. He never even knew you were around."

"Then why was he in the woods by my place?" Gus asked.

"That's not your place," Auntie Zanne said. "It belongs to Josephine Gail. My best friend in the whole world. And you were right. She doesn't know where her land starts and where it ends."

"But even with that, she didn't try to find the coward's way out," I said. "And shoot him in the back."

Coach Williams narrowed his eyes. "You shot my brother in the back?"

"Probably about ten yards out," Catfish said, the first time he spoke. But it seemed he remembered what we'd talked about when I did the autopsy.

The coach lurched forward like he was going to pounce on Gus, fists balled and fire in his eyes, Catfish and Rhett moved quickly to hold him back.

"You are a coward," Coach Williams spat out the words. "And thank God that Texas law don't hold too kindly to people who kill. But when they kill you, I'll be there to look you directly in your face."

"C'mon," Pogue said to Gus. "I think I have enough on you to take you in."

Gus kept a watchful eye on Coach Williams as Pogue handcuffed him. He didn't give any resistance and seemed grateful for Catfish and Rhett holding him back. It made me wonder how tough this guy was and if he had shot his other victim in the back as well.

"Wow," Floneva said. "Gus is a killer?"

"Puts a damper on your plans with him, huh?" Auntie Zanne said.

"What?" Floneva said. "I don't know what you mean. I came here for the music."

"Then you've come to the right place."

"I hate to say this at a time like this," Rhett said. "But, I don't know if we'll be playing tonight. We don't have a fiddler."

I saw Auntie's eyes light up and I knew what was coming. I looked over at Catfish and he, knowing my little secret, started grinning.

"You're not screwed," Auntie Zanne said. "You've got a fiddler player right here."

"Who?" he asked.

"Romaine," she said.

"You can play?" Rhett asked, shock written into his face.

"Oh, she plays a mean fiddle," Auntie Zanne said.

"And the piano, and violin, too," Crawfish said.

"So," Rhett said with a sly smile, "you wanna do this set with us?"

"Of course she does," Auntie Zanne said.

I drew in the breath. "I guess I could. But, I don't have a fiddle to play," I said. "And I'm not using that one." I pointed to Gus's instrument he'd left behind. For all I knew, the wood chips I'd found during the autopsy had come from when he made that thing."

"No need," Auntie said with a big grin. "I have yours in the trunk of my car."

"You do?" I said and gave her a mean look. "Why?"

"I just thought after hearing a little music tonight and seeing everyone on the dance floor, you'd get the bug and want to play. I had it tuned up for you and everything."

"You're full of surprises," Rhett said and walked over to stand by me. "I like that in you."

I sidestepped away from him.

Rhett chuckled. "Okay, Babet, go get this lady's instrument."

"On my way," she said. "And for the record, Sugarplum," Auntie Zanne said, turning to me and taking my hands in hers. "I never thought it was Julep who left that body at my funeral home. I just needed to create a diversion. I just couldn't abide by anyone causing Josephine Gail more anguish than what she was already going through. I wanted to keep Pogue's mind occupied while I tried to figure it out."

"You could have just let Pogue figure it out," I said.

"Now what would have been the fun in that?" she said and winked.

Epilogue

Sometimes in life, you get so focused on what you're doing now, and what you want your future to be, that you lose sight of the past. Especially when you feel like you have to outrun it.

That little revelation not only went for Gus, it went for me too.

What was wrong with me coming from a small town? Losing all of my past just so I could make myself out to be something and someone else all of a sudden just seemed wrong.

Playing the fiddle that night at the festival opened up a floodgate of memories. My parents. My love of playing instruments. My life in Roble. It all came swooshing back in with a jolt that almost knocked me over.

I was still going to go back to Chicago, I hadn't changed my mind about that, but it didn't mean I had to forget the people at home who loved me. Or make them feel bad because I had them thinking, with all my hankering to hurry and get away, that I was ashamed of them.

I mean what else could they think when I was always complaining and letting them know how fast I wanted to get back "home?" And then, not letting those people in Chicago, who I had yet to hear from, know the truth about me.

I guess I had my own set of secrets and lies...

But unlike Coach Chip Williams and his wife, Taralynn, I was contemplating coming clean.

Chip Williams was devastated over the loss of his brother, yet he and Taralynn had gotten us all together after the last set and asked us to swear that we'd never mention to Amelia anything about her "uncle."

Was that her Uncle Ray or Uncle Chip?

I didn't like the thought of being a part of any of it.

The two planned to take the knowledge of Amelia's real father to the grave with them. I didn't understand how they thought that could be best for her. Perhaps they were more worried about what she'd think of them after their years of lies and deceit than they were about giving her the knowledge of who her biological father was.

I believed that who we are is based on what we know about ourselves. We attribute our idiosyncrasies, habits, likes, and dislikes many times to whom we share our genes. How would I understand my love of music if I didn't know about my father's soulful guitar playing and my mother's beautiful singing voice? Or appreciate my Louisiana French Creole heritage through my cooking and speaking the language if I didn't know about it. No one wants their real parents' identity kept secret. Still, I agreed with the rest of them not to say a word.

It turned out that Gus wasn't as good at keeping his secrets, though. He did a bad job cleaning up the crime scene. The wood chips in the motel room trashcan matched those on Ray Williamson's shirt. Gus never emptied the formaldehyde in the back of Aunt Julep's funeral home, and the lab was able to match it to that used on our squatter. And Gus' DNA was all over the clothes he'd dressed Ray in—so sloppy.

But Angus "Gus" Garrison didn't wait for lab results to come in to convict him, he was too busy confessing long before then. It ended up that Ragland Williamson had kept a file full of information on the first murder and the Harris County DA offered Gus a deal to come clean. It appeared that the DA's office had a conscious and felt bad it had convicted the wrong man, especially since Ragland had told them repeatedly that they had.

And my Auntie Zanne had a new hat to add to her list of vocations: amateur sleuth. That made her poufed hair stand up that much higher. She couldn't wait until the next time she had the opportunity to use her newly acquired skills.

Meanwhile, she kept a teapot of boiling water whistling on the stove just in case she caught me off guard and could trick me into drinking a cup of her "staying" brew.

ABBY L. VANDIVER

Wall Street Journal Bestselling Author, Abby L. Vandiver, loves a good mystery. Born and raised in Cleveland, it's even a mystery to her why she has yet to move to a warmer place. Abby loves to travel and curl up with a good book or movie. A former lawyer and college professor, she has a bachelor's degree in Economics, a master's in Public Administration, and a Juris Doctor. Writer-in-Residence at her local library, Abby spends all of her time writing and enjoying her grandchildren.

The Romaine Wilder Mystery Series
by Abby Vandiver

SECRETS, LIES, & CRAWFISH PIES (#1)
LOVE, HOPES, & MARRIAGE TROPES (#2)

Henery Press Mystery Books

And finally, before you go...
Here are a few other mysteries
you might enjoy:

I SCREAM, YOU SCREAM

Wendy Lyn Watson

A Mystery A-la-mode (#1)

Tallulah Jones's whole world is melting. Her ice cream parlor, Remember the A-la-mode, is struggling, and she's stooped to catering a party for her sleezeball ex-husband Wayne and his arm candy girlfriend Brittany. Worst of all? Her dreamy high school sweetheart shows up on her front porch, swirling up feelings Tally doesn't have time to deal with.

Things go from ugly to plain old awful when Brittany turns up dead and all eyes turn to Tally as the murderer. With the help of her hell-raising cousin Bree, her precocious niece Alice, and her long-lost-super-confusing love Finn, Tally has to dip into the heart of Dalliance, Texas's most scandalous secrets to catch a murderer...before someone puts Tally and her dreams on ice for good.

Available at booksellers nationwide and online

Visit www.henerypress.com for details

THE AMBITIOUS CARD

John Gaspard

An Eli Marks Mystery (#1)

The life of a magician isn't all kiddie shows and card tricks. Sometimes it's murder. When magician Eli Marks very publicly debunks a famed psychic, said psychic ends up dead. The evidence, including a bloody King of Diamonds playing card (one from Eli's own Ambitious Card routine), directs the police right to Eli.

As more psychics are slain, and more King cards rise to the top, Eli can't escape suspicion. Things get really complicated when romance blooms with a beautiful psychic, and Eli discovers she's the next target for murder, and he's scheduled to die with her. Now Eli must use every trick he knows to keep them both alive and reveal the true killer.

Available at booksellers nationwide and online

Visit www.henerypress.com for details

LOWCOUNTRY BOIL

Susan M. Boyer

A Liz Talbot Mystery (#1)

Private Investigator Liz Talbot is a modern Southern belle: she blesses hearts and takes names. She carries her Sig 9 in her Kate Spade handbag, and her golden retriever, Rhett, rides shotgun in her hybrid Escape. When her grandmother is murdered, Liz high-tails it back to her South Carolina island home to find the killer.

She's fit to be tied when her police-chief brother shuts her out of the investigation, so she opens her own. Then her long-dead best friend pops in and things really get complicated. When more folks turn up dead in this small seaside town, Liz must use more than just her wits and charm to keep her family safe, chase down clues from the hereafter, and catch a psychopath before he catches her.

Available at booksellers nationwide and online

Visit www.henerypress.com for details

MURDER IN G MAJOR

Alexia Gordon

A Gethsemane Brown Mystery (#1)

With few other options, African-American classical musician Gethsemane Brown accepts a less-than-ideal position turning a group of rowdy schoolboys into an award-winning orchestra. Stranded without luggage or money in the Irish countryside, she figures any job is better than none. The perk? Housesitting a lovely cliffside cottage. The catch? The ghost of the cottage's murdered owner haunts the place. Falsely accused of killing his wife (and himself), he begs Gethsemane to clear his name so he can rest in peace.

Gethsemane's reluctant investigation provokes a dormant killer and she soon finds herself in grave danger. As Gethsemane races to prevent a deadly encore, will she uncover the truth or star in her own farewell performance?

CPSIA information can be obtained
at www.ICGtesting.com
Printed in the USA
LVOW13s0022010618
579130LV00010B/629/P